Letters to Middleton

Letters to Middleton

Middleton Series #1

PATRICIA GARCÍA FERRER

Copyright © 2021 Patricia García Ferrer
All rights reserved
Original title: Cartas a Middleton

Cover design: Germancreative
Cover images: Depositphotos.com
Author's photograph: Author's Archive

This is a work of fiction. The names, characters, places and events depicted are either the product of the author's imagination or are used in the context of fiction. Any resemblance to real people (living or dead), companies, events or places is purely coincidental.

First edition: November 2021
ISBN:
No part of this book may be reproduced in whole or in part, or incorporated into a computer system, or transmitted in any form or by any means, electronic, mechanical, photocopying, recording or otherwise, without the prior written permission of the author. Infringement of the aforementioned rights may constitute an offence against intellectual property (art. 270 et seq. of the Penal Code).

For you, always

Middleton Post. February 6, 1868

Dear readers,

The biggest scandal in the county has arrived on my doorstep. As of this moment, Louise Welling's carelessness of the previous summer is forgotten. Lord Williams and his family have fallen into disgrace. Rumors were rife that the eldest son of the former cantankerous Coby Williams had been unlucky at gambling, but I can confirm that there is no family fortune left that has not been squandered. Apparently, and as confirmed by reliable sources, a certain gentleman owes not only his fortune but that of some other kind-hearted friends. Pity his children and his beloved wife.

Lady Middleton

Middleton Post. June 20, 1876

Dear readers,

Everything seemed to indicate that the eldest of the Westworth daughters would never marry. It was not a secret, but a resolution which she herself, Margaret Westworth, had reiterated with conviction on more than one occasion. Social occasions, balls, and fan games were moments not worthy of her attention. But this time, no matter how much the young woman longs to get away from the intricacies of the salons or the whispers of the town, her father longs for her to continue the Westworth line, and her life is about to change. Perhaps the culprit behind these precipitous events is Lord Westworth, or perhaps a handsome gentleman from the north who promised to awaken the slumbering hearts of the county's young ladies.

Lady Middleton

CHAPTER 1

June 17, 1876
Middleton, England

"I cannot believe that Lady Middleton is the only thing you are interested in reading from the town paper," said Margaret Westworth, as she threw the scrap of paper indignantly on the dining-room table. There is nothing with any seriousness in her remarks to be taken into account.

"Lady Middleton returns with news? " the youngest of the Westworth sisters rose energetically from the table to retrieve the sheet on which the succulent and newly published gossip was collected. As she went, she rattled the table-cloth with impetuosity, throwing some of the rolls which had been so carefully and thoughtfully arranged in a tower upon one of the trays. The glasses almost spilled their contents, and Margaret, knowing her sister's energy, gripped the table tightly to keep them from going after the great earthquake.

"They insult our intelligence." The indignation of the eldest of the sisters grew by the moment before the enthusiasm of the other members of the family. She could not believe such hurtful words about herself could be of so much interest.

"Sister, these pamphlets are not written for women," said Rose Westworth as she held Middleton's leaflet over her head, proud to be the biggest fan of that section of the local paper, "Economics, cattle and land sales.... Uninteresting. However, the Lady's section....

"If everyone knew who Lady Middleton was, her bold and shameless remarks would be of no interest, don't you think?" Margaret sowed doubt and reflection among her sisters, who quickly looked at each other and returned to sharp, biting words." No woman in her right mind should have time for unsubstantiated rumors.

Margaret was, to her misfortune, the most sensible of Mr. Westworth's three daughters. She had for years cultivated her mind by the power of speech in books and letters. She was capable of dealing with most subjects which might interest gentlemen, and of entering into judicious conversation with them. However, she lacked some, or many, of the social skills required of a lady. She had never pretended to be one, and though the mysterious Mrs. Middleton would go out of her way to expose her shortcomings and her lack of interest in capturing a husband, she would remain true to her beliefs.

"You are angry because the author of these lines always finds a moment to criticize you." suggested the middle sister with a slightly haughty tone.

Every morning, when the social season came round, the same scenes were repeated over and over again at breakfast, and Grace was tired of her sister's lecturing them on their unwisdom in believing those words.

"Don't be foolish, Grace." the hint of Margaret's interest in being featured in the society pages was a joke between sisters that they well knew was nonsense, for the elder sister wanted to grab the attention of that woman's viperous tongue as much as adulterers needed to be recognized.

"And what do you wish us to spend our time on, dear sister?" Rose asked mockingly as she raised her teacup to her mouth with refined delicacy, causing Grace to laugh and Margaret's frustration to grow. This is

Middleton, nothing exciting happens at Middleton. Never." dramatized the youngest of the family.

Rose was a free spirit, eager to fly away from the four county estates, but she had never, in her eighteen years of life, set foot beyond Robert Pulman's land. To her, Lady Middleton was a breath of fresh air. It is possible that for her tender age she knew the secrets of most of the Middleton locals, and of some who came from beyond the borders of the town.

"Deep down you admire her. Admit it." Grace insisted, looking at her older sister.

"Admit that I am interested in the gossip of this town?" the color in Margaret's face began to change from a pale color to one befitting a person with little desire to speak decently any longer.

"If you had married Mr. Martin last year we would have had the chance to find entertainment at social events and recreation with other conversations. However, we are obliged to lose another season. " criticized Grace.

"Now it's my fault?" Margaret questioned angrily as she kept staring at her sisters.

The argument between the sisters had reached an alarming level of tension. Margaret's outstretched neck gave way to a crimson face. Her younger sisters' provocation had paid off because Margaret's anger was evident.

"Yes." shouted the two sisters in amused chorus.

Rose and Grace stood for a second in silence after realizing the lack of grace they had tried to convey to their sister. They both stared at Margaret, and from the tension in their bodies they could tell that the older of the two was about to explode. Perhaps they had been too hard on their older sister. Just then, Margaret broke the silence with a loud laugh and her sisters followed suit.

"No doubt Lady Middleton has the ability to learn all the intimate secrets of Middleton society, and for that I admire her." Rose confessed as she finished her chilled cup of tea.

"Rose, my dear, you should admire people who have contributed something more interesting to the world and not a string of gossip and assumptions about affairs." Margaret decried her sister's behavior and shallow hobbies.

"Let the poor thing be infatuated and obsessed with what will make her happy, there is not much entertainment to occupy our time either, shall we say." suggested Grace at Margaret's criticism of Rose's behavior.

"Someday, I'll find out who Lady Middleton is." promised the youngest of the Westworth family solemnly. She was tenacious and constant in those things which captivated her interest, so she would certainly succeed.

With this firm promise made by Rose, and breakfast over, they all retired to their chores. Rose went out into the garden to gather the fruit of the rose hips, whose branches were too wild, for the cook at the residence to make delicious jams. Grace resumed reading "The Lady of the Camellias," a romantic novel that her aunt had given her weeks before. And Margaret went to her bedroom.

After the death of the mistress of the house some years ago from severe fevers, young Margaret had been obliged to represent the family in society. For her, however, it was more of a punishment than a blessing.

Far from finding pleasure in ballroom dancing, voluminous costumes or seductive games with fans, the eldest of the Westworth sisters just wanted to get through another season without being the focus of prying eyes.

In spite of her stern attempts to keep out of the limelight, her pale complexion and long dark hair were always commented on at every social gathering, her company requested at every dance, and her words flattered in every conversation. The mothers of all young gentlemen of marriageable age adored her social position, her fortune and, of course, the sensuality with which her hips and breasts accompanied a pretty face.

The elders of other families were grateful for her wisdom and formality, for she could match any male in confidence and assurance. The young unmarried men both craved and rejected her coarse and biting remarks about their gender. It was bad behavior for any young woman of good family and reputation who wished to marry in any social circle.

But it was her defiant demeanor that made her such an attractive young woman to the handsome young men, who each week tried to approach her father to curry his favor. However, despite the intentions of Margaret's aunt, her dear father, and her late mother, Margaret Westworth had no desire to find a husband. She did not wish to give her life to any person who was not worthy of her heart, and would therefore wait for the right time, even if it deprived her sisters of the possibility of entering society, and of finding relief and amusement in social intercourse.

In a few days the new social season would begin, and young ladies all over the county would be ordering new dresses, shoes, and ribbons to decorate their bodies to please the eyes of interested parties. And there was Margaret Westworth, sitting on her bed in her swanky bedroom, looking out of the window with a neat letter in her hand, and wondering why she should wait any longer.

CHAPTER 2

19 June 1876
Middleton, England

The end of spring was a long awaited time for every family in the county. The cold winter and the restless spring were behind us and the warmth began to rise each morning. The fires in the hearths were replaced by carriage rides, walks in the parks, and wonderful ballroom dancing. And, of course, it was the beginning of the season of social events.

"Dear Margaret, I have been waiting about three hours for Mrs. Pickman to attend to me in the shop. I have already ordered all your dresses for the season. I am sure that if we can get rid of those coarse manners of yours, and you get used to saying nice words, or rather not to talk so much, we may get a good husband for you this season."

Beatrice Miller was the only aunt of the Westworth sisters. A strong-willed and temperamental woman with only one mission in life: to win the marriage of her late sister's three daughters.

She had given her word on her dear sister's deathbed, and so, year after year since Margaret's debut in society, she had tried to fulfill her promise of securing for her a worthy and advantageous marriage. The great reluctance of her eldest niece, however, was a drawback which she had not counted upon, and which gave her more than one headache.

"Dear aunt, it would be wiser of you if you decided to give up this task for the good of all." Margaret admired her aunt's efforts to find her a husband, but deep down she resented the fact that her terms were not accepted. No one understood her reluctance to remain unmarried.

"No, Margaret, it is you who should stop sabotaging all our attempts to find you a good match," her aunt commented angrily as she tapped her shoulder lightly with her hand-embroidered fan. I don't know if you've noticed, but you're twenty-four years old and after turning down two suitors whose proposals were most honest and sincere, I don't think you have any more chance of finding someone who wants to be with you. Every young man in this county knows your temperament. "Beatrice looked triumphantly at her niece believing she had uttered the exact words that would get Margaret to yield to her requests, but she was wrong."

"Maybe that's what I am trying to achieve." Margaret replied proudly as she crossed her arms indicating to her aunt that the battle was over.

"Oh, my dear, don't talk nonsense. It is possible that the family's well-to-do position may have given you the wrong idea of your situation, but would you deprive your sisters of a family just because you do not wish to find a husband?

"But..." Margaret hated it when her aunt tried to make her feel guilty for the lack of solidarity she was showing towards her sisters. Her words made her feel bad because they made her debate between her duty to herself and to her sisters.

"You well know that they cannot enjoy certain social privileges as long as you are not betrothed or married. Your father's business is profitable, but do you think they will be able to support three unmarried daughters for many years?"

The young Westworths' mother had passed away years before, and though they were still very young and the grief would always be there, Margaret could not help feeling hurt whenever she saw her dear aunt angry with her. The resemblance she shared with her mother was great, and when she looked into her mother's eyes she felt that she was letting down the person who had given her life, too.

Her aunt enjoyed a good position in society and as, unfortunately, she had not been able to conceive any children, she had consolidated her motherhood by taking care of her sister's three daughters and for this Margaret was very grateful.

Margaret's aunt was right, she was always right, to her chagrin She could no longer punish her younger sisters for her decision to refuse any male attention. Of course she had appreciated the overtures of those young gentlemen during the past season. They were gentlemen of good reputation and family who would guarantee her a life away from financial worries. She had known both men for years and had engaged in numerous conversations and shared dinners in their homes. The respectability of their intentions was beyond question. Margaret knew, however, that she could not find happiness at either of their sides.

Her late mother confessed to her one day, shortly before she died, that happiness in marriage is something that is built little by little, day by day, with delicacy and effort. But Margaret didn't want to wait so long to feel her body vibrate when she met this person.

On the other hand, she also longed to experience the love and passions that awaken bodies and hearts to find the right person. She had never felt her heart beating wildly, her stomach shrinking, or the shyness of a crossed gaze. The love books she treasured so dearly from her mother showed her a path that had been unknown to her until now. She longed for it. She longed for it. But perhaps, not with anyone she met in the county.

Although she was torn between the longing to find true love and the freedom to rule her own destiny, she was convinced that the truth would be revealed to her at some point and she would know which path to choose. But until that time came, she had to fulfill her duties as a daughter.

" All right, aunt, I will attend Mr. and Mrs. Abbey's concert. " Margaret finally yielded to the pressure.

"An excellent decision Margaret." said an ecstatic Aunt Beatrice after achieving her goal. "I have a feeling that this season will be the one. I'm sure a young gentleman will catch your eye and you will be able to give up that negative attitude."

"I hope so, aunt."

The days passed too easily at Westworth House in the early summer. Beatrice, Margaret's aunt, whose residence was only a few minutes away, was in and out of the great Westworth house on countless occasions.

Boxes of headdresses, high-quality muslin gowns, elaborate embroidery, and simple shoes were some of the humble investments the family had made through her. Margaret didn't understand the point of buying new dresses when the previous season's bespoke suits were waiting in pristine condition.

It seemed that all the ladies found pleasure, according to their dear sisters and their aunt, in buying new accessories that would decorate their bodies and make them more conspicuous than other young ladies in the county and, of course, more beautiful in the eyes of gentlemen of marriageable age.

Of course, Grace and Rose were excited about the big season. Their aunt had informed them that next year they would debut as the prettiest young ladies in the whole county, as their sister was to find a husband during the coming season. Because of this, they were obliging and proper in their treatment of their sister. They didn't want to pressure her, nor take her comments as a joke. A big gamble on Beatrice's part.

To Margaret's surprise, Friday had arrived. The concert at the Abbey residence was the event of the summer, no doubt about it. Not only did it mark the beginning of the social festivities, but it determined the fashion that would govern the whole season.

Her sisters had not been invited. Mr. and Mrs. Abbey had only extended the invitation to Mr. Westworth, Margaret, and Beatrice Miller. So the young ladies were embarrassed.

Mrs. Abbey enjoyed the fortune of her husband's textile business quite comfortably and this was reflected in the ostentation of her entire residence and herself.

So when Margaret entered on her aunt's arm and accompanied by her father, she couldn't have felt more out of place.

Despite the comfort that the family income afforded her, she had been brought up in moderation and financial prudence. She would never be short of money if she remained at her father's side, but she was not given to boasting about it to others. Fortune and the social recognition it brought could be fleeting, and that, unfortunately, she knew all too well.

"What do my eyes see? Is it Margaret Westworth?" asked Mrs. Abbey, in a jocular tone, as she approached Margaret and her aunt.

"When your aunt confirmed that the three of us were going to the concert, I could hardly believe it. Mr. Abbey couldn't believe it either, but here you are, gorgeous as always." Mrs. Abbey mentioned excitedly.

"Thank you very much for the invitation, Mrs. Abbey." Sometimes, social etiquette allowed for the snide remarks of uneducated people to be silenced, so Margaret was quick to thank her for the invitation.

"Of course, a young girl as beautiful as you can't miss an event like this. It's the best concert of the season, but of course, I'm not saying it myself, look at everyone in the audience."

Mrs. Abbey was vain, self-centered, and a person with a certain predisposition to comment on anything or anyone who attracted her attention. Of course, her advantageous position in society thanks to the business and income her husband provided allowed her certain luxuries and to be forgiven for her impertinence.

The trail of Margaret's coral-colored dress was followed by all eyes in the room as her figure passed through the rooms. The comments were whispered, barely audible but annoying. The gossip section of the paper had warned, or rather revealed to the whole county, that the young lady did not wish to marry, and had thus made her the centre of malicious comment.

Margaret's delicate, slender body was admired by the mothers of many of the young Middleton girls. Her fair complexion in which a blush was allowed to show, her long, untamed hair, her small, coquettish breasts, and even her curvaceous hips were a delight to behold. Her aunt had chosen a dress that was tight in the parts to be highlighted and flowing at the hips so that her niece's figure would shine in the crowd.

Aware of the reaction the young woman was provoking in the gentlemen in the room, Beatrice Miller watched the glances that came as they moved around the room. Some of the young men had interrupted their conversations to avert their faces, and even the ladies were curious and envious.

"Without a doubt, dear niece, you are the most beautiful young lady tonight," Beatrice Miller remarked with scant humility, as she fixed a slight wrinkle she had found in her niece's gown. I would not be surprised if young gentlemen lined up to ask for your hand for the ball."

"It's possible that such an event happened a few seasons ago, but now I'm sure there will be other, more interesting young women."

That was true. Over the years, the rejection of other young men and the confirmed rumor that she did not wish to marry made her an attractive young woman to any gentleman. However, her appearance that night and the beauty and simplicity she conveyed conveyed something very different.

"You underestimate the power of the forbidden." said her aunt as she loosely opened a fan so that she could bring air and intimacy to the conversation.

"What do you mean?" Margaret asked curiously as she repeated the same gesture as her aunt with the fan.

" A colt that is hard to catch is more exciting than a tamed mare." Her aunt's voice was a whisper that came to her ears like a great unknown, for she was unable to decipher its meaning.

"I don't get it."

"You'll understand." resolved her aunt, fanning hard to get more air into her face.

Margaret could not make sense of her aunt's words. She didn't seem to understand where she stood in the metaphor her aunt had used.

But whatever her intention, it was no help to her to get through that long and tedious night in which she was sure to have to smile and thank invitations from people she wasn't interested in.

From her position, Margaret surveyed everyone present and was able to recognize some familiar faces. She was glad to see that the elder Johnson had recovered from his riding accident and that his leg was healthy again. It struck her that Penny Jones had lost quite a lot of weight and she considered that the rumors about their engagement breaking off might be true. She hated to give Lady Middleton the nod, but apparently that mysterious lady had ears everywhere. But most of all, she was glad to see several people with whom she had a close relationship at the end of the room.

At the back of the room, stood Thomas Rogers, a gentleman only a few years older than Margaret who had been secretly in love with her for years. The young man was the eldest son of a family with close ties to Margaret's, since they had been fortunate enough to grow up together. When the time came, Thomas had asked for several dances during the season, and even, after what he thought was Margaret's good nature, had asked Mr. Westworth for his daughter's hand.

As tradition dictated, and after assuring himself of the truth of the young man's intentions, Margaret's father had accepted, desirous of further strengthening the ties with his dear friend Rogers. However, the liaison did not take place.

The young man raised his glass in the air as a salute to Margaret, and she returned it with a slight nod. The people inferred, after the fatal outcome, that the young man had an unhealthy hatred for Margaret, but nothing could be further from the truth. Thomas's interest had turned to friendship after understanding Margaret's reasons. She felt the need to justify to the young man, whom she considered her friend, the reasons for her rejection. This made Thomas respect her even more. From that moment on, the two had resumed their friendly relationship as if nothing had happened. Thomas tried hard not to show his feelings to his friend, and Margaret tried to pretend that she didn't notice some of the soulful looks that came from her friend.

Mr. Abbey announced the beginning of the concert, and urged his guests to take their seats in the great hall which had been so elegantly and carefully prepared by his wife and the servants. There were only about twenty chairs for the ladies, while the men had to stand. In front of the guests' area were the musicians who were preparing themselves and their instruments for the evening.

The gentlemen were stationed behind the chairs and around the chairs along the wall so as not to miss any of the details. Margaret took a seat in the second row next to her aunt and other young ladies.

The concert began and everything fell absolutely silent. Although the young woman was not a fan of social gatherings, she had to admit that enjoying a good concert was something worth getting out of her isolation for.

Margaret closed her eyes and let the music intoxicate her. Silently, her heart swayed and danced to those notes. She felt that those chords spoke to her, only to her, and invited her to talk and share secrets. It was a gift to be able to enjoy that moment.

After a few minutes, when the first of the songs ended, Margaret opened her eyes to applaud. A woman's applause should be demure, but sometimes Margaret forgot her manners and got carried away, as she did at that moment. When the whole audience fell silent again to begin a new tune, Margaret turned her face to look for her father, and her gaze met two brown eyes that watched him intently.

For a few moments, Margaret didn't blink. She just looked and let herself look. The owner of those eyes was a tall, handsome young man who would undoubtedly steal the sighs of all the young women during the evening. Margaret forgot to breathe and for a moment, she felt what she had hoped for, her stomach shrunk.

She felt a strange bond with those eyes and the young man who wore them. The young woman turned her face sharply to focus her attention on the concert, but she could not. She couldn't focus on any of the songs that followed. She closed her eyes to try to let herself be carried away, but that face kept coming back to her mind.

To Margaret's own surprise and embarrassment, the gentleman kept admiring her face every moment she clandestinely sought his gaze. She could not help feeling like a little girl. She would turn her face expecting him to be looking at her and at the same time, criticize his behavior for being unbecoming.

However, she was fascinated.

The stranger must not have belonged to the county, for she knew each and every heir and son of the surrounding lords at her aunt's great insistence. So, when the whole hall was filled with a general applause from the audience at the cessation of the music, Margaret, holding her aunt's arm, sought a place where she could talk over the concert with other guests.

"Beatrice Miller, I beg your pardon for the intrusion, but I would like to introduce you to someone."

At the same time that Margaret and her aunt were conversing freely with other ladies in the room, Mr. Abbey had walked up to them, accompanied by a young man. Margaret turned to them and was speechless.

His eyes.

It was him.

CHAPTER 3

19 June 1876
Middleton, England

"Mr. Bright, I have the honor to present Mrs. Beatrice Miller and her lovely niece, Margaret Westworth."

Margaret knew she should accompany her aunt in greeting the newcomer but her body was unable to respond. This disoriented the young woman, who always knew how she should behave in every situation and felt in control of every moment.

"Ladies, William Bright has just leased the old Knight house, and after receiving your visit only a few days ago, I felt that the rest of Middleton should enjoy such pleasant company," Mr. Abbey introduced the ladies. I hope they will make you feel at home.

"I thank you again for the invitation, Mr. Abbey. I did not expect this kind reception when I have scarcely finished signing the papers with Mr. Knight." thanked Mr. Bright very politely.

"Don't talk nonsense. Mr. Knight wouldn't rent his family home to anyone who wasn't trustworthy so, if old Knight trusts you, we should too. There's no harder man than old Knight."

Margaret had not heard any of Mr. Abbey's words, her gaze and her whole body no longer belonged to him. They had another owner now. Mr. Bright. However, the young man was looking at the different people in the group during the conversation, almost ignoring the presence of poor Margaret.

"And tell us, Mr. Bright, what has brought you to Middleton?" asked Margaret's aunt curiously as she came towards him gradually drawing her niece nearer. He was an unattached young man, it seemed, who might be a suitor for her young niece.

"Business. I have recently inherited my late father's title and business and have decided to settle in Middleton and invest in a new area."

Mr. Bright's voice was firm and sure, confident and direct. This attracted the attention of Margaret, who was accustomed, on occasion, to deal with young people of limited linguistic resources or lip.

"In Middleton?" asked Beatrice Miller curiously. It was well known throughout Middleton County that it possessed one of the strongest groups of businessmen and the most prosperous businesses in the area. But she was struck by the young man's enterprising initiative in an industry controlled by middle-aged men with far more business experience.

"Of course, don't be surprised Mrs. Miller, before settling in this county I commissioned market research and the results were very encouraging. The local market offers ample business opportunities and I hope my age will be the impetus for me to stand out." Bright's voice was very self-assured. Margaret was surprised at how fast his lips were moving and how little he had understood about it all despite being in his element.

"A great opportunity for you, no doubt. And am I to presume that Mrs. Bright will arrive in the course of the week?" Beatrice Miller's prying had no bounds, nor did she understand modesty. Her remark, awkward and impolite towards the young man, was enough to engage the interest of Margaret, who had hitherto witnessed the scene like a motionless doll.

It was obvious that his aunt's intention was to know whether there was a Mrs. Bright or whether, on the contrary, he might be an interesting match to be reckoned with. There was no ring on his hands to show that he was attached to a lady, and the mere absence of a lady from his arm communicated too much to Aunt Beatrice.

"I must confess to you, Mrs. Miller, I have not. I have not yet found the person to share my life with. My father was ill for years and I had to take over the family business, but... " he said, shifting his gaze from Mrs. Miller's wrinkled eyes to Margaret's flaming, lively gaze. "I hope Middleton will allow me to establish more than just a thriving business. I have my hopes pinned upon it."

"Then you will find no better place than Middleton to marry in. Our county is very varied and you are sure to meet a young lady who will catch your eye." Beatrice insisted as she lightly tapped Mr. Bright's chest with her fan eliciting a smile from all present. She wanted her niece to react in some way. She had never seen her so absent or so unwilling to enjoy a conversation about business as that one.

"No doubt."

There was so much force in those words that Margaret felt her whole body tremble as they were spoken. As her eyes remained focused on the floor of the room, she cursed herself for not having been able to utter a single word in Mr. Bright's presence. She did not understand how she, who had always been confident and self-assured, now felt like a frightened little bird. She was sure that any chance of a word with him would have vanished on the evening breeze.

"If you'll excuse me, I think I've monopolized your attention for too long tonight. I should feel guilty if I deprived you of other people's company." apologized Mr. Bright.

"You are very polite."

Although Mrs. Miller was desperate to find a life partner for her niece, she did not encourage the young woman to converse during the meeting with Mr. Bright. Deep in her heart she knew that her niece, inexperienced in the ways of love, would not be able to attract this young man.

There was something in his manner, in the way he had provoked her with his words when he spoke of his dual intentions in settling in Middleton that alerted Beatrice Miller that perhaps this man was too much for her niece.

Thomas Rogers approached Margaret to invite her to enjoy the next song. Of course, the young man waited for Margaret to receive and accept other requests before soliciting her attentions. His pride as a man did not wish to be hurt when society's comments branded him as still in love with the young lady. Therefore, he concluded that three dances were enough.

Margaret with a big smile accepted Thomas's hand and together they approached the dance floor to dance with other couples. At times she had wondered if in some way she might not have been happy with the young man. He was attentive, polite, and possessed a facility for conversation, though he was also shy and sweetly awkward. He could have been a good husband and their marriage would have been full of laughter like the ones they were sharing on the dance floor. However, something very important was missing. Passion.

As soon as the dance was over, Margaret felt a presence as she bade young Rogers an affectionate and joyous farewell.

"Miss Westworth, will you accept my invitation to the next dance?" asked a deep, serious voice from behind her.

"Yes." Margaret replied without thinking as she turned around to check that she had not been mistaken in her inquiries as to the owner of that mysterious voice.

Bright offered his arm to the young woman to return together to the track. There, as per protocol, they separated to take their places facing each other in two rows. When the music began to play, all the dancers paid their respects with a simple bow and began the dance.

Margaret felt unable to initiate conversation with her partner as her mouth was as dry as sand. She had never been in the presence of someone so intimidating and to her surprise, it was disconcerting. She, who prided herself on controlling conversations with her dance partners and even, instilling a slight fear in them that would lead them to keep their distance from her, now felt like a fawn. Scared.

"Do you like to dance, Miss Westworth?" asked Bright at last. His words elicited a response from Margaret who looked up to gaze again into those brown eyes.

"Of course." replied relieved the young woman who appreciated the initiative of her dance partner, but tried to reproduce the piece exactly to avoid being the center of comments and gossip for a possible error of steps.

"And have you enjoyed the previous pieces?"

"I have certainly been fortunate in having excellent dancing partners," commented Margaret in an animated manner feeling more comfortable with the conversation as she saw that Mr. Bright was commenting on trivial things that she could control. "Mr. Rogers is very skillful."

"Of that I have no doubt." replied Mr. Bright roughly. "It has been striking to observe how they exchanged glances and smiles in spite of the fact that I have heard that he turned you down last season. Let me tell you that it is not a very polite attitude on his part, to encourage the feelings of a young man in love in that way.

"I beg your pardon?" Margaret was incredulous at the stranger's accusations, and for a moment, alarmed at the rudeness she had noticed in his words, she lost track of the steps she was to follow in the dance.

That simple but scathing remark was enough to rouse Margaret from her stupor. If there had been a moment when she had wanted to make the brown-eyed young man's attentions her own, it was all forgotten when a surge of anger prompted her to start an argument. The young gentleman hardly knew her, and he had dared to judge her without any compunction.

Mr. Bright had no right to judge her, and with his remark he had started an argument which Margaret was prepared to win.

"You mustn't apologize, but pay attention," Bright went ahead to comment. The young man you were dancing with is still in love with you and accepting his hand for the dance does nothing but encourage you to continue to expect his smiles. You should not be so selfish, allowing him to find someone else willing to accept your attentions is the benevolent thing to do."

Bright's reproach didn't stop the dance between the two of them, even though Margaret had made some mistakes in her turns and clapping. She couldn't believe it. She had overdone it.

"Who do you think you are to say these things to me?" At last Margaret had come to her senses and with a strength that came from within her body she rebuked the young man, "You are not my father to scold me or have more moral attitude than me. Do you think I haven't noticed how you enjoy the looks of all those young women? You're fascinated. You like to be the center of attention. You can't reproach me that other men might find me attractive or desire my attention."

"Of course, every woman in this room wishes they were on this dance floor with me now, and yet I am with you."

Bragging about how he was able to catch the amorous glances of the young women in that room was not a very gentlemanly attitude for a young man, much less in front of a young lady.

"And should I be grateful for that, Mr. Bright?" Margaret asked, shocked at her dance partner's overbearing comment. It annoyed her that he thought himself so superior to her.

"Certainly, no doubt about it. However, I am here with you." Mr. Bright's ego was such that Margaret doubted if the rest of the guests would fit in the room

"Why?" the doubt consumed Margaret.

"Because they don't enjoy music like you do."

"What do you mean?" Margaret longed for the answer, and at the same time was repulsed by the interest with which he awaited her. The man's haughty attitude was odious, but she could not help feeling captured by his gaze.

"At first I thought I was asleep, but then I realized I was experiencing the music in a different way." he had noticed Margaret during the concert. Their exchange of glances was not accidental. "Maybe we should ask them to play for us privately, and I'll show you the power my eyes awaken."

Bright took advantage of the proximity that the piece offered, to take with force and determination the hips of his young companion — who took that initiative as the rupture of the elegance and education of every gentleman. Margaret, angry and frustrated by the gentleman's attitude, tried to stop the dance.

"You are a scoundrel." accused the young woman between her teeth to avoid attracting the attention of the rest of the attendees.

"He hasn't seen anything yet."

Middleton Post. June 20, 1876

Dear readers,

Yesterday marked the start of summer in the county and with it, the long-awaited husband-hunting season for mothers. Of course, there is no season without the soporific concert of Mr. and Mrs. Abbey. A select group of guests were able to enjoy, if I may say so, an optimal social gathering for the search for an advantageous marriage. To our surprise, and that of more than one young man, the eldest of Mr. Westworth's daughters, Margaret, a veteran of the social seasons, delighted all present with a beautiful coral dress and a radiant smile. We don't know whether the reason for such happiness was the amusing dance she shared with Rogers, the young man whose heart she so severely broke last year, or the intense but heated dance with a new and mysterious young man.

This season is going to be interesting, girlfriends.

The hunt for the newcomer begins.

Lady Middleton

CHAPTER 4

20 June 1876
Middleton, England

Margaret had scarcely been able to sleep once she had arrived home after the concert at the Abbey house. Her father, oblivious to any rumors or happenings in the Abbey household, only wished to go to bed to get out of his uncomfortable, tight shoes. For her part, Margaret's aunt appreciated every invitation her niece had accepted as a symbol of her commitment to the family engagement.

She was elated at the attention he had paid her and his confidence in the promising future of this season had brightened her evening and made her return with a big smile. Margaret, however, was not going to keep a happy memory of that first party of the season thanks to a conceited gentleman who had thought himself morally superior to judge her and, moreover, to make her feel fortunate that he had invested his time in dancing with her.

"Damn William Bright. How dare he insult me like that, does he even understand the nature of my relationship with Thomas? It is insulting, demeaning that he treats me as if I were a young woman who wishes to create longing in men. I have never encouraged Thomas to think there was more between us than friendship, and he has respected that. Margaret paced back and forth across the room, trying to quell her foul mood as she revealed her indignation to a long-lived night "Bright is vain and presumptuous. There's no doubt about it."

What had happened to Bright only laid bare the belief that Margaret had consolidated over the years that some souls are confusing to know, for outward beauty sometimes masks the darkness of the soul that possesses it. Margaret felt deceived and angry, for she had thought those eyes were worthy of a noble gentleman and not such an ungracious young man.

Such a haughty attitude was likely to attract the attention of young girls eager for love and attention, but Margaret, who had taken care to occupy and cultivate her mind to higher purposes than marriage, would not be so easily deceived by pretty eyes.

Morning came before Margaret knew it, and with it, the commotion in the great hall. She sent for one of the maids to help her dress and without any energy she went downstairs to meet her sisters.

"Rose, don't say anything, please." Grace's pleading voice was heard by her older sister even before she entered the dining room. Apparently, Grace and Rose were fighting over the morning paper.

"She needs to know. Lady Middleton speaks expressly about her, she needs to know."

"What should I know?" Margaret asked as soon as she entered the drawing room. Her sisters were suddenly speechless and neither were able to tell her sister that Lady Middleton had labeled her a striking and provocative young lady, or at least, that was her sisters' understanding.

"Come on Rose, what are you hiding back there?" It was a common pastime for sisters to run after each other while keeping secrets or letters. It was usual for Rose to hide the mail her older sister received. Every week the postman would deliver a letter to one of the maids and every week, the same scene was repeated between the girls.

Margaret ran after her sister round the table, and her sister laughed as she aired the page of Middleton's paper.

"Trust me sister, you don't want to read today's paper. " confirmed Grace, as she ate her breakfast calmly and nonchalantly while her sisters scurried around the room.

After several minutes, Margaret managed to steal the paper and turned her full attention to finding the damned gossip column of the local paper. Line by line her anger grew until she could hardly bear the astonishment.

"*...or the intense but heated dance with a mysterious new young man. Signed, Lady Middleton.* "How dare she insinuate that I accept the attentions of several men! What would that absurd woman know of me, Rogers, or Bright?" she suddenly fell silent, and when she seemed to have calmed down she tore the accursed paper into several pieces.

"Bright? So the mysterious young man Lady Middleton speaks of is real, quite a find!" proclaimed Rose as she jumped up and down like a young girl in love. "If you're angry it's because perhaps the lady is right."

"Reason? Reason? Oh, Rose..."

Margaret was completely beside herself.

I couldn't understand how a woman who might not have been present at that evening could have witnessed Bright's intense but embarrassing moment.

It was true that she had longed to share a dance with him, it was true that Margaret had trembled when he had held out his arm for her to rest it on, and it was true that she, though she would never admit it, had enjoyed every twist and every touch. Much to her regret that intensity had morphed into something darker when Bright had evidenced to her his alleged disregard for his friend's feelings or his lack of decorum in the social act when it came to closing his eyes.

"Margaret, Thomas Rogers may not have been the right young man for you, and the mysterious Mr. Bright may not be either, but let us tell you that the distant companion in your letters, neither is he."

"Excuse me? "Margaret asked dumbfounded as her sister covered her mouth with her hands.

Grace instantly regretted her words and clapped her hands over her mouth as Rose averted her eyes. The middle of the Westworth sisters had hurt her elder sister with her unfortunate remark about the recipient of her constants.

"What did you mean?" Margaret's feelings turned from anger to disbelief at the lack of respect for her privacy shown by her sister. Margaret looked at Grace and, expecting an explanation or apology for such a blunder, Grace opted to take the high road. She swallowed hard and crossed her fingers that she could say what she had long wanted to say to her sister without hurting her deeply.

"Sister, you have been waiting ten years for a young man who is not coming back." hurt created, Grace continued to tell her sister the truth. "Maybe you should allow someone else to own your affections. Move on and allow yourself to fall in love or maybe, just maybe, let someone else fall in love with you."

"You don't know what you're talking about." replied Margaret angrily as her eyes were torn between hysteria and tears.

With a blunt manner and without another word, Margaret left the room, leaving behind an embarrassed Grace, who still couldn't believe what she had just told her sister, and a speechless Rose, who, for the first time in her life, was at a loss for words.

The eldest Westworth, who had never been seen to shed tears after the death of her cherished mother, now broke down in soul-rending weeping. Margaret knew that her sister had spoken those words with no malice. But the secret of those letters was hers, hers alone, and she did not wish others to pry into them or to assess the truth of the sentiments they reflected.

More than a decade ago, a scandal ruined one of the Westworth's friendly families. This forced everyone to seek new opportunities in another county, but the scourge of gambling, betting and debt had tainted the members of the community. Lord Williams, his wife and three children left, and with them, the only true friendship Margaret had ever had.

Months later, Henry Williams, the middle child of the couple, sent his first letter. The young friends, in secret, had exchanged hundreds and hundreds of letters with confidences, anecdotes, and, above all, they had forged something that for Margaret was much deeper. On many occasions, she had wished that Henry would return to Middleton and occupy the old family home. But he never did, and she had been afraid to ask him, for she knew that family shame was a stigma Henry had inherited from his father, even if he did not share his terrible fondness for gambling. That is why, after hundreds of letters, Margaret had secretly given her heart to a young man she last saw at the age of eleven.

In the silence of her room, Margaret cursed herself for not being able to recognize that she could never consider another man as valid to be by her side except Henry even though that could never happen.

What her father, her aunt, her sisters, and even all Middleton demanded of her was but a utopia in their minds, for inside Margaret her heart had been given over to years of letters and confessions.

In one of the drawers of his wardrobe, inside a box, were the letters he had so lovingly kept. Sometimes he read and reread them to check that he had not lost any detail.

After perusing the last letter to regain the thread of the conversation, Margaret picked up several sheets of paper and her pen and began to write.

Dear Henry,

I would like to start today's letter by asking about your dear sister. You indicated in your last letter that she was not in good health so I hope that the good weather we are having may help her, although under your care, she will be better much sooner. Of course, how is your brother Marcus? I hope he is not giving you too much trouble lately.

How much I miss her! I barely have any memories of her but I am sure that she grew up with you full of love and brotherhood.

Summer has arrived in Middleton and with no stopping it, it's been filled with dresses, concerts, horse-drawn carriages and fake smiles. Last night I had the mischance to attend the first event of the season. The Abbey's, who I don't think you remember, put on a wonderful concert at their house. They are people who boast of their fortune and who resolutely accept any and all compliments. And I must confess that the concert was a treat for all music lovers, although it was everything else that continues to create a certain distaste in me.

After what has happened in previous seasons, I am still the target of comments and rumors. Sometimes I wish another young woman would be the one to catch the spotlight for another scandal that would overshadow my unwillingness to marry. But this town doesn't seem to want to change.

And, to add insult to injury, I was judged in a most indulgent manner by a gentleman who had just arrived at Middleton. His conversation was animated at first, but he soon revealed the very dastardly nature of his inner self. Quite frankly, a blight on this town.

There are still several months to go before the end of the season, and I had hoped with all my heart to avoid such an outcome, but I fear I have put off my duties as a daughter and as a sister for too long. I am my father's heir, and though he has had the misfortune of not having a son to carry on his legacy, I owe it to myself to marry so that I will no longer be a burden to him or my sisters. Of course, I will not give my hand to any gentleman who asks for it, as I have shown on previous occasions. This person must be upright in morals, cultured in conversation and sweet of heart.

I know I don't need to ask you not to judge my decision because I know you won't, but it is with much sadness in my heart that I must admit that the time has come. However, I still hope with longing that you can come to Middleton to save me from this unfortunate fate.

I sincerely hope you are all in good health at the beginning of the summer and I count the days until we can see each other.

A warm embrace,
Margaret Westworth

After writing those intense and revealing words to her friend Henry Williams, Margaret gently folded the sheets of paper into an envelope. She sealed the lines with wax and the family seal and wrote the address on the outside in neat, delicate handwriting.

Someone knocked on the door.

"Margaret, may I come in?" asked her sister Grace in a breathy voice.

"Yes..." Grace came in relatively slowly and saw her sister, lying on the bed with her face unhinged and a heaviness in her soul. Not only had her sister's harsh words taken their toll on her heart, but admitting to

Henry the painful truth of having to continue to follow the dictates of reason and accept a husband had completely shattered her.

She had only desired one person with all her heart in secret for years. At first, she hadn't realized it behind the innocence of his words, but as time passed, Henry's warm and soothing words had touched her in a very special way, cultivating deep and irreplaceable feelings. And now, at this very moment, she was giving him up for the sake of her family and her sisters' well-being.

"Sister, I didn't mean to say those words. Please forgive me."

Margaret's sister ran to the desk where she was and kneeling down took her hands in hers and wept, apologizing for her behavior.

"You're right, Grace." Margaret confirmed, cupping her sister's face in her hands. The young woman was in tears and although Margaret's own heart was broken, after admitting to Henry that she must accept the fate her position had in store for her, she did not want her sister's grief to taint their relationship. Her feelings for Henry had belonged to her in secret for far too long and, to her mind, they thought they had gone unnoticed by her sisters, but they had not.

Both sisters looked at the letter lying on the bedroom table that Margaret had so carefully sealed.

"For years I have believed that Henry would return to Middleton and dare to ask father for my hand, but he has not, and now".

"Excuse me ladies, you have a visitor. You are expected in the lounge." Said the housekeeper

The Westworth sisters were surprised at the announcement. It was an early hour in the morning, to make matters worse, too disrespectful an hour for a social call. Perhaps it was their Aunt Beatrice?

As they reached the lower level of the house, Margaret heard her father talking on the other side of his office, but continued on to the sitting room across the hall.

"It will then be a pleasure to us to have you present at dinner tomorrow at our humble home." Mr. Westworth's voice became clearer as he opened the office door.

Mr. Westworth was apparently accompanied by another person who was expected for dinner, but Margaret did not know his identity. It was certainly not her aunt, for she was in the drawing-room with Rose. Grace and Margaret greeted their aunt, and with some rapidity they all arranged themselves in the drawing-room to await Mr. Westworth and the visitor.

A few moments later, the girls' father entered the room with a brown-eyed gentleman.

Him.

When her dark hair and mischievous smile crossed the threshold of the room, every hair on Margaret's body stood on end. No one but Beatrice Miller witnessed the reaction of the young woman who from that moment on would eagerly capture her attention.

"My dears, I would like to introduce you to Mr. Bright. He will be joining us for dinner tomorrow as our guest, and I hope, of course, that he will enjoy our hospitality."

As decorum dictated, Mr. Westworth introduced his daughters to the visitor, and to the delight of two of them, joy filled the room. Their sisters, caught by Mr. Bright's beauty, were full of joy to enjoy his company for the evening, for it was not usual for them to have a variety of visitors at Westworth House.

"Father, are you sure it's wise to host a gathering at our house during the week when the social season has just begun? The other members of the community might be offended if they are not invited.

None of the possible motives her father could give her would lead her to agree to share a room with the gentleman again. After their meeting the night before at the concert, Margaret had decided to keep as safe a distance from him as possible and, above all, as the various social events would allow.

She could not believe that the man had been so kindly invited to her house after the ill-advised and petty behavior he had displayed the night before. But, as was obvious, that detail was not known to his father, who surely, without reservation, would have censured his guest's impudence.

"Don't be a prude, niece. This is a dinner party in our social circles. No one but Mr. Bright has been invited, it is understood that it is not a grand dinner but an intimate family gathering.

"But..."

"Margaret, my dear," interrupted Aunt Beatrice as she frowned and hardened the tone of her reproach to her niece," it would be advisable to utter no more words if you do not wish to offend our guest. You would be well advised to utter no more words if you do not wish to offend our guest.

Bright, who stood beside Mr. Westworth, smiled in amusement. The remonstrance of the girl's aunt and father afforded him an entertainment and an excuse which he would be ready to redeem to his advantage later on.

For her part, Margaret, indignant and annoyed within herself, had accepted silence as a form of obedience, though not of acceptance. Her nemesis looked across the room at her with a face of curiosity and provocation mingled with innocence and chivalry.

The rest of the Westworth sisters were introduced by their aunt and tried to make the guest feel more comfortable through questions about the weather during the morning, the way he had arrived at the house or even his shoes. No topic of conversation of any relevance or that would hold Margaret's attention.

When Bright bade farewell to the Westworth family, he addressed words to all the members... except Margaret, a fact that did not go unnoticed by Margaret or her Aunt Beatrice.

CHAPTER 5

June 21, 1876
Middleton, England

Margaret struggled to understand why her aunt and father were so willing to open their doors to Mr. Bright. After all, they had scarcely known him from a slight conversation at a social gathering at the Abbey home. They could not possibly have had time to form a strong opinion of him that would encourage them to invite him to more social events.

His sisters, unlike herself, were full of compliments ranging from the young man's apparent beauty and strength, to his his bearing and education. Compared with the other young gentlemen of the county, William Bright was worthy of attention and of being mentioned in the society pages. To Margaret, Bright was still insolent and ill-mannered, a fact which was reinforced by the absence of a formal and polite farewell at the previous morning's visit.

Margaret refused to accept that part of the blame for his unpleasant treatment was hers, but she suspected that his absolute and manifest refusal to accompany them to dinner that night was a reason for the young man's redress, and therefore for his anger. But what could Mr. Bright expect after his words at the ball?

He had accused her of being a young woman disrespectful of

other people's feelings without evidence or any knowledge of her person. Such lack of judgment or reflection was questionable, and Margaret felt it her right to be hurt and angry if she wished. The gentleman had not, at any time, shown the virtues which surround and should be shown by a decent gentleman.

"I hope, dear Margaret, that you will be able to show better manners in front of Mr. Bright this evening than you were able to use during yesterday." reproached Beatrice Miller sternly, to her niece "I am not able to ask you to nod at our guest's every remark and smile without reason, but I do not think it is too much to ask you to behave like a lady and engage him in cordial conversation."

"Aunt, I'm sorry if my behavior yesterday was undesirable." Margaret tried to apologize to her aunt because it wouldn't be the most coherent thing to contradict her.

"The desirable one?" Beatrice asked incredulously as she closed her fan. "I pray the young man did not misunderstand your words. Rumors that the elder Westworth is stubborn, obstinate, and rude will not contribute to the already arduous task of finding a suitable husband for you."

"I fail to understand why I should impress Mr. Bright. I have a pretty well formed opinion of him, and believe me, he does not want my affections, nor do I need what he can offer me."

"Of course, my dear. Of course." stated Aunt Beatrice opening the fan again to provide some air, or at least, so her niece thought.

Aunt Beatrice had gone to the family residence beforehand and while she helped her niece to dress she watched him carefully.

She couldn't believe the innocence she showed and inside she laughed serenely and cursed for not being the protagonist of such an unexpected possible romance.

Almost at dinner time, one of the maids announced the arrival of the expected gentleman. Dressed in a three-piece suit and a very smart hat, Mr. Bright entered the house. Mr. Westworth returned his greeting as the former removed his hat. The three sisters and Beatrice responded with a rehearsed curtsey.

"I must confess to you, Mr. Westworth, that it is a real pity we cannot have this dinner out of doors. The weather is delightful." At that instant, he turned his attention to Margaret, and she, meeting his gaze, froze. "Though it cannot compare with the exquisite young ladies with whom it is my privilege to dine tonight."

"Mr. Bright, please don't be so flattering. We do not deserve such words. "Blushes had come over the inexperienced faces of Mr. Westworth's little daughters, who had been greatly upset at the young gentleman's attentions, but fortunately Aunt Beatrice was able to reciprocate the gentleman's flattery.

"Farther from the truth, ladies, it's a pleasure. No doubt about it."

"Let's not stay in this part of the house, it's not so cosy. Please, Mr. Bright, let me ask you to join us in the living room. We shall be more comfortable there, and we can enjoy a pleasant conversation."

Mr. Westworth had always had a great appreciation of the company of his daughters and sister-in-law, but on this occasion it was the first time in a long time that he had been able to enjoy the company of another gentleman in his home, and he was not going to waste an opportunity of playing cards.

The ladies were seated in the different armchairs of the living room and, expecting to participate in a warm conversation, they waited for their aunt, as the oldest lady, to initiate the conversation and determine the main topic.

"We hope you had a good journey on your way to our home. We are delighted to be able to enjoy your company."

"In fact, it has been a most pleasant journey. Before moving to

Middleton I used the horse every moment. However, the peaceful life and closeness of the homes in this county has afforded me a pleasant walk. They have a very beautiful property."

"You have been fortunate enough to lease Mr. Knight's house. That property is the envy of the whole county." commented Margaret. The young woman, who loved the countryside and nature alike, tried to spend as much time as possible outdoors. Taking long walks, reading by the old trees and even helping to grow a small vegetable garden on her property. So when her long walks allowed, she would secretly go to the Knight estate to admire the expanse of its grounds.

"I couldn't agree with you more on how lucky I've been." Bright replied with a big smile on his face. His attitude had softened since the day before and he was proving to be flattering and even charming.

For a moment, it seemed that Margaret and Mr. Bright had found a common topic of conversation that did not generate tension between them.

"I'll wager there's no property like it in all Middleton." said Mr. Westworth with enthusiasm.

"I find no pleasure in gambling, but I would tell you that it is too large an estate for one man alone. I wish my brothers to come and live with me in a not very long time."

"Have you any brothers, Mr. Bright?" asked Rose cheerfully.

"Yes, of course. There are several of us. We grew up together, but unfortunately, in recent years, I haven't had the pleasure of their company. Sometimes business takes you away from your loved ones."

"I agree with you there, Mr. Bright. Building a business and turning it into something prosperous and profitable is not easy. God knows what sacrifices I've had to make in the past, but it was worth the effort."

"They say that the greater the effort the sweeter the reward."

The conversation with Mr. Bright was animated, and there was scarcely time for awkward silences. He was a young man with a facility for words, and there was no public more anxious to know than the Westworth family. They were not fond of rumor or gossip, but they considered it of vital importance to know their friends if they wished to continue to receive them in their home.

Margaret relaxed over dinner at Bright's pleasant manner with her sisters, her aunt, her father, and even with herself. For an instant, she forgave the young man for his ill-fated contact during the concert and the harsh words he had attributed to her. Perhaps it was the heat of the evening and the glasses of brandy or the dizziness of the dance that led to such an ill-advised remark. Perhaps there was something else about him that he had not been able to see with the naked eye.

Dinner, of course, was too copious and everyone agreed to return to the great hall for a little digestif.

"And tell me, Mr. Bright, would you care to play a game of cards with me? I rarely have the pleasure of enjoying this game of chance."

Mr. Bright looked at each of the people he shared the room with, he didn't seem very enthusiastic about the request at first, but as he smiled he asked Margaret to join them.

"But I have hardly any experience at cards. Besides, it's not very nice for a lady to play, it's a man's amusement." Margaret tried to excuse herself in every possible way. In the first place, because it was true that she had no skill at card-playing, for she had hardly devoted any time and effort to it, and, in the second place, she did not want to have the chance of the young man's new image changing her mind again.

"Luckily, no one outside the family is present at our soiree except me, of course, so your secret is safe."

Margaret looked at Bright hoping his request wasn't serious, but the calm smile on his face and the young man's arm raised toward her inviting them to join them told her otherwise. The young woman rose from her seat to settle herself across from her father and the young man. And with that, the game began.

Margaret was not a great gambler, for clarification, we might infer that she was not even a gambler. She did not tolerate gambling for fun, but she had learned to observe her father and other guests. For that reason, when several cards came into her hand she knew how to deal with them.

"Tell us, Mr. Bright, do you intend to remain at Middleton for a long season, or are you only passing through?" -the first to take sides in the conversation was Mr. Westworth, who had deftly dealt the cards from the deck, and was awaiting his guest's move.

"It will all depend upon the course business takes." he said as he looked up from his cards to Margaret, who found herself paying attention to the young man's poor ability to place the deck in his hand. At his surprise, Margaret ducked her gaze.

"Then we sincerely hope that your business will be prosperous because, although I don't know you in depth yet, I consider you to be a very interesting and educated young man.

"Thank you, Mr. Westworth, I hope your opinion is shared in the same way by others in the county. I would hate to be the center of ridicule, negative opinions or even rejection."

"Rejection?" asked the master of the house in surprise. "I am sorry to inform you that you have settled in a village, therefore you will now be the centre of comment, especially from the mothers of young ladies of marriageable age, but I doubt if I can consolidate a bad opinion of your person. You are a very handsome young man, isn't he, Margaret?"

Her father's words echoed in her head in different ways, but without commanding her to give an answer to such a question. When she gathered enough courage, the young woman spoke up.

"Father is right, Mr. Bright. It is with a heavy heart that I must confess that one of the things that shapes the character of a small community like this is its facility for creating gossip and spreading it. Besides, at the height of the social season, a gentleman like you will not go unnoticed."

Bright was surprised by the young woman's blunt remark. He had openly and clearly confessed that he found her attractive, or at least that he caught the attention of young women. It was a big step in his approach to the girl. He wanted to provoke a response from her and for the moment she was receptive to his attentions.

"From what I've been able to gather, there are a lot of people attending social events in Middleton."

"Yes, of course. The concert at Mr. and Mrs. Abbey's is one of the most popular of the season. No doubt those who enjoy the sympathy and affection of the couple are invited to attend.

"Certainly" Mr. Bright had understood the hidden message behind the words of the master of the house. If the Abbey family were so influential in the town and county, it was to be expected that the whole community would try to gain their attentions.

"Dear Margaret, it's your turn."

"Certainly, father." replied Margaret, trying to fix her attention again on the letters in her possession.

Margaret discarded one of the cards from the set she was holding, and then her father did the same. Mr. Bright took his time in choosing. He silently pored over the cards on the table under the watchful, nervous eye of Mr. Westworth, who was anxiously awaiting his turn.

"I hope to have invitations to the rest of the events, I would hate to be stuck at home when the community brings so much interest and joy to me."

"Don't worry about that, Mr. Bright." commented Margaret to cause relief in Bright's concern "If you received the Abbey's invitation to their concert, rest assured that the rest of Middleton will appreciate your presence. No doubt you will receive multiple invitations."

"You are very kind, Miss Westworth."

"Take heed of my dear daughter," interrupted Mr. Westworth, as he calculated the chances of hitting the card he wished to throw on the table," she knows the ins and outs of seasons in society.

When it was her turn, Margaret threw away the last card in her deck that didn't interest her, and in doing so, she created a winning combination. She revealed the resulting cards to the rest of the players who, amazed at how the newcomer to the table had dethroned Mr. Westworth.

"Look at that, Mr. Bright. We have a potential player before us!" shouted Mr. Westworth enthusiastically at the skill his daughter had shown. Pride.

"Don't say that father, it was just luck."

But luck was with Margaret for the next three hands to her dear father's bad loss.

"My dear daughter, I had hoped that the respect and affection you bear for my person would allow you to let me win just once." reproached Mr. Westworth with some embarrassment, as he was watched by the curious glance of Mr. Bright and his daughter.

"And would you feel good, father, if I had let you win?" she asked with a certain amused air to provoke a response from her father as she winked. She knew her father was not famous for either admitting to cheating at the table or accepting other people letting him win.

"Of course I do," said the master of the house with great alacrity, which caused a hearty laugh from Bright and Margaret. Soon Mr. Westworth joined them.

After several games of cards, Mrs. Miller called for the attention of the players to enliven the conversation she was having with her nieces, who were sitting on the sofas and were bored.

Soon the conversation became animated, and they were all able to enjoy some of Middleton's anecdotes and the events of the concert at the Abbey house. Margaret was enjoying Mr. Bright's visit, which led her to think that the tense moment she had shared with him had perhaps been the result of tension rather than of debauched or presumptuous behavior. Thus, as the evening began to take over, Margaret felt unhappy.

Young Margaret had to excuse herself to go to the toilet.
The tension that had slowly grown during the evening and the heat from the corset of her dress made Margaret feel more and more heated.

She refreshed the back of her neck with some water and repositioned a few strands of her hair that had come out of her hairpins. Before leaving, she looked at herself in the mirror, her cheeks were slightly flushed from the heat and her face reflected a mixture of curiosity, uneasiness and expectation.

As Margaret exited the bathroom, she bumped into the hard body of William Bright, who was waiting anxiously in the hallway. The young man gently grabbed Margaret as she tried to pull away from him and gently tucked one of her light locks behind her ear. The touch made the young woman uncomfortable, and she took a step back at Bright's bold behavior.

"That was unseemly, Mr. Bright," Margaret said, her voice strained but breathy as she tried to recover from the event. The proximity of the gentleman had surprised and inhibited her at the same time. With a tremor in her hands she tried to smooth the folds of her skirt.

"It may be that all the skill you show in play, dear Margaret, you lack in experience in love."

How was it possible that the young man could so radically change his behavior? Margaret had left the living room, leaving behind a proper, polite guest, and now there in front of her, in the darkness of the hallway of her home, stood an unseemly man.

How dare he say that to her when they had enjoyed such a pleasant conversation during those previous moments?

Whatever the answer, Margaret's mood had changed completely. His body, which had slowly managed to relax, was now as tense as a spring and as hot as a fire. Bright's touch had left her trembling, and it was something the gentleman had evidenced.

"You should learn, my dear, to play better. You must hide your feelings more easily than your cards." Bright decided to break the silence Margaret had interposed between them to laugh at the way she had responded to his action.

"Perhaps, Mr. Bright, you do not wish to have as much experience as you seem to show. It is ungentlemanly of you to boast of your conquests."

"Bragging? Who bragged? "Bright was confused by Margaret's comment. At no point had there been any reference to conquests, but Margaret needed to show that she wouldn't be intimidated if Bright tried to bully him like that.

"You yourself, Mr. Bright. If you suggest that my feelings are so easily revealed, it is because you have had the opportunity to provoke and test the reaction of more impressionable young men. And of course, you have enjoyed their misdeeds."

"I must confess that you have not been as impressionable as other ladies but yes, I have managed to generate a reaction in you that has captivated me."

"Women are not cards that you can put together in a deck and discard them when you don't need them."

"You are no letter, Miss Westworth."

Unexpectedly, and barely realizing that the tension of the moment had brought them within inches of each other, he grabbed Margaret's hips and pulled their bodies together as one, sealing them with a kiss. As expected, Margaret didn't know how to respond to this. Her body was tense and conflicted, and as she allowed William Bright's sensual lips to discover every nook and cranny of her soul, she thought of the reasons he had given her for hating him.

Margaret let out a sigh and that provoked a reaction in the young man who pressed his body even closer to hers and with a certain delicacy, ran his right hand over her face at the same time that she clung to Bright's hard torso to avoid falling to the ground. Margaret couldn't breathe. She couldn't think. Her whole mind was plagued by a young man and his intense kisses.

It was the first time her lips were loved, tasted, glorified. She felt so confused by everything she was experiencing that she didn't know how to react. She opened her mouth and let Bright play with her, reaching a state of complete daze.

Slowly and with a slight moan that came from Margaret's throat, William released his lover from the embrace that held her. She still had her eyes closed and was dazed and intoxicated by the moment.

He, for his part, found a certain pleasure in her state. He looked at her with his eyes wide open, not losing sight of the beauty that dominated this innocent woman who had just given him one of the greatest gifts of all.

Middleton Post. June 22, 1876

Dear readers,

I couldn't be more excited and pleased by the rumors that have reached my humble ears and that I so eagerly wish to share with you.

Mr. Bright was invited to dinner by none other than Mr. Westworth. It is well known to all that the eldest of his daughters is in her last social season. Although this is not a truth that has been spoken aloud, we all know that there is not much chance of her finding a husband at her age. Will that be old Westworth's intentions? Will Bright fall into the snatching and devastating nets of Miss Margaret Westworth? Perhaps we should ask young Thomas what he thinks about this possible relationship.

I'll keep an eye on the news

Lady Middleton

CHAPTER 6

22 June 1876
Middleton, England

Lady Middleton's impudence would have eclipsed Margaret Westworth's attention and fury if her whole mind had not been focused on that kiss. Her lips burned as well as her cheeks. William Bright returned to the drawing-room after their meeting, leaving her stunned. Her legs, shaky and sluggish, could not of their own accord make it to the drawing room where the rest of her family waited impatiently. It took her several minutes to compose herself, to regain her composure and make her way back to the living room. Only a few moments after they were reunited, Mr. Bright took a polite farewell with barely a glance at Margaret or a word of encouragement before he departed.

It was that silence that confused the young woman. What had that kiss meant? It had certainly been an unplanned outburst on his part, the result perhaps of provocation between them. There had been obvious tension during the card game, and Margaret understood that some of the comments he had offered her father were aimed at her.

But he didn't understand how he hadn't said a word after their meeting. Had it not been satisfactory?

Margaret was unable to divert her attention from any of the tasks that usually occupied her time in the morning. She replayed that shared moment over and over again. Silently, when no one was watching, she touched her lips as she closed her eyes. It was as if they still held the memory of the night, as if they longed for him. They wished to be possessed again. And Margaret longed for it too.

The man had aroused an interest in her, it was obvious. His lack of decorum and formality, and of course, the reaction he generated in her was enough to give him a preferential place on her list of candidates. This was against all norms. That meeting should not have taken place. No company, no chaperones. She had broken every social norm. If someone had found them, it would have ruined them both, and they would have been forced to unite their lives forever. Was that what Margaret wanted?

"It was a pleasure to enjoy Mr. Bright's company, wasn't it Margaret?" asked Mr. Westworth to his daughters at luncheon, "He is a very polite and courteous gentleman. I am sure his good sense will lead him to set up a thriving business in the area. It would be interesting to help him."

"Of course, Father. Mr. Bright is intelligent, gifted in speech and oratory, and has interesting anecdotes to share. A worthy guest, no doubt," Rose expounded. Margaret's sister looked uneasy at the previous evening's visit, and her sister's predisposition to Bright's smiles made the elder of them all the more angry.

Rose would be impressed by any young man who showed the slightest interest in her.

She was not given to reflection or questioning or censuring her behavior, but let her feelings come out when they needed to and that, in some circumstances, had brought her more than one problem.

"A great friendship, no doubt "commented the father of both "If the rules between gentlemen and education has not died I hope to receive an invitation from you, it would be the right thing to do."

Mr. Westworth's announcement caused excitement in Rose and great awe in Margaret. Would she have to see him again? How would she react to being in front of him? She had no answers to any of her questions, but only one thing was clear to her, she dreaded and longed to see him again.

"Margaret, this afternoon we might take a walk to old Knight's estate, perhaps we may hasten such a letter. What say you, sister? "Rose's desire to provoke a meeting with the young man who now occupied Margaret's thoughts left her confused.

"Decided, we'll go this very afternoon without delay" decided Grace amused. Besides, Bright confessed that he finds pleasure in walking around the property.

"You will come with us, won't you sister?"

"Of course, I will go with you. I wouldn't miss an opportunity to admire the property in question."

After teatime, and in a very pleasant temperature, the three sisters set out for a walk through the village towards old Mr. Knight's property.

Margaret had not been able to successfully gather her hair. Her fingers were trembling and she was unable to comb her hair to make herself presentable. Nor did she wish any valet to see her in this state of nervousness and jump to strange conclusions. It was just a walk.

Margaret had always admired the estate. In the centre of a vast expanse of countryside stood a small lake and, just beside it, a beautiful house. It could not be said that Mr. and Mrs. Knight were lacking in fortune, for the house was in impeccable condition, and it was well known that the interior decoration was exquisite. But it was not the interior of the house that appealed to Margaret's senses, it was the nature that surrounded the property.

Suddenly, Grace grabbed her two sisters by the arm and dragged them at a run to the entrance. They crossed a long dirt road that led to the front door and were met by one of the servants.

"Good morning to you, can I help you with anything?" asked the man with extreme politeness and bowing his head respectfully.

"We are Mr. Westworth's daughters. Last night we had the pleasure of welcoming Mr. Bright to our home and after our daily walk we have decided to return his visit in the hope that he would be able to show us around the property.

Although the young man had promised to accompany the sisters through the grounds to show them every nook and cranny, no date had been set.

"I am sorry to point out to you ladies that Mr. Bright has left the property and I am unable to indicate when he plans to return."

Had Mr. Bright left? He had made no remark during the evening to indicate his immediate absence from the town. It seemed that his desire to establish a business in Middleton, and to find a companion in life, encouraged him to remain at the Knight residence.

"It's a real pity," said a very dejected Rose.

"Excuse me, sir. Has Mr. Bright left any note or errand for any of his neighbors? "the question slipped carefully out of Margaret's mouth. She did not wish her sisters to hear her sad tone. She was sure the young man would have left behind him some lines explaining his departure.

"I'm afraid not, Miss Westworth," replied the servant, who seemed more interested in ending the conversation and returning to his duties than attending to the young ladies who seemed dejected by the departure of their handsome master. "I have no note to deliver."

No note? At that moment Margaret's world grew a little darker. William Bright and she had shared, in her view, an intimate if fleeting encounter, and though Bright's petty behavior prompted her to think it obvious that he would not leave a note for her, she longed to believe in the good and polite words he had shown at dinner.

A struggle gripped Margaret, who didn't know if Bright was a libertine toying with her or a gentleman who didn't know how to handle the situation.

Grace and Rose took their sister by the arm and encouraged her to go home and enjoy the evening. Margaret, for her part, let her sisters talk about the forthcoming events and dances at Middleton while she thought of the young man.

Margaret wanted to go home and lock herself in her bedroom. Luckily, the next social gathering wouldn't take place until Thursday, so she would have time to recover.

She had not discovered how profound the young man's influence was upon her until her heart was overwhelmed by the butler's words.

Part of her wanted Bright to be the one to open the doors of that house and, offering his arm, show her around the property. But on the other hand, she hated him for leaving without leaving a note.

Had their meeting the night before meant so little that he was able to leave without leaving a few lines for her? He might not dare to go to her house to make his situation clear, but at least a few words. Nothing. There was nothing.

Had their kiss not been satisfying? Margaret may not have been skilled in the arts of love, but she had felt a special connection between them during that kiss and even before, when their eyes had shown the desire growing between them.

But maybe it was for the best. Maybe she had exalted what that moment had meant by making it more important than it had been, or maybe it hadn't even meant anything remarkable in Bright's mind and heart.

It made the eldest Westworth feel so bad that when she returned home she was a nervous wreck. She slammed the door of her room and her footsteps echoed loudly on the wood. She had never been so upset before, and it surprised her. She couldn't believe the reaction the young man had aroused in her and for that she hated herself. She was always the one in control, the one who rejected young men who weren't right for her, and now she was the one being rejected.

If Bright had experienced the same emotions in that encounter that she had, he would have found a compelling reason to stay in Middleton, but no, he had left. Margaret's innocence had played a trick on her. Bright had told her outright: he had more experience in the field of love. And now she had been one of his conquests.

The realization of this ignited Margaret's insides, and whatever affection or desire she might have felt for William Bright turned to hatred.

She hated how the young man had made her feel and she was angry at herself for letting her guard down and giving the young man the power to confuse her and leave her that state.

Margaret looked at herself in the mirror, fixed her hair that had been undone after the walk, breathed in, and promised herself that neither Bright nor any other man would play with her.

This might be her last season in society, but she wasn't desperate enough to lose her nerve for a man whose attentions were clearly elsewhere.

Middleton Post. June 23, 1876

Dear readers,

I feel hopelessly despondent today. Mr. Bright seems to have departed Middleton as swiftly and mysteriously as he appeared a few days ago. His stay, brief but intense, has been like a hurricane which has dazzled and bruised our hearts in equal parts. Will Miss Westworth feel the same way?

Lady Middleton

CHAPTER 7

26 June 1876
Middleton, England

Margaret had paid no attention to Mrs. Middleton's hateful words that had been published days before, so the rumors that Bright's departure had left a devastated Margaret were completely dispelled when the young woman was seen strolling joyfully and jubilantly with her sisters several days later.

All Middleton was preparing for the ball that was to take place in the parlor of the Rogers' great house. The Rogers were a very fortunate married couple in the cotton business. Mr. Rogers had a close and long-standing relationship with Mr. Westworth, and thus the children of both marriages had been brought up together in the county. Hence the relationship between Margaret and Thomas Rogers was so close. It seemed that years of childish play had turned to purer and nobler feelings on the part of the young man for his friend, even if they were not reciprocated.

The arrival of the invitation announcing this special ball was not long in coming. Enclosed in a beautiful ivory-colored envelope were the neat words of Mrs. Rogers and her express desire to share with the family a pleasant and jovial evening.

Margaret's sisters helped her sister to dress up with the maid so that she would look as stunning as possible that night.

The carriage set off with Mr. Westworth, his sister-in-law, and Margaret in it. Any man of wealth and father of a large family might find society balls dull and tedious, and Mr. Westworth was to be no exception, though he well knew that he must pluck up his courage. Not only because this was to be his dear eldest daughter's last year of society, but because there were still two more daughters to be married off. Mr. Westworth, with a smile of resignation, and with a certain enthusiasm for the reunion with his friend, put on his white gloves in the carriage, and gave the order to depart.

The Rogers' mansion was a sight for sore eyes. Margaret was accustomed to its balustrades, its arches, and its grand gardens, but it was the people inside that she most looked forward to seeing. Thomas's sister Katherine was one of her closest friends, and they had been close since the cradle. The recent events of the previous season had not dented their relationship and Margaret was thankful for that.

"My dear Mr. Westworth, how glad we are that you are able to come!" expressed Mrs. Rogers warmly, as she met the guests at the gate." Margaret, you look very pretty young lady.

"Thank you very much, Mrs. Rogers." Margaret replied with a big smile on her face. Mrs. Rogers was a nice and loving person, and always treated her as a daughter.

"I think he's talking to his brother by the fireplace in the living room," Mrs. Rogers said as she gestured with her arm inside the room.

"Thank you very much."

Margaret began to walk slowly toward the parlor of the house in search of her friends, leaving her father and aunt behind. Almost as soon as she heard their voices, words came to her from the lady of the house.

"Mr. Westworth, it is a pity Margaret has no affection for Thomas, she is so noble and polite. How I should have longed to call her daughter."

Those words brought a feeling of sadness to Margaret's heart, and she paused before entering the room. Across the room stood Katherine and Thomas, two young men with rather similar features that left no doubt of their kinship. She watched Thomas silently. His features. His movements. His smile. And from the bottom of her heart, she wondered the same thing. Why couldn't she feel anything for him when he had all the makings of a devoted and devoted husband?

Margaret knew the answer.

It wasn't Henry.

"Margaret, dear friend, how long have you been there?" Katherine asked as she went out to meet her friend to invite her to join them. "I'm so excited that we can meet today. Have you seen the lovely dress my father gave me? Do you like the muslin on the skirt? Yours was bought outside of Middleton, wasn't it?"

"Come on, Katherine, don't crowd Margaret." Thomas, knowing how intense his sister could be at times came to his friend's aid. The guest, with a smile, returned the young man's gesture.

The evening was going on as normal, dancing and laughing until Margaret's aunt, accompanied by a man, approached her.

"Margaret, my dear. I would like to introduce you to Robert Kingston, the eldest son of Mr. and Mrs. Kingston, your father's friends."

The tall, dark, scowling young man made a small bow with his feet together, which was followed by Margaret's greeting. The young woman was not sure how to judge Robert Kingston's appearance. He seemed dashing and handsome at first glance, but she found it odd that she had not heard of him during her debutante years or met him at other family functions.

"Robert has just arrived from London. He has been studying law at university and has graduated with honors..

"Say no more, madam. Or it will seem that my merits are greater than my title grants." The gentleman tried to show humility by refusing Beatrice Miller's flattery as prudence dictates.

"If that is true, Mr. Kingsman, you need not be ashamed of them. I consider the cultivation of intellect to be a step towards socialization and progress," Margaret expressed with complete honesty. The young woman did not know whether the blush that was now on Kingsman's cheeks was the result of the aforementioned flattery, the heat of the summer afternoon, or the tension of the moment, but it was evident that the gentleman was uncomfortable.

"Splendid, I have no doubt you will find pleasure in discussing it," Aunt Beatrice replied quickly as she realized that the conversation between her niece and the new guest was going to be on more intellectual than superficial topics. Satisfied with her pairing, she prepared to leave the young couple. "If you will excuse me, I must greet Mr. and Mrs. Abbey."

"Of course, man must work his mind as a mandate for the betterment of society and be able to reverse in it an improvement."

Once Beatrice left to greet other guests at the party, Margaret experienced a certain comfort in the presence and conversation with Robert Kingsman.

The gentleman possessed the gift of the gab, was judicious and reasoned sensibly, which pleased the young lady greatly. It was unusual to find a gentleman with such facility in conversing with a lady.

After a long and animated conversation, Robert asked for several dances and Margaret gladly agreed.

To her surprise, Mr. Kingsman showed unparalleled agility of foot, and his dancing skills were admirable. They continued a lighter conversation amidst the twirling and crossing of partners without Margaret's being able to keep from breaking into a radiant smile of the most innocent happiness.

Although Margaret's aunt and her own father were kind enough to introduce her to three more suitors during the evening, they did not want to exceed their hosts' confidence or hurt their feelings about young Thomas. Margaret, of course, chose young Rogers to enjoy his company for several musical pieces because, above all else, he was her friend.

But after finishing each of the pieces, her gaze returned to the young man with whom she had danced at the beginning of the evening, who was conversing with other gentlemen.

When the evening was over, the Westworth family gathered up their belongings and made their way to the carriage, but not before bidding a cordial farewell and thanking their hosts. In the carriage, on the way home, Margaret was lost in thought. Her mind was restless, excited, throbbing. She had enjoyed the evening, every dance and every guest. But for an instant, a small instant, a handsome young man with full lips came into her thoughts.

Fucking Bright.

The days passed in Middleton, and to Margaret's astonishment a new letter from her dear friend came to her hands after several weeks without news.

Dear Margaret,

Thank goodness my sister is in better health and already enjoying the outdoors, the garden and other age-appropriate distractions. I am happy to see her smiling again, there is no greater gift as a sibling.

I must apologize for my silence. These last few weeks my duties have kept me busier than I would have wished and I have found it impossible to focus on our dear moments.

I am sorry for the pressure that has been placed on you and your family, but I think it is a very mature decision to take responsibility. I admire your courage and bravery and applaud your selfless heart. Being the heiress of a family that enjoys a position like yours is not easy and sometimes we must accept our duty.

I must confess that with each passing day I find it more difficult to come to Middleton and keep the promise I made to you as a child to be by your side. Like you, my obligations to my family are also important and I must prioritize them.

I sincerely hope that during these months you can find someone who is worthy of your attentions and your heart, because the lucky one you choose will have Middleton's most precious jewel.

A hug,

Henry

Henry's letter left Margaret in a sea of confusion. Weeks had passed since her last letter, and though she had longed to read the words of her dear friend, the coldness and remoteness she had noted in every line had taken her by surprise. Henry, the young man to whom she had given her heart for years without his knowledge, was encouraging her to find a worthy gentleman to wed and confirming that he could never return to Middleton. She did not know if the reason was the stigma surrounding his family, his real family duties and responsibilities, or that he did not really belong to her.

She did not know what to think, for her heart was broken in a thousand pieces. She had placed too much hope in Henry. Margaret wondered again and again when things could have changed between them without her hardly noticing. What could she have done to make her friend change his mind so quickly. For years they had been inseparable and even, a silent alliance had been forged between them in which no words of love had been exchanged but it was obvious that deep feelings flowed between them. Feelings that could lead to a marriage.

All these doubts shook the heart of young Westworth, who now found herself sailing on an uncertain sea, for the debate that was brewing in her heart was not desirable for any lady in her position.

Several days after the ball at Mr. and Mrs. Rogers's, Mr. Westworth received a somewhat unexpected visitor. Margaret heard the voices coming from her father's office as she approached his door. She found it reprehensible to eavesdrop on her dear father, but she could not help being tempted.

Suddenly, the door burst open and, with a jolt, Margaret found herself face to face with Kingsman.

"Miss Westworth, good morning. It is a delightful morning. don't you think?" Robert stammered as he turned the brim of his top hat on himself. He looked into her eyes without losing contact hoping she would not withdraw them, but afraid that she would.

"Of course, Mr. Kingsman. Of course."

"Would you be so kind as to join me for such a pleasant morning? Perhaps a stroll in the gardens of the property?"

Margaret froze. From inside the office, her father nervously watched his daughter's response. His eyes were vivid and anxious.

"Of course" -two words which served as an invitation and encouragement for the gentleman, with a broad smile on his face, to extend his arm towards the elder Westworth.

Mr. Westworth instructed his sisters that they should accompany the young people on their walk at a safe distance that would afford privacy but that they might be easily observed.

"You may wonder, Miss Westworth, at the reason of my visit, and the conversation I had with your father before. It is my earnest wish, and I have been most politely, and with your father's consent, to court you. Our first meeting, your company and conversation were much more than I had expected and I must confess that I find your presence welcoming and exciting. I understand that it is too early to stir your heart, but I desire nothing more than to awaken your affection, Miss Westworth."

Without realizing it, the eldest Kingsman had stopped the walk beside Margaret, and taking her tenderly by the hands, had confessed his feelings to her. The confession was not unfamiliar to the young woman, but it was from a man she hardly knew.

She still felt undeserving of another person's attentions, and, as with Thomas, she felt blissful. The families at the ball vouched for her provenance and decency, and so, when she heard the young man's heartfelt words, her heart trembled.

Margaret's body trembled as she gazed at the man and cringed at each thing her mind revealed to her as she stood beside him. As independent as she wanted to appear to the rest of society, she had to fulfill her mission as a daughter. Unfortunately, she was not going to be fulfilled as a woman through the written words of Henry's letters, nor through Bright's slippery arms, and she certainly could not provoke false feelings for her friend Thomas.

Mr. Kingsman was, at first glance, a decent and well-meaning man. Correct in his manners, with a cultivated mind and a fluent and versed conversation. He was a skilled dancer, a lover of nature, and a lover of literature. Qualities which Margaret found admirable and necessary in her companion in life.

She may have been giving up many adventures, her childhood sweetheart, and her best friend, but she had a higher duty to perform, one that transcended her own personal interests.

So, looking up at the man who stood before her baring his soul, she smiled.

Middleton Post. June 26, 1876

Dear readers,

After several days of uncertainty and some unconfirmed rumors, I can say, without a shadow of a doubt, that Mr Westworth's eldest daughter Margaret is being courted by Magistrate Kingsman. Both from very good families and with a promising future, let's hope that they will make the news in the future with the announcement of their marriage.

What will be Mr. Bright's opinion on the matter? Will we find a young Thomas Rogers devastated by the news?

Lady Middleton

CHAPTER 8

July 12, 1876
Middleton, England

The weeks followed one after the other, and before she knew it, the heat was one of the most prominent features of the walks and evenings. The increasingly crowded social gatherings Margaret attended only made it clear how lucky she had been to find a young gentleman who complemented her and whom she enjoyed.

Mr. Westworth was delighted at his daughter's disposition, and his aunt, of course, was overwhelmed with the excitement of a possible close liaison between the young couple. Her dear niece, married. Nothing could make her happier, though she also knew that she still had a responsibility to Grace and Rose, the youngest of the family, who would perhaps prove more complicated than Margaret herself. They were all different from each other with peculiarities that made them unique, but Beatrice Miller knew well that she had a tricky mission to accomplish the moment her niece left her late sister's residence.

For her part, Margaret had been struggling for the past few weeks with too many ghosts and feelings trying to come to the surface. On the one hand, the love she felt for her great childhood friend, for whom, although she hadn't seen him in years, she felt something very special.

The one with whom, through his letters, she had traveled to far-flung parts of England, shared intimacies and dreams, frustrations and sorrows. The one for whom he would leave his family name behind just so they could not consider him unworthy.

And on the other hand, and what angered Margaret the most, the passion Bright had conveyed to her with a single kiss. She, sensible and calm, had been able to tremble like a child when he had provoked her. She had never been kissed, and though Bright had been and would be the owner of her first kiss, his absence and lack of news during the last few weeks had made clear his total lack of intentions toward her.

Kingsman was polite, courteous and affable, but he wasn't affectionate like Henry or intense like Bright. However, she felt it was a viable option and a fair and respectable marriage. If Henry encouraged her to marry someone else and leave their shared past behind, she would have to focus on another young man who could fulfill her as a person even if it betrayed the feelings she'd had for years. Bright was not a reliable person after recent events, and no other gentleman in the county could live up to Margaret's expectations, so Kingsman might prove to be a good life partner.

For that reason Margaret had accepted every one of Mr. Kingsman's invitations during the last few weeks. They had shared long walks in the grove, rickshaw rides to the river, visited the town library together, and even found pleasure in cricket.

"Mr. Kingsman, this is a game run by the devil, there's no way you can get the ball into that hoop."

"It is not impossible, dear Margaret. Let me help you."

The gentleman stood behind her and gently, but with physical distance, embraced her and led her hands to the cricket bat Margaret was holding. The young woman was able to feel her companion's calm breathing on her shoulders and the evening breeze swayed some of her tresses that danced over her face.

"You should hold the bat with light force, but without choking it. Spread your legs a little wider to give yourself a better foothold. When you are ready, watch the direction in which the ball should flow. Slowly move the club back and forth without losing sight of the target and when you are ready... "Gently, Margaret pushed the ball with the club and it moved forward. As bad luck would have it, it was halfway across the arc.

"See, I'm too clumsy for this game."

"On the contrary, miss. If you notice. " said Mr. Kingsman breaking the embrace with the young woman" although the ball has not quite completed its path, the trajectory is correct. Look at that. "Kingsman hit the ball softly and it went into the arch" I just needed a little more force.

"I'm sure next shift I can make it."

"There is no doubt in my mind."

They both looked at each other and smiled warm smiles. Margaret found amusement in the company and in the games which Kingsman so skillfully controlled. It was the first time she had discovered cricket, but she had found a certain satisfaction in its practice and in the gentleman's manner of teaching.

"Shall we try it again? "asked Mr. Kingsman.

The good relationship between the two was something Margaret's sisters had discussed on several occasions with their aunt and their own father.

Everything seemed to indicate that a big wedding would soon be announced, but to rush into the announcement when it had not yet been made official by the bride and groom was not appropriate. Beatrice Miller was secretly writing a few lines for the record in the local paper when the time came. Even the gossipy and obnoxious Mrs. Middleton had found time in her busy schedule to devote several entries in her column to the young couple whom she already considered engaged.

The good humor of her aunt and even of her father was evident to Margaret, and, suspecting the motive, nothing made her happier than that she might at some time announce the longed-for union, but Mr. Kingsman had made no proposal.

That very morning they had received at the Westworth residence an invitation to the ball from Mr. and Mrs. Lonsdale, a couple who, though they had not all the grace or friendship of Mr. Westworth, were influential in the town, though they had a reputation for giving the dullest parties.

"I do not consider dancing at the Lonsdale's the most appropriate under the circumstances, dear Margaret." Beatrice indicated to her niece with great assurance.

"What do you mean, Auntie?"

"I think your skin is too pale today" he said gently touching Margaret's face "and you had better take rest, the summer is very long and I would not wish you to acquire an unhealthy propensity."

"Don't talk nonsense, Aunt Beatrice, I feel perfect. In fact, I would be much better if the wretched corset you ordered for this season did not press so tightly on my chest, hence my whitish skin. Tonight I shall go to the ball without delay. Besides, I gave my solemn word to Mr. and Mrs. Lonsdale and Mr. Kingsman. I cannot break my promise."

Aunt Beatrice seemed nervous and anxious and obstinate in her determination to prevent her niece from attending the ball. For several minutes she gave various reasons why Margaret should stay at home: the weather was not suitable, influential people were not going to attend, her friends had other prior engagements... To her chagrin, Margaret was determined to be true to her word.

"I reiterate that it would be best if you stayed at home on this occasion. The last few days have been very busy and I'm sure there is some homework or reading waiting for you at home."

"Don't insist, aunt, really. Once I give my word I must keep it. It would say nothing for it if I withdrew it at the last moment, would it?"

"All right," admitted Aunt Beatrice with some regret in her heart. It was strange that her aunt should discourage her from attending a social event and thus missing the opportunity to meet a future suitor. The surprise was even more pronounced when everything seemed to indicate that a few more meetings would bring about the longed-for news. Undoubtedly, an atypical behavior.

Having finished dressing, Margaret made her way downstairs where her father and aunt were waiting. The walk to Mr. and Mrs. Lonsdale's residence took no more than fifteen minutes, during which time Aunt Beatrice was constantly commenting on Mrs. Lonsdale's unfortunate grace in decorating the curtains in her drawing-room and the fabrics that draped the sofas. Margaret, to the astonishment of her father and aunt, was anxious to reach her destination, and was the first to alight from the carriage when it stopped on the gravel of the drive.

"Miss Westworth, allow me to help you, please." The servant held out his hand to help her out of the carriage.

Margaret surveyed the exterior of the residence. It was a place that once might have been splendid, but over the years had lost much of its beauty and notoriety.

"Father, Aunt Beatrice, I'll wait for you inside."

Her aunt and father stood for a few minutes outside the house as they greeted other guests who, like them, had just arrived.

Margaret walked with some haste into the Lonsdale residence, and there she found much of the Middleton community. Some of the more illustrious or renowned members had not yet arrived, or perhaps it was better to presume that they would not make their presence known, to avoid being included in comparisons with Mr. and Mrs. Lonsdale. To the fortune of the hosts, several couples stood in the centre of the great hall ready to begin a piece played by a humble orchestra.

Margaret sought out Mr. Kingsman in the crowd as she wished to exchange views with him on the latest newspaper articles about the textile industry that were affecting the area. Margaret was happy to have found a person who would allow her to engage in conversation on a variety of topics not restricted to the narrow social parameters established for a lady. She hated to talk about the fashions of the moment, ribbons, silk fans and other topics. She longed to discuss subjects she considered more important to the welfare of her family and Middleton.

"It would be a real honor to be the person you are looking so hard for, Miss Westworth, "said a voice behind her back that made her turn quickly.

"Then let me tell you that you are fortunate, Mr. Kingsman."

With a big smile on her face, Margaret held out her hand which was taken by Mr. Kingsman who gently put his hands around it.

"She is perhaps today the most beautiful angel at this celebration." said Mr. Kingsman quietly as he shyly admired his dancing partner. Though they had shared so many moments in the past few days that he should have left the barrier of shyness behind, there still shone a certain childlike, modest enthusiasm in the gentleman's eyes. It touched Margaret's heart.

"I hope I can enjoy the title of best company in equal measure tonight." Margaret replied sheepishly. She had never been good at being the object of other people's compliments, let alone, accepting them. A blush began to creep into her cheeks. After years of attending social events she should be used to compliments but the false belief that she didn't deserve them made her reluctant to accept them willingly.

"There's no question about it."

The two young guests smiled and, taking advantage of the innocence of the moment, Kingsman held out his arm for Margaret to take and together they made their way to one of the groups. Aunt Beatrice and Mr. Westworth were quick to take a close look at the sweet meeting of the happy couple and with great joy in their hearts, let them enjoy relative privacy without stares or surveillance.

"It is true that the development of these new machines in the capital is speeding up the processing of cotton, but nothing can replace manual production," confessed Mr. Riverton vehemently as he drained the last drop of brandy from his glass.

"I'm with you, old friend. Craftsmanship brings a unique and differential value that mass production can never stop to take care of."

"Gentlemen, I believe you are right about the care and attention to detail required for manufactured goods. However, the revolution that machinery has brought to the industry facilitates mass production, which makes it possible to buy raw materials at lower prices, thus increasing the profit margins that entrepreneurs make. And as I understand it, this is the aim of the market."

"It may be, Miss Westworth that your father has joined the group of businessmen who advocate machines over people, but well I reckon".

"I believe that machines are not a substitute for people in everything. Mr. Westworth has implanted machinery in those processes that are tedious and harmful to his workers and has assigned those personnel to jobs that require more attention or care," Margaret replied with confidence and conviction. Her father was a sensible and humane businessman, he would never dismiss a worker in order to accommodate a machine in his work at the risk of depriving a family member of her daily livelihood. Mr. Westworth truly cared about his workers and their families.

"Miss Westworth is right, gentlemen, labour will not be replaced by machines and, fortunately, you will have laborers for long years to look after your business, but we cannot deny that profit margins have increased." Mr. Kingsman replied.

Margaret turned to Mr. Kingsman to thank him for endorsing her views on industrialization when she realized she was smiling like a child, since she had been able to discuss industry with other men without being belittled. That filled the young woman with satisfaction.

After a while, Margaret began to feel overwhelmed by the heat of the evening, by some of the drinks she had taken to cool herself and by the hubbub of the dancing, so, bidding Kingsman farewell, she wandered to one of the windows for some fresh air.

The night was beautiful. Only a shy waning moon was in the sky accompanied by hundreds of thousands of bright stars that created a delicate mantle. Summer had granted no respite since its arrival and just a light breeze ran across the face of the young woman while two gentlemen discussed and enjoyed a few cigars and a few glasses of liquor.

Unaccompanied and having lost track of time, Margaret decided to find one of the residence's toilets to freshen up her neck and return to the ballroom with the rest of the guests.

She asked for help from one of the staff, who politely pointed her to the washroom. After pouring some water over a porcelain bucket delicately painted with floral motifs, Margaret wet the back of her neck and neck and looked at herself in the mirror in front of her. She brushed back a few stray strands of hair and stepped out of the bathroom.

She closed the door to the washroom and on the way to the great hall all the hairs on her body stood on end. She didn't know why, but she felt a shiver capture her body and make her stop.

"Dear Margaret, I am glad to see you again."

CHAPTER 9

July 12, 1876
Middleton, England

Bright.

She recognized that voice the moment he uttered the first of his words. It was a voice coarse and deep, cajoling and brazen. A voice that had spoken her name several times before with a sensuality that could have made many a lady lose her virtue.

"Damn you," Margaret thought.

Thousands of different curses crossed Margaret's mind and they had Bright as their target.

He had been missing for weeks and now he was there, in front of Margaret. In an impeccable black suit, with his mischievous smile and a look that could knock a woman's socks off. With his full, kissable lips. Staring at her. Only at her. All of him was a provocation to Margaret and her body had alerted her even before she saw him. Long days had passed since they'd last seen each other, but in Margaret's eyes he'd gained attractiveness and bravado in equal measure.

Standing in front of her she hoped that her greeting would be well received by the young man and that she would not so indiscreetly demonstrate how she would drink the winds for him.

But Margaret, proud and wounded like any other young woman, tried to play down his presence. With effort, she pretended that she hadn't noticed that slight tingling in her stomach or that tenderness in her limbs.

"Did you miss me, Margaret?" Bright asked as he reached out to take the young woman's hand in his and bring it to his lips. Margaret's senses crossed into oblivion as her whole body jerked as she felt the touch of Bright's lips that she had missed so much.

He could not imagine how something as chaste as a kiss, which many other young men had done in the same way on her hand, could arouse so many emotions in him. Feelings that confused and alerted her at the same time. They were alone, without a chaperone, in the middle of a semi-dark hallway at a large party. Margaret was convinced that it was that forbidden feeling that animated Bright.

"Mr. Bright, I'm sure the ladies here will be glad of your return. It has been several weeks of absence."

Margaret couldn't help but let her resentment show in those words. Bright's departure, without warning or note or credible excuse, had left her bewildered, especially after his passionate kiss. Realizing that perhaps her words had come with more hatred than indifference, she tried to make amends, but it was too late.

"I am flattered if all these young ladies have had thoughts of me," said the gentleman presumptuously, as he slowly advanced towards Margaret trying to close the distance between them with the clear intention of creating a moment" but I am more interested in whether I have been able to cause you regret, dear Margaret."

"Regretful?" Margaret tried to play indignant, "I think you overestimate the effect your presence may have had on me. These past few weeks have been enlightening and hectic. I have barely had time to think about my chores in the garden long enough to spend time with you."

"Don't lie, Margaret," Bright said approaching her closer with a challenging look. Margaret's presumed indifference had caught his attention and provoked him. Although several guests strolled casually through the halls of the residence and even bumped into the young men, no one noticed the closeness of their bodies or how Bright, almost in a light whisper, said to her, "You may not have had time to think about me, but I am not able to forget your lips and I would like to make them mine again."

"It's a real shame then that you continue to attach importance to that insignificant moment, Mr. Bright."

"Insignificant? I wouldn't call our kiss insignificant, especially not after I felt your legs shaking."

The closeness Bright was showing and the lack of decorum in his words was alarming Margaret. She knew that, when the time came, she would be lost. She must remain unmoved by his appeal and his provocations.

"I see that bragging about your conquests is still the main course of your conversations. Don't worry, I'm sure any lady in the room will find your attentions entertaining and be delighted to feel your warmth."

"But you don't?" asked the gentleman in confusion as he subtly scratched one of his ears as if he had been hurt by Margaret's indifference.

"Certainly not" she wouldn't let Bright beat her to that game. She may have been an inexperienced gazelle, but Bright had certainly made her gain knowledge at an accelerated rate.

Margaret looked up to meet Bright's eyes. They glowed brightly, and like a firefly drawn to the light, Margaret couldn't help but feel captured by them. They devoured her passionately without so much as a word. Part of her would have let herself go as far as Bright's roguish behavior would have challenged her, but another part, the proud and cautious part, needed to fight the emotions this elusive man made her feel. She would not fall for him again.

Bright took another step forward as he gently touched Margaret's face, trying to soften the young woman's hard countenance. He noticed Margaret's resistance and to him, it was like a reward, for if she was being surly, it was because their previous encounter had made more of an impression on him than she insisted on denying.

"You've got some nerve, Mr. Bright. Excuse me," Margaret scolded, her tone changing as she realized how he was trying to provoke her and how he expected that reaction from her. He, amused, gave her a triumphant smile in return. Margaret continued through the large hallway until she came to another that seemed to connect the residence to the garden.

Before they reached the front door, a strong arm wrapped around her hip and led her into one of the adjoining rooms. They entered quickly and the door closed behind them. Night had come without them noticing, and the whole room was dark with no trace of a presence in it, only the warmth of a timid fire.

Bright carefully pushed Margaret until he had her back to the door and making her body a prisoner in his arms, he glared at her furiously without touching her.

Margaret could barely breathe. It was possible that she didn't even know if her body was capable of such a thing because her whole being was focused on the only light that shone brightly in that room: Bright. Margaret feared everything that the night's previous experience could teach her in the art of love and at the same time, she desired him without shame. She wanted Bright.

"I have not tasted such sweet lips. No face so jovial and full of character. There is no woman who can arouse these same emotions in me."

"I..."

Bright eliminated the distance between them and captured her lips. It wasn't a soft kiss or one filled with devotion, but it was need that took over. Bright was claiming her as his own.

It was the second time she had received a kiss and both times it had been from the lips of the same man. It stirred something inside Margaret. It may have been curiosity at first, for she longed to know what secrets his kisses hid, but there was something more intense growing in Margaret's loins. Passion. She craved to know the skills in the art of love that Bright had acquired and she wanted to enjoy each and every one of them.

A part of Margaret knew it was the hatred she felt for the young man that fanned the flame of those feelings, but she couldn't help it. Her words said one thing and her body said another.

So when Bright prompted Margaret's lips to open and introduced his tongue so he could taste her that much more, she allowed him to do so. Her limited experience seemed to be forgotten when she placed her hands on Bright's chest, which he took as a clear invitation to deepen their encounter. So he cupped her face intensely and drove her into madness.

Margaret's body burned with desire and the fire grew hotter and hotter with her companion's touch. She wanted Bright to show her everything that a woman and a man shared in intimacy.

If he had asked her at that moment, she would have given in. It was that precise statement that clouded Margaret's mind and made her lose her concentration. She tried to pull away from Bright, but he was pulling her closer and closer. Margaret's strength was on the verge of failing in that instant when she was asking to be separated from Bright, and he was still passionately loving her lips.

"No, that's enough. Stop." Margaret summoned what little willpower still coursed through her body to break that moment. There was nothing that hurt her soul and body more, and she felt real pain when

Bright pulled away from her, but she needed to bring serenity to the moment.

"This will not happen again, Mr. Bright." Margaret said with bated breath and a raised hand. Somehow, she hoped his arm would establish the distance between their bodies so that he would not come after her again, or perhaps, so that she herself would not throw herself back into the arms of this gentleman.

"Yes, it will happen again. It will happen every night we meet. Because you want me, Margaret. I feel it." Bright took small steps forward until he stood before the nervous, angry Margaret. "Your kisses are sweet and innocent, but they are full of desire."

Bright's slow, calm voice was intoxicating and her nerves were on edge.

"No, it will not be so. My attentions now are for Mr. Kingsman. You forfeited your possible right by leaving without warning."

"If I had stayed," Bright's voice became serious and looking at Margaret he waited to ask his question, "would you consider me worthy?

"That we shall never know. Now, please, I must go."

Margaret needed to go back to the great hall, get some air and collect herself. No doubt he was right. She wished their kisses could last forever, but it couldn't be repeated. It was a mistake.

She had given her word to Mr. Kingsman in accepting his courtship, and it was neither acceptable nor wise to be alone in a room with another man. The exposure to censure and criticism was too much to bear. Bright couldn't let her go. He grabbed her, but this time, gently and tenderly. He pulled her back closer until it met his chest. He entwined his arms about her and, as he took in her quickened breathing, he brought his lips to her ear and the words flowed out.

"Then why are your legs shaking?

In that instant, Margaret knew. She was in love with Bright.

Middleton Post. July 13, 1876

Dear readers,

I am overcome with emotion and my pulse barely allows me to write with the calm and serenity that characterizes me even if you cannot appreciate it, but I will not let the truth go unsaid.

Mr. Bright, who hastily and mysteriously left Middleton weeks ago in the middle of the social season, was seen yesterday. Although he chose one of the dullest events for his reappearance, it may well complicate the future liaison between Miss Westworth and the young Kingsman.

Let's hope so because then I'll be happy to keep you informed.

Lady Middleton

CHAPTER 10

13 July 1876
Middleton, England

If anyone had entered the room to discover the young people in such a compromising situation, the possible liaison between Margaret and Mr. Kingsman would never take place. They would be obliged, by the rules, to marry immediately, to avoid the gossip of young Margaret's possible loss of virtue.

The air had changed in that room. The accelerated breathing of both lovers had warmed the room by the desire that was born from their bodies.

Margaret didn't want that. She was angry. She was indignant at being so weak before this gentleman.

Upset by Bright, by the boldness of the first kiss they exchanged, by his unexpected departure, and by allowing their passionate second encounter.

She had hardly been able to sleep that night. Lying without sheets on the bed and wandering around her small room on many other occasions, the young woman recreated the encounter in her mind.

She didn't blame Bright for indulging her passions, she blamed herself. She was always an example of strength and serenity, and yet one look from this gentleman could disarm her. It robbed her of her reason, and all she could think about was his lips.

She thought of the passion in his kisses and the warmth in his eyes, those brown eyes that had so sweetly teased her time and time again. Eyes that had already become burned into her mind.

But in all that sleepless night, Margaret had no thought for Kingsman or for her dear friend Henry. And for that, she felt the guiltier.

Henry Williams's letters, resting in a box in her closet, throbbed in the wood and reminded her of the promises exchanged. For years they had been her encouragement to endure the demands of society and the lessons her aunt had tried to impose on her over the years. Henry had been her companion during those years, her friend, and with the arrival of maturity, she believed she had found a kindred spirit. But his last wish expressed in the letter was clear: he wanted her to move on and find a husband who would make her happy. He would not come back for her because he had to put his family's needs before his own. Margaret hated that, but she understood it because she was making the same decision herself, but it didn't make it any easier.

It gnawed at her insides not to know whether at some point he had also had feelings for her, or whether, on the contrary, it had been an unrequited love for many years. She thought she had seen certain signs during the countless letters they had exchanged, but she could no longer be sure of anything, since she had never had the courage to ask him so indiscreetly about his feelings.

On the other hand, she felt guilty and bad for disregarding Kingsman's attentions. He had nobly and loyally promised her that he would treat her well and make her happy, and she, by allowing Bright to invade her thoughts and dreams, was relegating him to an inferior position.

No, she wasn't going to allow such a thing. She wasn't going to let Bright own her body or her thoughts. He didn't deserve it. He certainly possessed all the qualities to make a decent young woman walk away from him: he was haughty, presumptuous, a womanizer, and had a great tendency to abandon young women. In spite of all the good words that businessmen had for him, he was not to be trusted. And that, no doubt, should have been enough to keep her away from him.

She wasn't going to let anyone play games with her, her feelings, or the welfare of her family.

And so she would.

She would keep any thoughts of Bright out of her mind and repudiate his presence as much as decorum would allow in order to keep him away. Or, rather, not to be tempted.

With the arrival of the first sounds of excited young ladies in the house, Margaret called one of the maids and asked her to help her dress. She went down to breakfast with renewed energy and with a serious countenance sat down at the large table to wait for one of the waiters to serve her breakfast.

"A great evening, my daughters, a pity you could not come. Perfect, no doubt," said Mr. Westworth, as he glanced with little attention at the paper. The young ladies' father was a business man, and had a flair for numbers and business arrangements, but he was scarcely capable of fixing his attention on papers or newspapers. He preferred to deal with people, and to have Margaret read the news and then tell him what was most important.

"Margaret, did anything interesting happen last night?" asked Rose restlessly and curiously. The young girls, they lived the excitement of the dances and the drawing-room gossip through the eyes and words of their elder sister and aunt. But contrary to what they longed for, their elder sister was coarse in words, and her descriptions were superfluous, with scarcely any interesting details.

Hearing that question, Margaret's mind flashed back to that moment with Bright. She felt the hair on her body stand on end as she remembered his touch, as she felt again how Bright's hands ran over her body with gentleness and passion. It was as if she were there again.

"No, nothing interesting. " she lied still with the taste of Bright on her lips and her cheeks burning, "Father, please, I would like to speak to you in your office after lunch."

"Of course, my dear," confirmed Mr. Westworth, folding the sheets of newspaper until they lay folded on the hall table.

"Father, give us the paper. I'm sure Lady Middleton has reviewed last night's meeting. We need to know any gossip."

"My daughters, you should follow your sister's example and avoid reading such nonsense. It is not proper," said Aunt Beatrice sternly as she finished her lunch.

"Aunt Beatrice, how can you tell us such a thing? We may as well confess that you were the first this morning to enjoy Lady Middleton's lines."

"It is not true, Rose," exclaimed her aunt indignantly. But it had been so. Beatrice had hurried to her brother-in-law's, for she knew that the postman was first at the Westworth residence to deliver the mail, and with it the paper. She was anxious to know whether Mrs. Middleton had reviewed or devoted a few lines to last night's party and Bright's return.

Aunt Beatrice had seen the young man reappear on one of the roads leading to the village, and it was certain that he would be at the Lonsdale family party. The hopes she had cultivated for weeks that her niece's attentions would remain centered on Mr. Kingsman would be dashed if she could see the young man. Her brother-in-law and the rest of the community might be deluded and unaware of her niece's preferences, but she wasn't. And, unfortunately for her, it was clear that Margaret had a preference for Bright.

She could not allow her niece's efforts, now that she had agreed to be courted by a man of good reputation who would lead to a happy marriage, to be disturbed by the return of that odious man.

Rose quickly got up from the table to grab the paper before her sister did. Roughly turning the pages she stopped at the society section to find her favorite emissary's column. There it was. She perused her every word as she looked up several times at her older sister. Surprised.

"Rose, you'd better not say anything." Margaret threatened loudly. Rose understood why, but still, she wanted her sister to confirm if these rumors were true.

"Nothing about what?" asked Grace not understanding the silent discussion taking place between her sisters "What's going on?

Grace turned her face from side to side asking questions, but none of her attempts got an answer and, frustrated, she kept silent and finished her breakfast.

Mr. Westworth retired from the dining-room to his office, and while he was arranging some account books on the table, he waited for his daughter's arrival. A few minutes later Margaret opened the door, and stood with decision before her father.

"Tell me, daughter, what can I do for you?" asked Mr. Westworth with interest. It had been some time since his daughter had requested an audience in his office, and he suspected that whatever she had to tell him was not connected with business or commerce.

"Father, I should like to speak to you on an important subject, which, by the very nature of it, needs to be discussed in private." The seriousness of Margaret's words caught her father off guard, and he put his spectacles in his coat pocket and gave her his full attention.

"I hear you."

Mr. Westworth tried to say something at the sadness of his daughter's words, but Margaret held up her hand for silence and calm. "I should have married a man long ago and started my own family, giving my sisters a chance to make their debut and enjoy the richness and variety that social life offers, but I have not."

"Daughter..."

"No, father, let me finish," Margaret pleaded, "So I have decided to leave behind all that holds me back, and though I feel that I will never be ready for the life that fate has in store for me, it is time to grow up. I should like to receive Mr. Kingsman's attentions in public and to be able to consider marriage with him if he should so request."

When he finished his speech, Margaret felt short of breath. Her mind was convinced that marriage was the best option at this point.
She had weighed all the possibilities after years of participating in social events, of dancing with dozens of candidates, of pretending to be interested in their boring comments, and even of putting up with their insistent mothers. She could no longer postpone her duty to her family.

Bright's pursuit and insistence would be stopped because, above all else, gentlemen would never dare to seduce another gentleman's fiancée and of course it would quell all the feelings that were welling up for him to focus all his attention on another man.

Besides, though her heart was divided, she also needed to leave Henry behind and give up her childhood dreams. On multiple occasions, Margaret had asked her pen pal to come to Middleton, but each time he had dodged the request.

By making this decision, she would choose wisely to whom to direct her attentions, and at last her heart would stop yearning for Henry and her body for Bright. Neither was worthy of her. And with that strong conviction, Margaret gave up passion and innocence to make way for sanity and maturity.

"Are you sure about that, my dear?" formulated her father with incredulity and admiration.

"Of course. I'm determined."

CHAPTER 11

16 July 1876
Middleton, England

The days following the revealing conversation between Mr. Westworth and his daughter passed quietly.

Mr. Westworth showed renewed happiness at his daughter's willingness to accept Mr. Kingsman's attentions. In his view, the gentleman was a man of good family, respectable reputation, with a flourishing career, and who had shown vivid attentions to his daughter.

Margaret had several visits from Mr. Kingsman. They had walked about the estate, picked flowers from the garden, exchanged views on their favorite novels, on their dreams, and many other subjects which came one after the other without their noticing it. Margaret's mind was flattered by the ease with which she could converse with the gentleman, and every day she felt happier with the decision she had made about him.

She may not have felt any affection for him but she was sure she could do it.

Life seemed to be getting back to normal, and the peace that had surprisingly settled into the young woman's life made her enjoy every meeting with Mr. Kingsman. Although every day she had to muster all her strength to keep Henry and Bright out of her thoughts, she forced herself to know and discover Kingsman's virtues.

That day, the gentleman in question rode in a carriage to the Westworth family residence and asked permission to take Margaret to his estate to show her his gardens and the shy lake it contained. Both Margaret and her father agreed and soon, she was ready to get to know the Kingsman's home and perhaps, in the future, her own.

During the journey, as usual, words flowed between them until they arrived at the Kingsman estate. The estate was twenty minutes from her family residence, and that pleased her, since, should she marry him, she would not have to travel a long distance to meet her father and sisters.

With the help of her gallant companion, Margaret descended from the buggy and marveled at all the simplicity that surrounded the residence. Margaret's attention was not on the great house before her, but on the garden that surrounded it. The young woman valued the freedom that nature offered above all things. On more than one occasion, when the strain or constraint of her social position had stifled her, she had run out of the house to discover the limits of her property and also of her own strength.

So she encouraged Kingsman to take her by the arm, and followed by one of her ladies-in-waiting, the young couple strolled through the gardens. Kingsman interrupted the walk on numerous occasions to relate some anecdotes which made Margaret laugh. Her companion, in spite of his serious countenance, was amusing and a great storyteller.

"Did you enjoy the ride, Miss Westworth?

"Of course, I must confess that you have a splendid, admirable property," confessed Margaret incredulously. The sparkle in her eyes left no room for doubt, and the remark seemed to please her companion.

"Thank you very much. If I may be honest, I was fearful of your reaction this morning," confessed Kingsman as he tried to control his slightly trembling hands. "I wanted and I wish very much to make you feel at home, Miss Westworth," Kingsman confessed as he tried to control the slight tremor in his hands.

"You are very kind, I thank you."

"I mean it with all my heart. I long for the day when I can cease to call you Miss Westworth, that I may call you Margaret. My dear Margaret."

Margaret stopped to turn her body to face Mr. Kingsman. The young woman was afraid of what was going to happen next. She was not naïve. She had experienced it on several occasions with other young suitors who wished to ask for her attentions and her hand, but this was the first time she had been inclined to accept them.

Despite this, she couldn't help but get nervous.

Mr. Kingsman was polite, attentive and cultured. She considered him an equal and so they discussed politics, culture and economics. He liked to walk outdoors and enjoy simple but fun sports and, above all, he made her smile.

Anticipating the moment caused her body to react. Soon the color rose to her cheeks and shyness forced her to look at the ground instead of at her host. She felt her mouth go dry as if she had swallowed a handful of that light sand she had never seen except in paintings.

The young man took her hands gently and softly, slowly ran over them until he became familiar with their touch. They were not the hands of a lady, nor were they those of a peasant girl.

Margaret enjoyed working in the garden and in the family orchard, and at the same time she had to pay attention to the appearance of her position and take care of her skin.

And though her skin didn't bristle at Kingsman's touch, she did feel her heartbeat intensify. Recapturing what little cockiness she had in her body and overcoming the shyness that had captured her at that moment, she looked up to find that his gaze had long since been able to look only at her. It haunted Margaret.

She hadn't noticed until that moment but Mr. Kingsman was handsome. His height was acceptable for a gentleman of his age as was his build and musculature but it was his face that caught Margaret's attention. His tender gaze, his cheeks that had now turned pink and his thin but captivating lips.

"Margaret, I feel that the last few weeks have brought us much closer and with each passing day, I am more convinced if possible that you are the one and only perfect companion for me. You will find that I have a little temper when I am obfuscating, that I am too permissive with the servants, and that I enjoy spending hours in the library without hardly noticing that time has passed around me, but I promise above all things that, if you will agree to be my wife, my one desire and my one promise will be to make you happy."

Everything stopped.

For an instant Margaret's heart was moved. She had never heard such beautiful words from any other man. She had hoped for years that some letter from Henry would capture those sentiments, but it had not. Kingsman had opened his soul and revealed his fears and hoped she would accept them and become Mrs. Kingsman.

Margaret treasured and appreciated every word the gentleman had spoken. It seemed to her a humble and sincere confession, befitting Mr. Kingsman. He did not show more than was there, he was transparent and open. He would never give hope or make promises to a woman if he wasn't willing to keep his word as a gentleman. Just the kind of person Margaret needed in her life. She was tired of the lies, the deceit, the silence, the back and forth of the gentlemen in her life. By accepting Kingsman she would have stability and a man devoted to her.

So Margaret took a deep breath and sincerely uttered the following words.

"Mr. Kingsman, you will find that I am sometimes obstinate and independent. I confess that I do not enjoy taking tea or attending social functions, I like the intimacy that forms with a partner at a dance, and, of course, feeling the air on my face as I walk. You will find more faults with me, for I warn you that I am not an easy going young lady, but I promise you that I will do my best to be the companion you expect."

Kingsman's joy was reflected in eager, lively eyes that took the young woman's hands more firmly in his, and, bringing them to his lips, ran over them with countless tender kisses. Margaret smiled like an infant excited by the new adventure on which she seemed to have embarked.

Mr. Kingsman's words were sincere, and though young Margaret's feelings were not yet romantic, she was sure that the generosity of Kingsman's heart would soon change her mind.

After the visit to the Kingsman residence, the young man accompanied Margaret to her still home in the hope that she had taken a liking to the property. Margaret had found the residence, which in some time was to become her home, very pleasant and comfortable.

On the way home the young couple were nervous, but at the same time uneasy and excited. They had hardly exchanged words since the confession and since Margaret had agreed to be the future Mrs. Kingsman. Margaret concluded that they were both too overwhelmed to talk further.

As they reached one of the main streets, Kingsman stopped to greet one of his father's closest friends who was also his godfather. They chatted for a few minutes and even though there was a light summer breeze blowing, Margaret felt her body burning. A slight tingle ran through her whole being and she began to get nervous. Looking up, she saw him.

Mr. Bright stood across the street, his back leaning against one of the park gates. Margaret, proud and self-confident, raised her head in a slight bow, which did not go unnoticed by the young man, who, with a cold look, returned her greeting by taking off his hat.

Damn Mr. Bright. Inwardly, Margaret still cursed the man's control over her. Even though she had forced herself to forget him and had decided to accept Kingsman, her body still trembled in his presence. He was hateful. So, with an air of superiority and pride, Margaret greeted Bright.

And from that moment on, she would be in control of herself.

Or at least, that's what she thought.

Middleton Post. July 17, 1876

Dear readers,

The most eagerly awaited moment of the season has arrived and I am the first to confirm the big news. Miss Westworth, the eternal spinster of the social seasons, is to be married to Mr. Kingsman. Rumors of the gentleman's attentions to the stubborn young lady were obvious, but we were all, including myself, sure that the intensity of the newcomer Mr. Bright's gaze would boggle the young lady's mind. In spite of all this, Bright seems to have been relegated to second place or almost forgotten, for Margaret Westworth will enjoy her last season as a spinster.

But my friends, summer is not over yet and something tells me in my wise woman nose that not everything is written in stone.

Something tells me that a lot can still happen.

Lady Middleton

CHAPTER 12

18 July 1876
Middleton, England

Rumors of a possible liaison between the young couple circulating the streets of Middleton were confirmed after a corresponding announcement in the society section of the local paper. Lady Middleton, through a few lines elaborated with little grace, had confirmed the relationship.

Of course, this great news brought with it a wide range of emotional reactions from those close to the young woman.

In the first place, the dear younger sisters could now enjoy the social life in which they would be given a little more attention as the next in the Westworth family of marriageable age. They would be able to attend balls, buy beautiful and expensive dresses, and meet young men to whom to give their hearts.

They, without a doubt, were the most excited about the future marriage. After hearing the news from their own sister's mouth, they had been all hugs and kisses with her. Happy, of course, she would have decided to give her hand to a young man she considered worthy, for they suspected that after the high expectations the young woman had for her pen pal there would never be anyone to live up to them.

And, secondly, for themselves.

Of course, the girl's aunt was one of the people who had been most enthusiastic about the marriage. She wished nothing but good wishes for her niece, and she knew that the young Kingsman, of good family and reputation, would succeed in making her happy. The official announcement of the betrothal brought a sigh of relief to Beatrice, who was still nervous about her niece's possible affections for the mysterious Mr. Bright who had so stirred the community since his arrival.

Aunt Beatrice's heart was somewhat confessed, but she wished by all means to prevent her niece from associating with a man of so little education as Mr. Bright, of whom it was said, among the ladies' gossip, that he boasted of the hearts he left in his wake. Mr. Kingsman, no doubt, would be a better companion for his dear Margaret.

And, lastly, his father. Mr. Westworth was at once happy and unhappy. On the one hand, he wished his daughter all the happiness she could attain, as he and his late wife had attained, but, on the other hand, he was grieved at his daughter's leaving the family home. For long years, he had applauded his daughter's temperament and impetus that set her apart from other young girls her age. She would leave behind the frivolous desires of society to seek a love marriage worthy of her.

But over the years, he also feared that this force would lead her to eternal spinsterhood, and he cursed himself for having encouraged it. To some extent, he had spoiled his eldest daughter for years because she reminded him of himself as a young man. He too had refused to marry and go along with his father's impositions, but when he met the right person he did not refuse the opportunity to embark on a great adventure with her.

However, his daughter had accepted a gentleman of great reputation and charisma and he was sure that if she had made that decision it had been of her own free will and desire.

"Father, will we be able to attend the ball at the Pullbrights' next Saturday?" asked Rose anxiously. The young girl had been restless ever since the news of her sister's engagement. She had carefully embroidered the note in the paper to remind her of the day when she might be free.

"I would like to speak to your aunt first to consider whether it is appropriate given the recent announcement of your sister's engagement. It would not be pleasant for all Middletons to think you are desperate to find a husband," Mr. Westworth remarked, trying to calm his daughter.

"But we are, father!" said the youngest of the sisters, almost shouting. Rose was eager to fall in love, to give her heart to a gentleman skilled in the art of dancing and predisposed to be wild like herself. Her father burst into loud laughter, rose from his chair and went straight to his daughter to place a familiar kiss on her forehead. Amid laughter and near tears, her father left the room.

"Margaret, you must introduce us to all the young people during the dance" the youngest sister's mood suddenly changed as her father left the room and stood silently with Grace and Margaret. Despite her father's reluctance she could not hide the excitement she felt inside.

"But Rose, you don't know yet if you will be able to attend. Father has said he must speak to our aunt first."

"Aunt Beatrice will say yes."

The three of them were silent for a minute and, following their father's example, let out a loud burst of laughter.

Margaret was happy for them. She felt guilty of having monopolized the attention of all Middleton for years during the social seasons. She was the first-born of the Westworth family, and a great match for any gentleman who wished to marry into a wealthy family. But to see now the happiness which her liaison produced in her sisters made any guilt she might have felt disappear, for her sisters had never held any grudge against her.

Now they would have their moment to shine and be attended to in public, to be the center of the gaze and criticism of the mothers of the unmarried gentlemen.

For the rest of the day they talked about some of Middleton's best positioned families, nearby towns, seasonal dresses and colors, remembered the steps to some pieces and tried to get the perfect blush color by pinching each other's cheeks.

As expected, Aunt Beatrice encouraged the two young ladies to participate in the social recreations and insisted on accompanying her nieces to town to buy dresses for the evening. She was nervous because she didn't know if the dressmaker would have time to make two beautiful dresses for the weekend with the high demand. However, she was willing to pay whatever it took to make her nieces look perfect.

In Middleton, of course, there were several women who were dedicated to the tailoring of dresses, but not all of them had the same skill and grace to create true works of art.

Rose and Grace, accompanied by their eldest sister and aunt, went into town to buy other things which, no doubt, were needed to complete her impeccable attire. Some ribbons, a few yards of excellent and expensive muslin to complement her dress, some beautiful fans, and some comfortable and safe shoes.

As might have been expected, her aunt got Middleton's best dressmaker to do the dresses for her nieces. Mrs. Jewsbury and she were intimate friends, and after long years as her regular and faithful client, it was only natural that she should establish such deference.

Margaret found satisfaction in these little moments with her sisters. For years, her independence and pride had denied them this moment, and now, looking ashamed of it but full of excitement, she accompanied her sisters so that they could enjoy a lively dance.

During their walk they met their faithful friends, the Rogers brothers. She was the first to greet the group of brothers who were standing near one of the windows of the village shoe-shop. The young girl ran up to Margaret, forgetting the delicacy and gracefulness that a lady should show, until she took her hands and, with great joy, congratulated her.

"Margaret, I am very happy for you. I wish I could call you sister, Margaret, but I want you to know that I am not capable of holding any grudge against you. We are friends."

Keeping up appearances and with some feigned cheerfulness, Thomas Rogers approached Margaret and her sister. He waited until both friends broke their embrace.

Thomas's sister ran nervously to the rest of the Westworth family, leaving Thomas and Margaret alone. For a moment silence fell between them. They held each other's gaze, but, unable to say anything, they stared at the stones in the street and the firmness of their shoes, waiting for the other to say something.

"Margaret, I wish you happiness on your engagement. Congratulations."

They were few but sincere words. Margaret knew there was no malice or resentment in her friend's good wishes. Though she knew there was sadness in his heart, and that it would be the end of his attempts to win her, Thomas understood his friend's decision.

Margaret, approached him and with a familiar gesture and with no other intention than to show support and affection to the young man, took him by the hands and invited him to share her gaze.

"Thomas, you are a caring, sincere and honest young man. During all these years I have felt your love and support and you have never judged me. I strongly believe that you are a great person and therefore I am sure that you will soon find the right woman. A lady who will not be able to let you escape and whom, God willing, you will fill with happiness."

"I hope God hears you, dear Margaret," Thomas cursed himself after he had finished saying those words. "I don't think it is right for me to call you dear Margaret, for now it will be Mr. Kingsman who will show his affection in that way."

That was true. Decorum dictated that affectionate or affectionate words should now be spoken only by the young woman's fiancé. That hurt young Rogers very much because, although he had always felt warm feelings for his friend, above all he had shared great moments with her since childhood and to call her in that way, comforted him.

But now, they both had to grow up.

"I am sure you will be blissful in your marriage, Margaret, if that is what you wish."

"Of course, that's what I want."

Was it true, was this marriage what she wanted? Of course, she had chosen it. She had accepted Mr. Kingsman as her mate.

She might well have refused his attentions and his courtship and sought a more congenial partner, but there was none. Bullshit. He did exist, but he would not deign to come to Middleton and try to ask for her hand.

She had written to Henry countless times over the past days and weeks, but had received no reply. She didn't know if the letters had gone astray, if the young man had moved away, if he hated her after hearing the news of their liaison, or, worse, if he had grown tired of her or forgotten her after all these years.

Either of the last two options hurt Margaret. To admit that her close, secret friend had forgotten her or hated her would destroy her happiness completely. But he had decided to go along with this silence, and though it pained her, he was the master of his decisions and she should respect that.

If he did not answer her letters, she had no way of communicating with him, so her friend had said goodbye.

CHAPTER 13

19 July 1876
Middleton, England

Margaret was anxious. It was the first social event she had attended since the announcement of her engagement to Mr. Kingsman, and she imagined that all eyes and comments would be upon her. One of the things she abhorred most was being the center of attention, and of course, given her unwilling personality, she had been the subject of much gossip. However, she had to face this decision like a lady. Accept the good wishes of her family, friends and acquaintances and relate to them.

Mrs. Middleton might even take her person as the centerpiece of a few more newspaper columns until her thirst for gossip was alerted by a new scandal. There was scarcely anything interesting going on in the county to quench the craving of the mysterious lady behind the pseudonym.

As the weeks progressed, the novelty of the liaison would fade into oblivion, and at last they could all focus on other matters. That would ease Margaret's nervousness and ease her tension.

Grace and Rose were more animated than ever. Since they had picked up their respective dresses in the village, they were unable not to quarrel about the maid. They both wished to be dressed first, to have their hair more neatly arranged, and even to have their muslin ironed on numerous occasions to prevent wrinkles. Margaret, leaning against the doorway of the room the two sisters shared, watched them with a big smile on her face. She was happy to see that she had succeeded in making her sisters happy.

Her aunt, on the contrary, was in a state akin to supreme happiness and the most extreme anxiety. For years she had undertaken the terrible mission of procuring a husband for her stubborn niece, and now she had under her tutelage two young ladies who would drink the winds for any young man who would offer them his attentions and flatter their dresses. This made Beatrice's task both easier and more complicated. Protecting them from themselves would be an adventure.

On the way to Mr. and Mrs. Pullbright's, Margaret could not prevent certain thoughts from wandering freely through her mind. Would she meet Mr. Bright? Had he heard the news of her future marriage? Would he be annoyed? A part of Margaret wished he would not come to the party, that he would understand that her future marriage to Kingsman was proof enough that she did not wish to continue these impetuous meetings.

On the other hand, she wished he would come to show her that she meant nothing to him, but at the same time she knew he would be looking for her dark eyes as soon as he got to the track.

Margaret was very confused and wondered over and over again how attraction or love could cause such a level of cowardice, confusion and naivety in a person.

"Margaret, please, you must keep your promise and introduce us to all the young people of the evening," requested her younger sister with much effusiveness. "Remember that I wish to dance all night."

"Don't be selfish, Rose. Am I not here?"

"Come on, dear sisters, don't argue. The three of us will go into the house, greet our hosts properly, and then look for a group of people we know."

"Why is it necessary to look for people we know? They're not interested in us, we want to meet new people," her sister replied angrily. She was too free-spirited and jovial to understand some things, but she was eager to meet new people.

"Rose, dear, you still have a lot to learn," said Margaret trying to calm her younger sister, "If we are surrounded by other people we will have a better chance of being introduced or younger people coming forward. If we are alone, the scene is more intimidating and the chances are reduced."

"Margaret, how do you know so much?"

"Because she's been attending and running away from dances like this for years. At this point, she's a master." Grace indicated confidently. She knew her sister had been forcibly forced to learn the workings of society regardless of her efforts to keep herself secluded from it. Grace knew Margaret would be happy taking care of her father's business but it was not to be.

The three sisters laughed in the carriage. Previously, Mr. Westworth, Aunt Beatrice, and Margaret had used one carriage to get about, but with the addition of the two new sisters to the family, space made it necessary to use two carriages for the convenience of all.

"Mr. and Mrs. Pullbright, it is truly an honor to have received your invitation."

"And a blessing and joy that the entire Westworth family and their beloved aunt were able to come."

Margaret made a slight bow which was soon imitated by her sisters.

"It is a pleasure to have you here, Miss Westworth, Miss Westworth. I hope you may find amusement in our dances and refreshment to your liking."

"It will be, Mrs. Pullbright, we are sure." Rose spoke those words quickly, still looking around the house for familiar faces. She took Grace by the hand and together they headed inside.

"Excuse my sisters, Messrs. Pullbright, I think the excitement has made them forget the rules of politeness."

"Don't worry, Miss Westworth," said Mrs. Pullbright, accepting the young lady's apology, with a big smile on her face. I still remember the feelings I had at social functions when I was younger. I was so nervous that I tripped over my left foot and spilled some of my drink on the jacket of one of the guests."

"My dear, that guest, that was me," indicated her husband.

"Really?" asked Mrs. Pullbright doubtfully of her husband. They looked at each other and a smile of admirable complicity crossed between them. It was very nice and enviable to see such simple but genuine displays of affection after so many years of marriage.

After bidding farewell to the lovesick Pullbright couple, Margaret sought out Mr. Kingsman among the guests.
She wished to alert him to the presence of her crazy sisters before they approached him with little delicacy to thank him for freeing them from the torture of social incarceration.

His friend, Thomas Rogers and his family were also at the party that night and of course, other of his father's associates.

In one of the adjoining rooms were several groups of gentlemen. Some were playing cards while enjoying a few drinks, and next to them, a group of gentlemen were engaged in a lively conversation. Among them, he recognized the face of Mr. Kingsman. As if sensing her presence, he turned his face and met her gaze. Kingsman smiled and politely said goodbye to the rest of the gentlemen and made his way to Margaret.

"I find this evening rapturous, if I may say so, dear Margaret." Mr. Kingsman's melodious voice was a treat to her ears. She struggled day after day not to blush at the gentleman's attentions and his beautiful words, and she was sure that some day, after many years of familiarity between them, she would manage to regard it as a matter of course.

Margaret blushed. Her compliments were sincere, for she could see true veneration in her companion's gaze. She had always wanted a man to look at her that way, and though she had hoped that her heart would react in a more intense and inordinate way, she knew it would only be a matter of time.

"Thank you very much, Mr. Kingsman. If I'm honest, it's the first time I've ever felt inclined to go to a ball, I wanted to ..."

"See me?" asked the gentleman curiously and with a certain mischievousness.

"Yes..." Margaret replied shyly as she gently took Mr. Kingsman's proffered arm.

"You cannot imagine how your words excite me, and, if I may say so, I think the best way to begin this evening is with a dance." The gentleman seemed pleased by Margaret's disposition and smile. Her enthusiasm had increased his impetus.

"I couldn't agree more."

Margaret and Kingsman made their way to the main hall and with other couples stood on the dance floor facing each other. The music started to play and all the dancers began their synchronized dance. Long years of dancing experience had made Margaret an expert even if she didn't want to be, but she had to admit that her partner's feet were more skilled than hers and she found pleasure in that piece.

As expected, all eyes were on them since it was the first social event in which both were seen together after the news of the wedding. If the news of the wedding had not been noticed enough through Lady Middleton's column, that dance would confirm any suspicion of doubt.

On the one hand, from the women, there were conflicting comments. Some of the mothers were cursing themselves for letting slip the opportunity of marrying their daughters to a man of so good a character and reputation. Others rejoiced that at last the eldest Westworth had decided to marry, and celebrated with a few glasses of wine. And, of course, some of the young ladies were angry at their unhappy loss.

Margaret did not hear any of those comments during the whole ball and evening because she did not care for them. She had always shunned criticism and gossip, and now, with so much news about her, it was best to omit it.

The smiles between them at the dance and the complicity that seemed to be present between the young couple excited everyone.

The end of the music ended the dance, but Kingsman requested the next dances and Margaret, determined to enjoy the evening, agreed and danced each one.

As the dance progressed, Margaret began to notice a slight pain in her feet so she sought rest in one of the chairs away from the dance floor. She apologized to her fiancé and even urged him to enjoy the company of other guests.

A part of her wished to get rid of such uncomfortable shoes and to be able to continue enjoying every dance, but politeness would not allow it so she had to resign herself. At that moment, assuming her resignation, she began to observe the rest of the guests to whom, until now, she had not paid the slightest attention.

There he was. A gentleman with eyes as dark as night. In front of one of the parlor windows. And though she caught his countenance from behind, she knew it was him. Bright. Next to a lady.

She was slender and with an elegant bearing. Her dress, a true delight and a perfect gift for any young woman who could wear that lace and corset. For a second, Margaret hated her. She didn't know her, but she hated her. Hated how Bright pulled his body closer to hers. How she unknowingly responded to his pursuit as if they were two objects destined to meet. That slight intimacy between them made Margaret jealous.

She couldn't help it, but her heart was pounding. It was as if she was not in control of her own impulses. She wanted to rush out of the room, to find a place to hide, to scream and cry at the same time.

Margaret cursed herself over and over again and picking up her small bag from the nearest table, she made her way to the large terrace.

There, several gentlemen were chatting animatedly about business. Margaret, who had come in search of fresh air, felt her heart grow more and more compressed when her ears caught a female laughter approaching the terrace. Turning, she found that same young lady accompanied by Bright.

The couple stopped.

"Well, we didn't expect to find anyone out here," said the young woman. "Perhaps we should find somewhere else to talk, Mr. Bright." Her suggestion was welcomed by the gentleman, who, slowly placing a hand on his hip, drew her body close to his.

The gentlemen on the terrace had not perceived the subtlety of the gesture, but when Bright's lips almost touched her ear, Margaret could not help turning her back at once. She put her arms on the balustrade and waited until they were gone.

It was another careless laugh from Bright's young companion that made her lose her reason. With her insides on fire, Margaret left the coolness of the night and hurried back into the hall past them like the devil in the air. There, with alacrity, she sought one of the main corridors that led to the garden. She longed to get lost, to run away, to run as fast as her body would let her, to silence her heart and stifle her spirits.

The sight of Bright showing such intimacy with another young woman had made her unhinged, and she was sure it had been more than obvious to Bright, which made her even sadder.

She couldn't allow herself to react that way. She couldn't allow herself to show such strong feelings when she had just danced with her fiancé. She couldn't.

She walked for a few minutes until she stopped at a stone bench surrounded by neatly trimmed hedges.

She couldn't stop thinking about Bright, about that young woman, about her laughter and that embrace between them. He was a despicable being. She hated Bright.

"Margaret," said a male voice that spoke her name with gentleness and fear. This voice materialized into a body that slowly took shape as it broke through the hedges.

"Go away, Mr. Bright. You won't find the company you're looking for here."

Margaret was unable to look him in the face. Her body, tense and rigid as stone, had her back to the young man who had sought her out. She had risen to her feet so quickly that she had hardly had time to think.

"Who says it's not you?" asked Bright. Margaret was so confused and angry that she could not appreciate whether it was mischief or doubt the nuance she saw in the odious gentleman's question.

"I'm certainly not," Margaret's voice was laced with irony. She wasn't going to let Bright get away with this. She would stand firm and straight, omitting any provocation on his part. "And now if you don't mind, I wish to be alone."

"I have no intention of leaving," Bright replied flatly, staring at a tense, rigid back in front of him.

"Why?" cried the young woman with slight fortitude as she turned to face Mr. Bright. Her face conveyed a mixture of pain, anger, and confusion.

"Why? Perhaps that question should be for you to resolve, Miss Margaret. You should be the one to explain to me the reason for your coarse reaction to my companion when it is quite clear that you enjoy yours."

"Should I excuse my behavior when it is clear that yours has bordered on censorship? Is your young companion aware of your long reputation as a conqueror?" The tone in which Margaret asked each of the questions was inquisitive and you could tell she was overcome with rage. She was overstepping her bounds in her remarks, but she did not care.

"Now I have a reputation as a conqueror? And who has taken it upon himself to spread such a reputation?" questioned a Mr. Bright incredulously.

"You yourself, of course. Do you think that...?"

"Oh, enough of answering with more questions, Miss Margaret. We both know you've been jealous of seeing me with her. It's been too obvious."

"I don't know what you mean, Mr. Bright. I have my priorities straight at the moment."

Of course she knew. Margaret knew distinctly what Bright was asking her. It was jealousy and envy that she appreciated in this recrimination. Mr. Bright had been jealous of Mr. Kingsman's attentions to her.

In the face of the young woman's silence, Bright decided to move on.

"How can you judge my company or my desires when you have decided to marry at the end of the season? You are not my mistress."

The heat of the discussion had caused Margaret to pace back and forth. Nervous she couldn't think straight, but Bright's bringing his engagement to the table, the ease with which he enjoyed another lady's company, and the bluntness with which he'd stated that she didn't own him, had angered her to an unimaginable degree.

"I am."

Without owning her actions, Margaret pounced on Bright, grabbed him by the lapels of his jacket and pulled him to her causing their lips to collide.

It was not a ladylike kiss, but rather a demanding kiss. Bright, surprised by his partner's spirit and momentum, responded to it. He allowed Margaret to accede to it. She opened her lips and the two melted into an encounter that, no doubt by the reaction of their bodies, was expected by both.

Margaret didn't know the ways of love. She had kissed Bright on two other occasions but now she was the one holding him tightly so that the distance between them would not increase, the one in control of everything.

A few gasps came from the inside of Margaret's mouth as Bright grabbed her hips tightly and guided her to one of the nearest trees. There, he gently pushed her body until Margaret's back hit the bark.

The desire that Margaret felt was increasing and lost in the intensity of the moment she embraced the young man placing her arms behind her neck and intertwining her hands. A clear invitation that was accepted by Bright and this encouraged him to go a little further.

It was like swimming in warm liquid and feeling part of it. Margaret didn't know how her legs supported her body, didn't understand why her arms had a life of their own or how her mouth demanded things in such a demanding way.

Bright broke the kiss between them and with tenderness and passion, placed multiple kisses on Margaret's neck. She lifted her head and with her eyes closed gasped.

"Bright."

His mind was only capable of thinking and saying her name. And it was that that drove Bright crazy, who, after hearing his name, took her face in his hands and pressed the kiss even harder. She was his. Completely his. Body and soul. Gone was the jealousy, the argument, and the bad words. He only wanted her for himself.

"Margaret, please. We must stop," Bright whispered with barely a breath.

"No," Margaret answered sharply and forcefully. She was not going to let that moment she had so longed for and hated come to an end.

One word was enough to make Bright lose his mind. Intoxicated by her sweet, innocent scent, Bright wanted more, so much more.

"Margaret, please. We must stop."

"Why?" asked Margaret at Bright's insistence. She didn't understand why he wanted to break up this wonderful encounter between them. It was obvious that passion was flowing between their bodies and she just wanted to show Bright how much she loved him.

"Let's talk. There are things I wish to tell you."

Bright had broken the kiss between them and with much pain and regret, their bodies began to pull apart. Margaret's ragged breathing and rosy cheeks didn't outweigh the tension Bright felt in other parts of his body.

Margaret felt lost and confused.

"We can't repeat this again. You must understand." Bright tried to calm himself and put distance between them as he watched a docile and eager Margaret still waiting for him on the log. It was torture but he had to get over it.

"Why?

"Because it's not mine."

"Of course I am," Margaret confessed as she took a step forward to return to her lover's side. She grabbed him again by the lapels of his jacket, but he caught her hands first and stopped her advance.

"No, it's not my name next to yours on the newspaper ad." Bright's words threw a vase of cold water on that scandalous encounter. She was right, though Margaret didn't think it was an appropriate time to bring that up, at least not after what they'd shared.

"You left," Margaret shouted in response. "You kissed me and left me behind. There was no note. No word or promise remained for me. What did you want me to do, wait for you forever? I've been waiting for a long time for love to come, but I couldn't wait for you without a sincere word from your lips."

"What do you mean?" confusedly asked the knight who now found himself between a rock and a hard place in front of Margaret.

"It's quite simple, Mr. Bright. Do you feel anything for me?" the words could not have come more simply and sincerely from Margaret's mouth. She was tense, confused, and obfuscated by Bright's slippery way of dealing with her problems.

For a moment that seemed like forever to both of them, Bright couldn't take his eyes off Margaret's. It was as if he was analyzing every part of her to figure out the best answer to that question. It was as if he was analyzing every part of her to find out what was the best answer to that question. However, it was the delay along with the lack of a simple answer that made the lady even angrier.

Margaret turned angrily and started to walk away from Bright. Her whole body was begging her to run away to avoid further darts from the insincere heart of this gentleman. How could he be like that?

"Please don't leave. Yes, you're right, I did leave but I wanted to come back to you," Bright confessed as he took her arm in his hands to hold her. He wanted her to understand him, to see beyond what his words were unable to say but her eyes were only asking for help from a person who needed more than silence to calm her heart.

"Oh, of course," replied Margaret mockingly, as she crossed her eyes and raised her hands in exaggeration." And I can tell that by the number of letters I have received during these weeks, can I not? By the promises you have conveyed to me, or by the feelings I should sense from you?" At last Margaret was able to reproach him for what she had been holding in her heart for weeks.

"Sometimes it's not that easy, Margaret. Being with you is hard," Bright replied, bringing his hands to his head to push his hair back. He was nervous, it was obvious.

"Hard?" Margaret's voice was rising by the moment as her anger grew at the incredulity of the conversation. She might not be a connoisseur of the intricacies of love, but she understood perfectly everything that hurt her heart.

"Yes, it makes everything more complex, deeper and sometimes things aren't...."

"Is that why you decided to make your life easier with that other young lady? Why is being with me too complicated?" Margaret asked angrily as she pointed at herself.

However, something grew in Margaret's heart after she asked that question. She hated herself for even asking it, but she knew the pain would be greater if she got an answer for it.

Bright's words were not long in coming.

"I am with another young woman because it pleases me, because I find her smile beautiful and because I need the company and warmth of a woman."

Margaret felt a pang of pain and humiliation. She felt that the moment they had shared was dirty, empty, for Bright was indifferent to sharing it with her than with any other woman. Her hand smacked Bright's face causing a resounding noise at its impact. He, stunned, looked up at her.

Margaret's eyes were glazed over.

"Has that been it for you?" Margaret asked in a sad voice but hoping the answer wouldn't come. "Was I just looking for the warmth of a woman?"

Margaret's hurt look snapped Bright out of his state, who realized at once the mistake he had made with such unfortunate words.

She tried to take Margaret by the hands to apologize, but the young woman was too angry to see reason and refused any further contact between them.

"Find that young lady and bring her here. I'm sure she'll melt in your arms. You do that very well, Mr. Bright."

Without finishing the conversation, Margaret regained her composure and left the place that gave them so much privacy to return to the house. Bright did not go after her.

CHAPTER 14

❦

20 July 1876
Middleton, England

The morning stirred in Margaret too many mixed feelings. She was in her bedroom after a sleepless night, with great fatigue in her body and regret in her heart. She had allowed Bright to touch her body, had trusted him enough to give him the pleasure of possessing her mouth and making him enjoy himself. She had been the one to seek him out. She felt jealous, felt her whole body hate the young woman who had enjoyed his attentions and wondered why she wasn't the one.

However, Bright had made it clear to her after their meeting that he was with whomever he pleased. He had made it very clear. That had infuriated Margaret because she thought they shared something special. But that had shown her that they barely knew each other. They had barely exchanged a few sentences since they had met, most of them provocative, but she had managed to pick up on something special in him. She didn't know many intimate details of the gentleman's life, and yet Bright had something primal about him that appealed to her.

It was obvious that she had been wrong in judging Bright's possible feelings or attentions. It had all been a sham. He himself had confessed to her that being with her wasn't easy, that that was why he sought out other young women. He harbored no romantic feelings for her beyond carnal need or pleasure. It wasn't enough for Margaret. She needed to establish a deeper bond that would allow her to justify her reason for skirting the rules with the gentleman.

Margaret knew Bright wouldn't go after her since, if they were both seen coming out of the darkness that area offered a young couple, the scandal would be a heavy price to pay. And she was engaged.

What a crazy idea! She was shameless. Those were the words Margaret kept repeating to herself over and over again. She had given her word to Mr. Kingsman that she would be his wife, and not only was she having feelings for someone else, but in her heart of hearts she knew that if Bright had asked for her innocence at that moment, she would have given it to him.

Recognizing that was an eye-opener for Margaret. She would not be that kind of woman. This all had to stop. For years she had rejected gentlemen as unworthy of her and now it was she who did not consider herself worthy of the feelings Mr. Kingsman had for her. She was ashamed of what her body had experienced and craved. Shameless.

He changed his clothes and went downstairs to the living room. There she found her exhausted sisters and a silent father. His sisters, though they were incessantly commenting on each of the dances they had shared with dashing young men and women of good character, showed the mark of weariness on their faces.

"Rose, I don't understand how you can eat so much. I can barely lift my fork. My whole body is sore." Grace slurred each word as if she was having an awful time pronouncing it. She was sure they would hardly have slept at all from their excitement after the dance, tired as they were, and that made Margaret smile. "Blessed innocence, I'm so hungry I'd be able to eat your plate and mine. Margaret, you didn't tell us the dances were so exhausting."

"Then she must be hungry because she danced most of the dances with Mr. Kingsman. You looked very well together, dear sister."

Margaret could barely pay attention to her sisters' words about the party the night before but when she mentioned Mr. Kingsman she calmed down.

"Yes, he's a great dancer, I must admit."

"Possibly one of the best at the party, if you'll let me say so. But young Lucas Jameson was also very skillful at dancing."

"Yes, I had the opportunity to dance with him as well."

"But it was second place, of course."

Rose and Grace began to argue over the attentions the various young men had shown them during the party. On the one hand, it was amusing to watch them compete with each other, but at the same time, the shrill voices were giving her a headache.

Margaret took advantage of one of the servants coming to the table to speak to her father to ask him a question.

"Mrs. Lemon, have any letters come for me?"

"I'm afraid not, my lady. I'm sorry."

Another day without news of Henry. Margaret looked dejected. "Mr. Westworth, Mr. Bright is here."

"Mr. Bright? We did not expect that young man, and certainly not at this hour of the morning," said Mr. Westworth, as he hastily folded up the paper. He checked the time again on his pocket watch, and it was scarcely eleven o'clock in the morning.

Bright? What the hell was he doing in her house? After hearing his name, Margaret's pulse raced.

It was utter impudence on his part to appear so early in the morning at a neighboring house, unannounced and unwilling, at least on the part of one of the young ladies who lived there, to be received. On the other hand, her sisters and her father would be full of praise for the gentleman, for she was sure he would show his most charming and obliging face.

But Margaret didn't need to look again at his handsome dark eyes or his indomitable chivalry to know that this was all a ploy to see her again. Margaret blamed herself as she dug her nails into the palm of her closed hand at the thought of how unclear she had been the night before when she had left their meeting, or how cruel he could be for trying to get close to her after what had happened.

Bright entered the dining room. Margaret couldn't help noticing that he also looked tired and that sad shadows had settled under his eyes.

He wasn't going to take responsibility for his appearance for anything in the world, he was the cause of his own misfortune. Both of their misfortune.

"Mr. Westworth, Mmes Westworth," he greeted each member of the family, removing his hat and bowing slightly. A very good morning to you."

"Mr. Bright, what a joyous and early surprise! What brings you to our home?" asked Mr. Westworth, between delight and surprise, to the new visitor. It was not proper.

"I should like to speak to Miss Westworth, if you would please." Bright turned his gaze to Margaret, who had barely been able to lay her eyes on him. The young woman was trying to show straightness and indifference, but her whole body was strained by that refusing look.

"With Margaret?" Mr. Westworth clapped his hands and motioned to his youngest daughters to join him in leaving the room. He looked delighted as well as curious. "Of course, we will retire to the drawing room."

"Oh, no, Mr. Westworth. I feel rather guilty for my boldness in coming to your house at this hour; I should not like to have your breakfast interrupted for me."

"You are very considerate, Mr. Bright. However, don't worry about the hours. We are, fortunately, quite early risers in this house, so feel free to come whenever you please," Mr. Westworth said as he encouraged his daughters to rise.

Margaret knew that she must be the one to take the reins and lead the young man into one of the sitting-rooms. Grace nodded to him to go forward, and Rose, in slight silence, laughed at her sister's innocent behavior.

Margaret was afraid to be alone with Bright, but she couldn't show her anger at him either, since that would have been a red flag for a bad encounter between the two of them in the past. And thank heaven, no one had witnessed the argument they had had the night before. Her very presence disturbed him. So, when they both entered the small room, they stood on opposite sides of the room.

The silence between the two played a game of cards for which neither had the right trump card.

Bright paced up and down the room. He scrubbed his hands, and on several occasions, he ran one of them through his hair to remove a few strands from his forehead.

Margaret, on the other hand, stood motionless by the fireplace staring at the floor.

"Margaret, I..." when Bright spoke those words, Margaret looked up at him to find that, like her, he was sad and tired. Bright was unable to say anything more. And for a few minutes silence again reigned in the room. Was that what he had come to her house for?

The young girl hated and hated herself for the reactions both her body and her heart were experiencing from being in the same room as Bright.

Her body longed to be in Bright's strong, dominant arms again, and her heart would only encourage her to do so. She longed to lose herself in those lips that had so sweetly spoken her name and enraptured her senses. But her mind absolutely refused to do so. It had wounded her pride to consider her one more of his conquests after their ardent encounter. And such disrespect would not be easily forgiven.

Having made up her mind to put a stop to any further damage to her heart, young Margaret took the initiative and approached Bright, challenging him with her eyes.

"Mr. Bright, if you have nothing to say I beg your pardon," Margaret indicated as she strode purposefully to the door to make clear her interest in his leaving, "but I have some chores around the house that require my attention."

"Wait, wait please." Bright reached out to gently grasp Margaret's hands as she passed him to leave the room.

Their bodies lay side by side. A heat like liquid fire ran through Margaret from her fingertips to the rest of her body parts.

"Margaret, please look at me."

Bright pleaded in a sweet, innocent voice for Margaret's attention. She trembled. She felt. Wanted. Needed.

She shivered from his touch. She felt the heat. Wanted his kisses. She needed Bright. Needed him.

She couldn't fool herself. She couldn't deny that there was no attraction between them when each of her bones had Bright's name carved into it by hand.

The moment she looked up, she knew she had lost the battle that was raging within her. His eyes were drawn to her lips. Sensual, full. She wanted to kiss them again and have them devour her. She imagined his arms around her again. Bright's hands uncovering areas of her body that burned with desire.

"I must apologize for the unfortunate words I spoke to you yesterday. You, Miss Westworth, confuse me."

"I confuse you?" These were not the precise words Margaret had expected to hear, which added to the tension that was already adding to her confusion. "Why are you here, Mr. Bright? Tell us so we can get on with our morning."

"Yes. You confuse me. You confuse my mind when I see your skin react like this to my touch." Bright's hands gently run down her arm as he delights in the way her hair ruffles as he passes "When I feel her legs tremble as I speak to her close."

"That's nonsense!" replied Margaret dryly and sharply. She hated that he took such liberties with her body.

"I am not finished. I feel like you're totally mine, that you want me like I want you. I feel that you are mine every time you let me kiss you. That you let me discover the virtues of passion for you. But then..."

"Go on. Tell me everything you think I am thinking or that is hidden in my heart. Enlighten me." Margaret's anger was becoming more and more evident, and the tension smothered the room with a fierce look.

"You're betrothed to Mr. Kingsman. You have given your word to another man, and yet you seek me. I feel how your gaze judged me when I was with that young woman. Your body told me that you wished to be the one to receive my attentions and to whisper amusing words in my ear. And yet you are not mine."

"You decided to make it so when you left Middleton after our first kiss. You left without a word, without an explanation, and without a promise. You couldn't expect me to wait for you if you can't tell me how you feel."

"Margaret, things are sometimes complicated." Bright insisted on the complexity of being with her over and over again and it abhorred Margaret.

"Things are not complicated, we make them complicated. I doubt that these hands are incapable of writing a few lines that can be sent in a letter."

"It wasn't possible for me." Bright concluded, trying to sound convincing and not taking his eyes off Margaret.

"It doesn't take much effort to write a few lines. I do it almost every day. It's liberating for the soul and the mind," Margaret said sternly. She wanted to make it clear that she was angry, and that however much he tried to pretend that he wished to be with her, he had made no promise to her, nor had he expressed any feeling that would cause her to reconsider her liaison with Mr. Kingsman.

"Besides, you're the one who forgave me. It was you who grabbed my clothes in the dark and lured me in. You keep contradicting yourself and confusing me."

"If I'm honest with you, your chance has passed, Mr. Bright" Margaret became much angrier when Bright accused her of being the cause of her situation. "You have shown me no quality for which I should even consider your words. And I certainly don't mind if you prefer to share your time with other young women."

"You can't deny to me that last night it was more than evident that you were jealous."

"Jealous?" she asked in alarm but trying not to raise her voice too high, for she was sure her sisters would be attentive on the other side of the door. "Why should I be? Mr. Kingsman is a polite, intelligent, and courageous gentleman. He has respected me and treated me politely at all times, we share many hobbies and opinions and I am sure he will make a perfect life partner."

"And I am not, or cannot be?"

"In all honesty, I don't know what to expect from you, Mr. Bright. The first time we met, you provoked me with unpleasant words. The second time we met, you kissed me. You knew the importance of that act, of that kiss, and yet you went away. And as I decipher from your words you are asking me to intentionally break my promise to a gentleman."

"I ask you to break your engagement."

Margaret let out a loud laugh that showed how frustrated she was with the situation. She hated it when Bright played games with her, and her earlier comment had been a drop in a very full bucket.

"I beg you not to laugh at me, please."

"Don't I laugh at you? You went knowingly. If you had left a note or explanation, I would have held you in better esteem or could consider you for a noble gentleman. You declare that you wish me to be yours but you appear in society with another woman on your arm and shower her with attentions." Margaret's fury was unleashed and nothing could stop her now. She had to let loose all that she had been keeping to herself for days. "But then, I can only imagine that he dupes a young woman and then abandons her. Undesirable behavior for a young woman of reputation unless, of course, that's what he intends to do with his actions. To ruin my reputation."

"That's not true, and you know it." Bright replied flatly as he shook his arms in denial.

"No, I don't. I don't know anything about you."

"And yet you want me."

"That's not true."

"Your body doesn't seem to listen to you because it wanted more of me last night.

"You must leave, Mr. Bright."

Margaret wished to end the argument. Her words would not end well, and before the two of them said anything they might regret even more, she wished to bid him farewell. So she left the safety of the fireplace and approached the door to the hall when she was intercepted by Bright.

"Not until you tell me you'll rethink your commitment."

"Not only will I not reconsider my engagement, but such bold and self-absorbed behavior only reinforces the opinion I had of you. You do not love me, Mr. Bright. You desire only that which belongs to another. Tell me, if I had not accepted Mr. Kingsman's proposal, would you find me as interesting? "

Bright didn't answer the multiple questions Margaret was reproaching him with which infuriated the young woman even more.

"Did it bother you to have that which you considered your property taken from you? Couldn't you feel more valued as a man if you displayed your charms on another willing young lady?"

Margaret stared defiantly at her unexpected guest. Her eyes sparkled with the intensity of the situation and the tension Bright always made her feel. For a few moments, Bright was silent, not taking his eyes off her.

"I'm sorry you have such a horrible opinion of me."

Margaret's harsh words wounded the young man who, without saying a proper goodbye, left the room leaving a proud Margaret with glassy eyes.

CHAPTER 15

21 July 1876
Middleton, England

After Bright's visit, Margaret felt guilty. She knew her words had been harsh. The gentleman had tried to apologize, and she, hurt and vain, had thrown a few fierce ones in his face. She had not been brought up to inflict pain on another person, and nothing could be further from what she wished, she knew she should make amends to the gentleman.

However, perhaps the harshness of her words would cause an irreparable estrangement between the two that would help Margaret to calm down, sort out her feelings and keep her promise to Kingsman.

It was best, no doubt, Margaret thought. It was her duty to secure her engagement to the gentleman whom she had accepted, and whom she felt sure could make her happy. In her heart of hearts she knew that no promise of engagement was contained in Bright's words of desire. He had only asked her to break off her engagement, that he desired her, that he desired her body, but he had not mentioned words of love or hope.

The regret in Margaret's heart was growing, for another day was piling up without a letter from Henry, and it made it clear to her that, though she had made her feelings plain to him, he would never come to her rescue. At times Margaret felt imprisoned by the demands of her position. It was evident that her father would not accept the young man she had always been in love with because of his father's recklessness in gambling and the reputation it would bring upon the young woman. On the other hand, the libertine disposition Bright had demonstrated was not the perfect label to assign to a young woman under the spell of passion.

All his logical deductions and the events of the last few days were explicitly pushing him towards Kingsman.

That afternoon, Mr. Kingsman came to the Westworth house to invite his fiancée for a carriage ride. Accompanied by one of his sisters, the young couple made their way to the Kingsman family estate.

"Margaret, I'd like to show you one of my favorite parts of the property."

The illusion the gentleman showed in his eyes was palpable, contagious, and though Margaret still felt twinges of guilt in her heart at having feelings for Bright and being betrothed to an honest and charming man, she couldn't help but smile.

"Of course." Margaret replied delightedly as her enthusiasm for the property grew.

The young woman accepted Kingsman's proffered arm and together they walked leisurely through the garden, enjoying every whistle of a bird, every rustle of the trees and their own animated conversation.

Margaret appreciated the care of the garden and as a great lover of botany and gardening, she enjoyed the beauty of the humble but generous grounds that Kingsman possessed.

It was all a blanket of color mixed with tall old trees and a few fruit trees. Margaret let go of her companion's arm to go to one of the most peculiar trees in the grounds, a beautiful chestnut tree. It was unusual to find a chestnut tree on this side of the country, and she was surprised.

After talking for several minutes about the story of how that chestnut tree had come to the family grounds, Kingsman and Margaret finally arrived at their destination.

"These are my father's stables. My late father had them built when I was just an infant, and when I was only seven years old he gave me my first foal."

Margaret had never been in a stable before, and she realized that she was not dressed appropriately for it. Although they were clean and neat, hay was scattered near the stall doors to feed the horses, shovels to pick up the cilia by the main entrance, buckets of water near the indoor watering trough, and in each of the stalls, there was a lovely whinnying sound.

"Take me by the hand. Trust me."

And so she did. Margaret let Kingsman take her hand and, following in her footsteps, they went into one of the cubicles where the horses were kept. The lady-in-waiting waited patiently at the entrance, but was close enough to come to her mistress's aid in case she needed it to think that she could not see her from inside the stable. The animal smell was strong, and not everyone could stand it.

Kingsman and Margaret stood beside one of the most beautiful specimens of steed the young woman had ever seen.
He had a noble bearing and was of great size. He was brown and his hair looked wild and untamed. Kingsman held out a brush to his companion and placed it in her hands. Guided by them, he encouraged the young woman to stroke the animal together.

"Trust me."

He did so. Together and in silence, they passed the brush again and again over the horse's back, which barely moved.

"This is Lucero, my partner."

Margaret then understood the trust that had been established between the animal and its owner. Years of relationship that didn't bother either of them. At the same time, she was amazed at the ease with which she herself had blindly trusted Kingsman.

There was something magical about that moment. Margaret closed her eyes and felt how the steed and she were one. His docility and his bravery. His temperament. She felt a unique energy flowing between them. It was wonderful.

Kingsman watched the young woman silently as she stroked the pony. A few moments ago he had left her alone to groom the horse and had secretly stood beside her.

When Margaret opened her eyes, she found Kingsman beside her. The knight slowly approached the young woman and without taking his eyes off her, placed a sweet kiss on her lips.

Margaret was taken by surprise, and without realizing it, she tensed up and jumped back a little.

"I'm sorry, Miss Margaret, I've overstepped my bounds."

Margaret's little startle had been misinterpreted by Kingsman as a show of effrontery. The gentleman, with an expression that crossed from humiliation to utter embarrassment, knelt down in front of her to apologize for his confusion.

"No, please, you haven't."

Though the gentleman's approach had come as a surprise, Margaret could not deny that he had chosen the perfect moment to offer such a token of affection. And, to her surprise, it had not been bad.

Those words made the gentleman smile, and, taking confidence again, he approached the young woman, who this time kissed him. Margaret didn't know if it was the first kiss that her companion offered to a woman, but, even if it wasn't, she felt flattered. It was hoped that the intensity of courtship would gradually flow between them and details like that were important for the passion to emerge.

At first, their bodies were stiff and tense as if they were pieces that couldn't quite find a way to fit together precisely, but when she was receptive to his lips and let herself be embraced by him, Kingsman was encouraged to deepen their kiss.

Margaret felt respected and loved in that kiss. Kingsman was giving her his heart to be hers, so that she could see it to the full and know each and every one of its secrets. It was the noblest thing she had ever seen. He took her not in anger but with affection and gentleness, as was proper for him.

There was no passion. There was no fire. It provoked no emotion in her except affection.

It was that thought in her arms that woke Margaret, who, putting some distance between them and still gasping for breath, looked at the one who was to be her life partner. Kingsman's politeness was impeccable and he tried to apologize to the young woman, but she would not let him.

Margaret could not go on with this farce.
She needed to put an end to all the lies she was trying to tell herself to do the right thing. She had to be honest, she had to be a good person because Kingsman didn't deserve that.

"Kingsman, please, you must not apologize to me. It is I who owe you an explanation." Margaret tried to calm herself and to make her companion understand that he was not to blame for her rejection. "You are a noble, wonderful gentleman with too much affection to offer a lady."

"Margaret, please..."

"Throughout these weeks you have shown me the honesty of your intentions, the ease with which we share concerns and even the affection you have for me. I am aware that I am not an easy person to love and that I would sometimes have to give in to my wildness and that I would be happy to do so, but I do not think I am the right lady for you."

"I do not understand. If this moment has made you uncomfortable, my dear, I beg your pardon." There was despair in the gentleman's gaze.

Without knowing how, Kingsman had gone from holding his young fiancée in his arms to being rejected by her. He didn't understand how a kiss had triggered all that conversation that would undoubtedly be definitive for their relationship "Seeing the gentleness with which you caressed Lucero transmitted too many things to me and I felt it was the right thing to show you my feelings for you."

"And it was very nice, Mr. Kingsman. I am aware that I shall hate myself for the rest of my life for what I am about to say, but I feel that I cannot reciprocate your feelings."

Margaret's confession was painful. It was evident that Mr. Kingsman had given his heart to her, and the kiss was a demonstration of his devotion to her.

"You need not love me at this moment, my dear, over the years love will come, I promise you." the assurance with which Margaret hated herself from that instant for what she was doing because the pain she was seeing in the gentleman's eyes told her that Kingsman's heart would break at any moment.

"Perhaps you are right. I love our conversations and my intellect is flattered by yours, but...."

"Don't worry, we have plenty of time to get to know each other. The doubts you feel are normal, I feel the same way on many occasions. But it's the nerves before the engagement and the wedding that cloud our reason. We don't have to get married right away, we can wait until I'm ready. I believe there is something very special between us and in time I assure you we can be a great couple."

"Yes, I agree, but I think something deeper and more instinctive would have to arise in our hearts, in our bodies, something more than the desire for companionship or familiarity."

"You haven't felt anything, have you?

Kingsman had uttered the words that Margaret had been so afraid to say. She did not wish to hurt the gentleman's feelings, but at the same time, she wanted to be sincere. In her heart of hearts she knew that this man, whose heart she was breaking and at the same time betraying her own pledge, was and would have been a faithful and self-sacrificing companion. But at the same time she was aware that nothing but affection would arise between them. He failed to arouse desire or passion.

She owed him the truth and was unwilling to base a future relationship or marriage on a lie, especially when other people's names beat in her heart. Kingsman looked at her with sad eyes fearful of her response.

"No, I didn't feel anything." Margaret began to cry. "I'm sorry to my soul, Mr. Kingsman. You don't know how sorry I can be."

Margaret was telling the truth. She was sorry.

"And I, dear Margaret.

CHAPTER 16

21 July 1876
Middleton, England

Margaret hated herself. She hated herself very much. By confessing her feelings she had ruined perhaps her only chance of marriage, for once the breakup of their liaison was announced no other man would want her. Her reputation would be damaged. But she could not offer Kingsman a life together that had begun with lies. She could no longer keep up the charade.

All her thoughts turned to a mysterious, coarse, vain gentleman who toyed with her and made her feel things that had never come to her from the pages of a romance novel. She hated Bright and she loved him. He was the only one who managed to drive her out of her mind, who drove her to the edge of her own reason. She barely knew him, they'd barely exchanged momentous conversations or talked about the future or sleep, but there was something very deep between them. It had taken her a few days to realize it, but after Kingsman's kiss, her suspicions had been confirmed.

He was her owner.

Kingsman was the first to leave the stable but not before asking the young woman not to make public, for the moment, the breakup of the engagement between them. Kingsman asked her to reconsider her decision for a few days and if she still did not feel that she could have feelings for him, he would announce the cancellation of the engagement.

Margaret admired the fortitude with which Kingsman had accepted her revelation, like a gentleman. This resignation was admirable and at the same time made Margaret suffer more for the hurt she was causing him and that the rules of politeness did not allow her to externalize to the gentleman the possible fury or anger she might feel.

The young woman asked Kingsman if he could drop her off at her dear friend's residence, for she wished him to help her clarify her thoughts. The gentleman could not refuse. Any chance for her to rethink her decision would be wonderful.

The journey home was silent, for neither of them were in the mood to carry on a conversation. The silence made Margaret uncomfortable as she was not used to it, especially in a house with two sisters arguing at every turn. She could not judge Kingsman for his lack of dialectic or expect him to be a more receptive person at this time.

Her dear friend and Thomas welcomed her unexpected arrival and, with a sadness evident to all present, Margaret and Kingsman said their goodbyes.

The gentleman turned around at the entrance to the residence and slowly disappeared down the main road that linked the property to the village.

To keep the heat of the day from taking its toll on the young women's bodies, Thomas encouraged his friend and her sister to enter the family residence, but Margaret suggested a horseback ride.
The request took Thomas by surprise and he refused outright because of the dangerous implications of such an adventure. No lady of his class was to ride astride a horse, only in a carriage.

"You're not a rider, Margaret." Thomas stressed as the young woman strode purposefully up to the family stables followed closely by her friend.

"Are you afraid that I might go farther than you?"

Margaret provoked her young friend to let her get on a horse. She had never done it before, and she knew that to sit on the back of this great animal would be too much of a shock, but a part of her needed to escape the conventions of her own class and, above all, of the moment.

She was sure that she had completely lost her mind by confessing her feelings to Kingsman, causing the breakup of their engagement, and hurting a good person. She felt unhappy, a horrible person, and afraid of what might happen next. It was all choking her, compressing her heart, and she needed time to think. She needed to escape from there, from the pressures of her whole world. She hated having to choose when her heart was a box of threads with hundreds of knots.

"I fear for your beautiful face and body, you should not propose such foolish things, my friend." Thomas tried several times to stop his friend by reaching for her arm, but Margaret was elusive and managed to reach her destination lend-lease.

"Okay, that's clear." Margaret stopped suddenly and turned around to place her countenance next to her friend's and uttered those words that every man dreads to hear from a woman's mouth, "You're chicken."

"No, I'm not."

"Prove it."

Margaret knew that provoking a man by questioning his manhood was the best way to get a reaction from him. She knew Thomas was absolutely right to refuse to let her, inexperienced and clumsy, ride a horse, but she could not back down.

For a few moments Thomas looked at his friend, and it was clear that there was a great debate within him until, at last, he bowed his head and agreed.

There was a winner. Thomas stepped forward to open the doors of the family stables and showed him the horses. Together with one of the grooms, they saddled two beautiful horses. A great horse for him and a beautiful mare for her. She must have been young, for she had not yet attained the proper stature of the species. She looked rather like the horse that Kingsman had allowed him to groom, but this time the mare had a beautiful black mane that had been carefully groomed. A fine specimen.

Thomas gave her slight directions on how to control the horse and made her promise not to do anything rash and to listen to him at all times if she was unable to control the animal. She nodded silently, though she wasn't really paying attention. She was just petting the mare while looking into his eyes.

With the help of one of the grooms, Margaret climbed onto the mare's back and as she had expected, she was very much imposed upon by the height and position from above. A part of herself felt at the animal's mercy, and on the other hand, she felt powerful. It was a reckless courage. Margaret knew it might be a great folly but her need to fly free was clouding her judgment.

"I'll race you."

Those were Margaret's four words before she encouraged the horse to gallop off. Thomas, surprised, began to shout at his friend when she left him behind. Not because she had taken the lead in the race, but because it was the first time she had ever been on a horse and it was foolish of her.

How had he allowed his adored friend to talk him into this? He was not objective about what Margaret was asking of him and he knew, she had played with it.

Margaret rode far ahead of Thomas. Her mare, as she had

predicted, was young and had too much energy that needed to be released. She could tell by the speed and the jumps to avoid some bushes. Margaret was regretting every moment that passed of that idea she had had. Part of her body ached and she knew she would have to pay the consequences later.

What worried Margaret most was how she would be able to stop the mare, for she had tried to pull on the reins on several occasions but the animal had not reacted.

Margaret's fear began to take hold of her inability to control the animal, and even though she heard her friend's cries in the distance for her to stop the mare, the animal would not budge.

Margaret feared the worst. She would die on that animal. The speed had shredded her hair and she was sure that some branches had grazed her face after she had passed too close to them. Her heart was pounding and she felt as if it might burst out of her chest at any moment.

She regretted that she had not listened to Thomas, that she had been stubborn and not heeded his directions. She didn't have the experience or the maturity to take that horse.

But, at the same time, she felt free. That animal was making her enjoy herself and releasing the tension she was accumulating.

A few small drops of rain, preceded by a great rumbling in the sky, gave way to a summer storm. This frightened the horse even more, and she quickened her pace.

Before she knew it, another horse came up beside her as she galloped, and strong hands pulled hard on the reins until the animal gradually slowed down. Both animals yielded to the other rider's commands and stopped.

Margaret remained on the horse, not quite knowing what she should do.

Her gasping breath and trembling hands waited for the rider to give her directions on how to proceed. In front of her stood a small cabin. Thomas had told her about it when they were just children, but they had never been so far into the forest as to see the fearsome ogre's house. A dark tale to strike fear into her, and with the desired effect, Margaret shivered.

Arms grabbed him by the hips and, without looking at his owner, lowered him to the ground. Margaret couldn't control her body's reaction.

"Are you out of your mind, Miss Westworth?"

It was Bright.

Margaret's gaze could not quite focus on the figure, but she recognized his voice and the strong arms that gently grasped him to check for serious damage. She carefully and carefully examined every visible part of his body.

Bright had rescued her.

They were both getting soaked and, without a word, Margaret let herself be carried by her rescuer into the cabin.

"We'll stay here until it lets up. It's a summer storm, I don't think it will last long," ordered the young man as he hurriedly lit the cabin's fireplace with four sticks that lay to the right in a basket. Some of the pieces were rotten with damp and time, but with some skill, he was able to light a warm fire. He turned to look at a trembling Margaret with fear in her eyes at what had happened. She had put herself in danger.

"How can you think of riding a horse like that? Have you lost your mind? Out riding with the sky crying rain and no company," Bright's inquisitive questions were accompanied by alarming cries that further emphasized the obvious state of panic in which the young woman found herself.

"I... I..." Margaret shivered. The moment her body relaxed from being under the protection of the cabin and Bright, she felt weak. The dampness brought on by the wet clothes and the tension and fear experienced on the horse now made her body shiver.

Bright suddenly reached over and wrapped his arms around her.

"Forgive me, I did not mean to shout at you. I have been so afraid to see you on the horse. I was afraid I wouldn't be in time to stop it," he broke away from her and took her face in his hands. "If anything had happened to you, I ..."

She couldn't finish her words because her lips were captured. Margaret broke the distance between their faces and pulled her body to his until they melted into a passionate kiss.

CHAPTER 17

21 July 1876
Middleton, England

It was the concern she felt in Bright's words that finally made her react. There was no reason to deny what she wanted any longer. She knew it wasn't right to feel this way about a man of dubious reputation, but still, she couldn't help it, her whole body and soul needed Bright.

Bright responded to Margaret's kiss, at first with surprise, for he was so furious with her that he hadn't expected such a reaction, and then with attention. Seeing her riding so wildly in the middle of the forest had made him lose his mind. And now he had her beside him, safe and sound, claiming his affection. It was he who took Margaret more tightly into his arms.

His hands roamed over her face, not wanting to miss a single detail of that moment. No raindrops running down her rosy cheeks, no laughter, no moans. They were hers. Only hers.

Margaret let herself. She allowed Bright to run his hands over her body. His touch provoked new reactions in her even with her clothes on.

She felt jolts of energy coursing through her limbs and knocking her senseless. For now, she had none. The coldness caused by the damp garments soon began to fade as a hotter heat was now supporting her legs.

Bright, intoxicated by the moment, ventured his hand down to Margaret's breasts. She gave a little gasp at his touch, but for nothing in the world broke the kiss between them. Slowly, the top of the dress exposed shy breasts that Bright devoured. He lifted the young woman up and captured her breast with his mouth, driving Margaret wild causing several moans of pleasure to escape her lips.

Margaret felt herself losing her mind as Bright pulled her into his arms in front of the fireplace. She had never been so intimate with a man before, and though she feared what might happen if they didn't stop, there was nothing she wanted more than to know the passion their bodies were arousing.

Carefully, they lay down on the floor and their gazes met. You could see how their chests were heaving and how their breathing was barely audible. Margaret was teasing, seeking the kiss of Bright who had decided to take a moment to appreciate the moment. He was watching her closely.

"Margaret... You're so pretty and wild. You know what could happen now, don't you?"

"Yes," she replied followed by a kiss. "I understand and I want you."

Those words were enough to make the young man lose his reason. He captured Margaret's face again with one of his hands and kissed her. He kissed her as he had never kissed her before, with passion, with devotion, with fear and longing. He wanted her to be his, in every way.

Margaret felt her body burning. Her heart was pounding and all she could think about was Bright's kisses. For the first time, Margaret experienced the heat in an area that was unfamiliar and forbidden to her and her parts were crying out to soothe that itch. There, with her breasts exposed under the body of a man with whom she didn't feel vulnerable or weak, she felt powerful.

She had read several times about the passion between a man and a woman, between the secrets they confessed to each other in the bedroom and the intensity of the moment. And she wanted all that and more.

Without owning her movements, Margaret ran her hand over Bright's chest and encouraged him to take off his jacket. He complied. Her breasts were already exposed and she wished with every passing moment that he could grab them again. Her nipples were stiff and she felt like they would burst at any moment if Bright didn't play with them. She wanted him so badly...

At no time did Bright ever take his eyes off the beautiful young woman in his arms because it was like looking at a goddess. Pure and true. All of her.

He read in his lover's eyes her desires and as if he were her slave he played with her. That made Margaret moan even more, and she arched her back and fretted as she felt a hardness growing between Bright's legs. She was provoking that reaction in him.

An animalistic roar came from within Bright who kissed Margaret again. He was melted by the innocence with which Margaret teased him, for he knew it came from a passion she was only just discovering in herself. Painfully, he broke the kiss that bound them together and lowered his body until his hand gently began to run down her leg.
From her ankles he slowly worked his way up her leg, slipping under her skirt. That surprise made Margaret raise her head, but Bright whispered to her to relax.

Margaret's body jerked as her lover's fingers reached her most intimate area. There, he fiddled with her hair. Margaret stirred slightly and tried to pull her skirts down again to avoid the contact, for she knew it was too unseemly. The embarrassment of the situation was beginning to creep into her mind, but the ease with which Bright opened those hot lips to release her heat left any trace of doubt behind.

Margaret moaned and Bright, intoxicated by the pleasure he was making his lover feel, was encouraged to continue playing with her.

He lifted her skirts higher and gently, deposited a few kisses on her thighs. This caused Margaret to beg him to stop.

But he did not, for he knew that it was shame and modesty that spoke, for her whole body was screaming for him to continue.

And so he did. In the heat of the moment, Bright slipped one of his fingers inside her. Margaret was lost. She was swimming between passion and madness. She was so hot that she couldn't help touching the top of her dress to remove what little was left of it.

It was indecently passionate.

"Take me."

Bright looked up and, looking at his beloved's pleading face, asked her again if that was what she wanted. She, between moans, cried out that it was.

The young man moved back to eye level with her and with alacrity, shed his boots, trousers and breeches and stood in front of her.

Margaret had never seen a naked man before, and the sight of that body with his erect member forced her to look away. That was not acceptable for a lady.

"Don't look away. This is me, Margaret, and this is what you make me feel just by looking at me."

He stood over her and, looking into her eyes, placed his member at the entrance to Margaret's innocence. It was all too natural and simple, as if fate had planned it that way. He had been the first to kiss her and he would be the first to make her his, so he had to be careful.

Patiently, he waited until Margaret's walls adjusted to him and, when they opened wide enough, he entered. He entered her, breaking through all the barriers that separated him from purity, and this provoked a scream from Margaret.

"I'm sorry, my love," Bright tried to apologize as he listened to his lover's complaint. He was afraid he had hurt her. "Really, I know it hurts, but it's only at first. I'll be careful, I promise."

"I know."

It was Margaret's trust that encouraged Bright to continue. Holding her in his arms was a unique gift to be treasured and so he tried to love her gently until her body relaxed enough to enjoy it.

Despite the pain he had felt penetrating her, Margaret wanted to experience the fullness of their bodies. To make real the stories she had read and the loves she had felt in the secrecy of her bedroom thanks to those tomes. With the first few thrusts, however, Margaret realized that this was far beyond what she had expected.

She was able to experience Bright in a way that was beyond her comprehension for their union had now surpassed the barriers of decency and propriety. He was hers.

At first Bright's tentative thrusts hurt, her body still tense, but gradually, as she managed to relax and enjoy her lover's caresses and kisses, she found the intimacy pleasurable.

Realizing that her body was relaxing, Bright grabbed one of her legs and flexed it so that his body and his cock would fit inside her better. Margaret's response was not long in coming and she arched her back in madness.

Bright quickened his thrusts and Margaret lifted her other leg until she was completely around her lover's back. Margaret felt her lover's member more intensely and was unable to decipher whether she was on earth or in heaven, for the pleasure was so intoxicating that her mind could not sense reality. Suddenly, and just when she thought she could experience no more pleasure, her body jerked and relaxed after a great moan. Moments later, her partner's movement stopped contentedly.

CHAPTER 18

21 July 1876
Middleton, England

Still lying on the floor, Margaret was breathing heavily on Bright's chest. He, lying on his back, fiddled with the strands of his young lover's hair that had come loose from their bun and flowed down her bare back as he reviewed with delight the moment they had just shared.

Margaret couldn't have been happier. She had shared the most precious thing with the man for whom her heart was beating and with whom she was in love. If they had been married and on a warm, soft bed it would have been more comfortable, but it wasn't, nothing could have been more romantic or more beautiful.

She still felt some of the burning in her body and longed to feel her lover on her again, but just the thought of it overpowered her modesty.

He understood what had happened between them, how she had given herself and how he had made her experience heaven together.

A few minutes passed in silence with only the crackling of fire and wood as companions.

Margaret's hand, still resting on Bright's chest, was so peaceful as she could feel his heart beating. She gently fiddled with a few curly strands of his hair as she watched his fingers tangle again and again.

Neither of them wanted to say anything, but Margaret knew she must leave soon because Thomas would be looking for her with concern, and she couldn't let the night catch her unawares. If anyone saw them leave the cabin together, or worse, if anyone came through the door at that very moment, the consequences would be dire.

Margaret wanted to tell Bright that she had broken off her engagement to Mr. Kingsman, that, even if the announcement wasn't official, nothing tied her to him. That, if he wanted her, they could be together. She wanted to be honest with him in the same way that honesty had led her to confess everything to Kingsman.

"I have always found your freckles adorable. They're like stars that fill your face with a unique firmament. If I could watch them for hours, I'm sure I'd be able to discover the secrets they hide." Bright gently ran his fingertips over his young lover's face, uncovering each of the spots that lively and delicately covered her face. She remained with her eyes closed as if to memorize the path he was tracing over her face. "You have such soft, sweet skin...."

It was such a familiar and tender feeling that she could only feel the warmth melt her insides. With her eyes closed she could only feel Bright's hand cupping her face. Gone was the challenging, bullying man who teased her to her heart's content. She was in the arms of a different man. She closed her eyes to enjoy this moment because she knew, first and foremost, that it would end as soon as they decided to return to mortal reality.

"Margaret..."

"I love you, Mr. Bright." those heartfelt words came from deep inside Margaret's heart without her even realizing it. She didn't know if it was the time or the place, but she knew they were right. She was in love with this man, with his kisses, his touch, his tense arguments and how confused he made her feel at times.

Lying next to him and still looking at him, Margaret tried to infuse the greatest of her feelings through her body so that Bright would notice the truth behind her words. She had been loved by him and no doubt he loved her back. Or at least, she wished he had.

"We should leave," Bright said, breaking eye contact between the two of them and pulling Margaret's arm away from him to lean back up. For an instant, the young woman felt cold and lonely as she lay alone on the floor of that abandoned cabin in the woods.

The young woman rose reluctantly to her feet and hurriedly began to put on her clothes. Her breasts, still warm, missed Bright's rough, experienced hands, but she had to enclose them within the thin corset.

It was not her body that was causing her the most turmoil but her mind and her heart. She had opened her soul to Bright by confessing her love for him and he had not only not returned her words of affection, but had decided to walk away from her, resolving that Margaret's words were lost in the wind. That wounded Margaret to the core, who had just given her body to a man who did not love her.

Bright, for his part, pulled up his shorts and pulled on his pants. As he put on his jacket, he looked at Margaret.

That sweet young woman had given him something too precious, her trust. And Bright had to return the favor.

"Margaret, this may not be the time to say this, but I would like you to break off your engagement to Mr. Kingsman. I understand that it can't be at once." Bright's request caught Margaret off guard, who, still rearranging her clothes, looked at him in astonishment.

"I beg your pardon?

Margaret was shocked. Part of her, loved the urgency with which Bright was asking her to break her future union with Kingsman. He wanted to claim her for his own. But, on the other hand, it was too selfish a request. Bright was incapable of expressing any feelings for her, and yet he believed he had the right to decide about her future marriage to Kingsman.

"Now that our bodies have joined, I can't allow another man to be able to touch you." Bright indicated insistently as he finished buttoning his shirt but without looking at the young woman.

At last Bright's intentions were revealed. There was no love or honor in his words, only pride. He felt he owned her now that they had shared something so intimate, but he was unwilling to make promises of love or formalize their relationship. This infuriated Margaret, who had no desire to feel possessed by anyone, and Bright had relegated her to a mere trophy.

"No, I won't!" cried Margaret, convinced that she would not give in. Her body may have experienced the greatest possible satisfaction in that cabin, but she wasn't going to let any man tell her what she should or shouldn't do. Bright didn't own her. He was an overbearing, self-important, conceited man. She'd thought she'd seen real concern in his eyes when he'd rescued her from her risky adventure, but she'd made it clear that this gentleman had stayed elsewhere in the room.

"What do you mean by that?" he asked indignantly and confused. He did not believe that the young lady would be so obdurate to his request after what had just occurred between them. Any lady, faced with the situation of losing face in public, would have accepted his proposal at once. It was the right thing to do.

But really, and to Margaret, Bright had made no overture to him, though in the gentleman's mind it was more than obvious that it must have taken place.

"What has this meant to you, Mr. Bright?"

Margaret's question was direct and blunt. The young woman needed to know what this encounter had really meant to him. It was clear that for her it was a complete surrender and a declaration of feelings. Bright opened his mouth several times, but he could barely manage a few mumbles. He was unable to express his feelings, if he had any at all.

This silence hurt terribly for Margaret, for whom their shared intimacy had meant everything. Bright looked at her in fear because he was afraid of her reaction.

And she, for her part, would not reveal to him that she was free to be with him because she had found that he did not feel the same way if he was not able to express it. Margaret had expressed her love for him by allowing him to take her virtue, but Bright couldn't put into words whether their meeting had been the result of carnal passion between any two people or the product of love.

"Tell me what I have been to you, tell me what everything we have shared has meant to you and I will be able to value your request."

But the words still didn't come out of Bright's mouth.

She looked at him terrified and pleading, begging him with her eyes for a word of encouragement, for a hint of feeling for her beyond carnal passion. But there was none. Bright stood petrified in place. His mouth opened, but nothing more.

Margaret, angry and hurt, moved toward the entrance of the cabin so Bright wouldn't see the tears that were about to fill her face.

"Margaret, please let me speak."

"I told you, Mr. Bright, that I was no ordinary woman. But it's clear that I am to you. I have just given my heart and body to you, to you alone. I've made it very clear what my feelings were, but if this meant nothing to you it won't mean anything to me either. Your cowardice is only equal to the gallantry with which you think you conquer the ladies."

"Margaret, please..." Bright pleaded with his voice cracking but it was too late, the damage was done.

"Now let go of my arm for you will get nothing more from me."

Margaret glared at Bright. He stared at her in surprise at the bravado of her words and knew that holding her any longer would not change her mind. So, with great regret, he opened his hand and released her.

The storm had left the valley, Margaret untied the reins of the mare Thomas had lent her and walked back into the forest with her. She dared not ride the animal again. She would have liked nothing better than to lose herself with her in the forest and let her humiliation and shame be lost with every tree she left behind. But she couldn't, she didn't have the strength to climb.

As expected, Bright didn't come after her. Coward. Bad-born coward.

An expression that brought tears to Margaret's eyes.

She had broken her bond with a wonderful man who adored her to give her body and soul to another, with a huge inability to commit. What had she done, she asked herself over and over again.

Her body still remembered Bright. She felt broken inside for having been so naïve, so foolish. She had been wrong to give her body and her heart to this man.

"Margaret, for the love of the most holy, where have you been?"

Riding from behind several trees came Thomas. He dismounted with great speed, left the horse and hurried over to the young woman. He looked at her and without hardly touching her found that she had no serious damage except for some slight cuts on her face and matted hair, her clothes were dry unlike those of Thomas who looked disheveled.

"Are you hurt? Tell me, Margaret, are you hurt?" It was obvious that his concern was genuine, and it pained her to see that the young man's hands stopped trembling when he gave up the search for damage. He looked carefully in all visible places to make sure there was no damage. Except for a few scratches on the young woman's face and a pride wounded by a now unconfessed secret, Margaret was fine.

"No, I'm fine."

But Thomas's concern soon turned to anger, and his words took on a harsher, more critical tone. "How could you do such a thing? How could you do such a thing to me? You can't imagine how worried I've been. You disappeared into the woods, you didn't answer and I could only imagine you lying on the ground. Oh, my God."

Thomas was very angry. He was pacing back and forth without looking at his friend. Margaret had never seen such a state of anxiety and worry in her friend before, so she felt bad.

He hadn't considered his friend's feelings at his stupid, foolish idea of getting lost in the woods, and the time spent in the cabin with Bright had only fueled the fear Thomas had felt at not finding her. It had hurt Thomas.

The hole she felt at that moment in her heart grew until it threatened to engulf her completely. It hurt so much.

"We must go back to the house." said Thomas imperatively and coldly.

Thomas could not look at his friend, and in a state of alteration which he was unable to subdue, he turned and, taking the reins of his horse, began to walk home.

"Thomas, I..." Margaret tried to apologize by approaching her friend, but his stride was determined and firm.

"I said we must go back, Margaret."

His words were blunt. Dry. Direct.

In all their long years of friendship, Thomas had never spoken to him that way and it hurt her too. Without a word, for she knew there was no way she could at that moment repair the pain she had caused, she let her friend help her onto the mare and together they rode home. Aware that the storm might return at any moment since the season was ripe for clearing and rain, they quickened their pace.

Once on the ground, the young man took the reins of both horses and lost himself in the stable. Margaret waited for a long time, but he did not come out again. She understood what he meant.

She said goodbye to her friend in the house, who asked her about the walk, and without giving details, Margaret walked back on her own. She had not been gone long enough to raise the alarm, and she hoped that Thomas would not say anything about her little getaway either.

Walking with her face lowered and crying like a little girl, Margaret returned home. Her body still ached. She had just shared a magical moment with Bright and her private parts were sore. The horse ride had done nothing to improve the situation, so the young woman was uncomfortable.

He cursed the rising of the sun, for during that day many hearts had been broken because of him. Mr. Kingsman had lost his betrothed, Thomas had surely lost confidence in his dear friend, and Margaret had lost her body and soul to a ruffian.

From across the clearing, his fists clenched in tension and anger, Bright watched as Margaret walked away with her mare. Her friend Thomas was escorting her back to his property, but he blamed himself for not being at her side at that moment.

He had been unable to tell her how much that moment had meant to him as well. But instead, he had only babbled like a small child.

"Fucking coward," he kept repeating over and over in his mind. Coward. Coward.

He wanted to run after her, to grab her arm, to pull her in front of him and make it clear that she wasn't just any woman. That she was his woman. His soul. His heart. That from the moment he saw her he knew he'd be a slave to her untamed hair and her smile. That the way she was unnerved by his provocations only increased his desire.

I wanted to reveal too many truths to her.

Too many.

But there, standing by the cabin, he watched her leave, believing that her surrender had been an act of debauchery. The young woman would censure his behavior and marry Kingsman.

He had let the only chance he had to be with Margaret wither away.

CHAPTER 19

22 July 1876
Middleton, England

In the silence of the night, Margaret had not ceased to recall all that had happened the previous evening.

She regretted every action.

Undoubtedly the breaking of her engagement to Mr. Kingsman was the most troubling thing to be faced during the coming of the day. Margaret did not know how much time she would have before the news became public, but she must try to explain again to her betrothed that though she felt no affection or love for him, he was a noble man worthy of any lady's attentions and affections. Any woman would be honored to be his wife. He was a gentleman of remarkable ability and kind heart, and also a great confidant. She was grateful for the charity Kingsman had shown in not insisting on an immediate disclosure of the breakup, for he knew that it would be detrimental to Margaret's reputation. And, of course, that he had not responded as an angry, broken-hearted man.

Margaret felt sorry for herself for not being able to appreciate the young man's attentions in a more romantic way.

Thomas, on the other hand. Her innocent and sincere friend had been badly hurt by her childish behavior. She knew that escaping from his sight would worry the young man, especially since she had managed to manipulate him into going out riding. Margaret was aware that Thomas would not be able to deny her anything and she took advantage of that. She was childish and shameless. The pain she had caused her faithful friend ached in her soul, for she knew that Thomas loved her as more than a childhood friend.

Bright. Hateful, wonderful Bright. Her body was slowly getting used to the absence of his kisses and hugs.

The way he had taken her on the floor of that cabin made her shiver with excitement. She craved his touch and his body and if she had refused, Bright would have obeyed. But she didn't, she wanted to give herself to the passion that was growing between them beyond all doubt.

But while for Margaret their intimacy had only further reinforced the feelings growing for Mr. Bright, he had shown her that his caresses could be shared by any other woman. He had boasted on several occasions of his popularity with the ladies, and at the previous party he had proved it, watching his smiles focus on another woman. But he believed she was above it all.

She thought in Bright's eyes she had a different glow but she had been completely wrong and it hurt her.

Silly, conceited girl.

She did not wish to think of the consequences of their meeting. Bright had asked her not to marry Kingsman not because he had feelings for her, but because, as the rule goes, if a man and a woman lie together, they must marry. It was only because of an ancient tradition.

To even think about the possibility of expecting Bright's child was overwhelming and suffocating, and to know that that might be the only reason Bright would have proposed that she break off their engagement made her even angrier. Like a good man he took responsibility for his actions, but he didn't want responsibility, she wanted love.

She wished that their union was for love because for her his surrender had been complete. Of body and heart.

The sun had long since filtered through the curtains in her room, and Margaret knew she had too much to deal with that day.

The young woman called one of the maids to help her get ready and went down to breakfast with her sisters. They were both sitting wearily in the dining-room. The ball at the Lonsdales' was far behind Margaret's mind, and yet her sisters had not yet recovered from the fatigue of hours of dancing and laughter.

"I can't believe my feet still hurt. I don't think I'll ever be able to feel them again, my poor toes!" dramatized Rose in an inordinate way as she could be heard to be shedding her shoes to ease the pain.

The youngest of the sisters had a penchant for overacting and overemphasizing minute details, but she was also observant like no other researcher.

"Good morning, Margaret, did you get any rest?" asked Grace, welcoming the young woman as she sat down at the table to have some breakfast. The sisters loved to talk over breakfast, but Margaret was in no mood to share confidences on this occasion.

"Not too much, really."

"I don't wonder at all, Margaret. I, too, would have my heart leapt if I were to be married. How thrilling it must be! Mr. Kingsman is a most respected and graceful gentleman. I wish I could find such a man for myself." Rose's enthusiasm was tender but overwhelming. She was a young girl who lived in love with the concept of love.

"Don't burden our sister, Rose. There's still a long way to go until the wedding. Aunt Beatrice is looking for the best dressmaker in the county so she can make you a wedding dress. It won't be cheap, that's for sure, but it doesn't matter because you both have access to a large fortune."

"Grace, don't say that! I'm not marrying Mr. Kingsman for his fortune, and you know that." Margaret looked angry at her sister's remark. Fortune was not one of the qualities Margaret contemplated in a candidate for her husband. She had enough fortune not to choose an advantageous marriage, but it was well recognized that the alliance between the two families would be profitable.

"I know, my dear sister. We are glad that you have finally found a gentleman who respects you, is polite and makes you happy. The truth is that in the last few days you look different. Like this morning, you look different.

Margaret jumped back in her chair. Grace was looking at her unblinkingly, and her remark had encouraged Rose to look at her closely, too. What could they see differently in her? Could they see that she had lost her virtue? No, that was impossible. It was not a trait that could be seen with the naked eye on a young girl's face.

"Don't talk nonsense, sister. Let me have my breakfast in peace, I have several errands to run today and I don't want the morning to be thrown at me." Margaret said sharply to put an end to the rumors between sisters.

Margaret finished her breakfast as quickly as she could and left the dining room, bidding her sisters farewell. She had been rough with them, but she knew that if she stayed much longer they would be able to get everything out of her, and of course her secrets had to remain hidden.

The first of the tasks was undoubtedly the hardest of them all, and Margaret needed all the courage she had in her heart to open the knob of the front door of the Westworth residence and step outside.

The morning was pleasant and mild, typical of a summer day. There were still some traces of the previous day's disastrous storm in the sky, but they seemed to be far behind Middleton.

The town was full of life at that hour and the members of the community were walking to and from in their daily chores and visits. It was hard for Margaret to see how life went on indifferent to the events that had taken place in the last few days.

Without thinking too much about the path she should take, her steps led her to a large house that she had so often visited and could also call home.

"I would like to see Thomas."

In the first place, her conscience begged her to excuse her lack of consideration for her friend. Losing her honor to a libertine was nothing to losing Thomas's confidence.

The young man was in one of the offices, reading some papers. He wasn't surprised to see Margaret, but he didn't smile when he saw her either. Dark marks under her eyes made it clear that Thomas hadn't had a good night either, and that made Margaret's pain grow, for she knew she had been the culprit.

"Thomas, please, I'd like to talk to you if you have a few minutes."

Thomas did not look up from his papers as Margaret demanded his attention. It was to be expected. She could not blame him when it had been she who had acted in a reprehensible manner. He had only tried to care for her, to protect her, but she, stubborn and childish, had had her way.

"I am aware that I hurt you a lot yesterday. I manipulated you, knowingly dared you to help me ride a horse because I needed to breathe and think about a lot of things. I can't imagine the anguish you felt when you couldn't find me in the woods. I certainly deliberately disobeyed you and I am heartily sorry for that. I have been a bad person and a terrible friend, Thomas. Can you forgive me?"

Margaret's voice broke with the last few sentences of apology and tears came to her eyes. She walked over to her friend's table and knelt down in front of him. She took his hands and begged him to look at her.

The pain she felt in her heart right now was great, and it tore at her soul. She hadn't been aware of the real pain she had caused her friend until she saw him in that state and could appreciate his indifference. Her chest ached so much that she could barely breathe. She only wished her friend could look him in the eye one more time.

"I'm really, really sorry, Thomas. I'm sorry to my soul. I shouldn't have played with you and your feelings. I'm sorry."

Margaret's crying was heartbreaking and Thomas, moved by his friend's apology, hugged her.

"I can swear to you Margaret, I have never been so distressed in my life. If anything had happened to you, I'd..."

If Thomas's voice didn't deceive her, Margaret noticed how her friend's words were beginning to take on a tone tinged with tears. The young man was crying, too.

Margaret broke out of Thomas's embrace because she wanted to apologize by looking into his eyes, but at the same time she knew that Thomas might be embarrassed by her tears. But he wasn't.

Thomas did not look away, nor did he wipe away his tears when Margaret looked at him.

"I know. Please tell me that I can still regain your trust and your friendship. Tell me that my apology is not too late and that my repentance will be heard" Margaret pleaded gripping her friend's hands tighter. The poor thing was a nervous wreck and her hands were shaking too much, but they were tempered by the firmness that Thomas seemed to be regaining. Her friend took her face in his hands.

"Promise me that you'll never do anything foolish like that. You won't put your life in danger. Promise me?"

"Certainly, I promise, Thomas."

Margaret's promise was sincere and true. She was not willing to hurt her friend in that way or any other way. She knew Thomas was a fine person and did not deserve any mistreatment that her words, actions, or heart could give him. She would do everything in her power to never again wrong him in her life. He was too important to her."

The two friends melted into a warm, tender embrace and Thomas offered Margaret his handkerchief so she could wipe away her tears. It had broken Margaret's heart to see Thomas cry and she promised herself that she would never do anything or let anyone hurt him enough to see him cry again. His face always looked happy and that was the way it should be.

For the rest of the morning, Thomas and Margaret enjoyed a long walk around Thomas´s property. Thomas's mother invested time and money in her garden, and although it was humble and simple, it was one of the most appreciated in the village.

After the walk, they both enjoyed an interesting game of cricket in which Margaret, displaying her lack of aim and skill, lost. It was impossible for Thomas not to laugh at his friend's lack of grace in the game, but it was only natural, for it was the second time she had picked up one of those wickets.

"If I didn't know you so well I'd say you let me win on purpose to win back my friendship, but I know you well enough to know that's not true. You can't help but be a mess in this sport," Thomas commented with a chuckle, trying to provoke her friend.

"How can I not be? This is the second time in my life I've played cricket. Mr. Kingsman showed me the rules and thanks to him, after a long time, I managed to get a ball in the hoop. But I think it was the rookie's luck."

"Does Mr. Kingsman know how to play cricket? Maybe I should invite him to play a game. It's fun to find someone who enjoys the sport and with whom to compete."

As Margaret waited for her turn to come she looked at her friend and said thank you for getting her back and seeing him smiling again. He was a great person.

It was almost time for lunch and Margaret knew that her father and sisters would be waiting for her to sit at the table so she said goodbye to her friend and he wished to accompany her home.

"Don't you trust me, Thomas?"

"I trust the protesting and insolent Margaret completely, but I don't know the origin of the horseman Margaret. So I prefer to leave you safe and sound at home."

They both laughed on the way home, happy. They recalled some of the best anecdotes of their childhood with Grace, Rose, and Thomas's sister, and at one point Margaret's stomach ached from laughing so hard.

Margaret said goodbye to her friend at the entrance to the property and asked him to get home as soon as possible, for she did not want his mother to reproach her for sending him home late for lunch. Thomas began to walk with his back to her, turning several times to wave his arm in farewell. Margaret radiated happiness, but the shouts and reproaches she heard inside her house told her that she would soon have to deal with trouble.

The cries of her sisters were her welcome letter as she opened the door of the residence.

"No, you told me I could wear your purple dress to the next dance, Grace. You promised," Rose protested as she strode down the aisles behind Grace.

"I told you 'maybe' I'd let you have my dress, but now I've realized it's the one I feel like wearing to dinner."

"You're hateful."

"Father, doesn't this color suit me better than her?"

Trick question. No matter what answer Mr. Westworth gave to that question, he was committed to hurting one of his daughters and earning her enmity. Margaret looked at him in amusement, trying to figure out what answer would get her father off the hook.

"I haven't seen any young ladies this season wearing that color. Maybe it's not appropriate for this season. But what do I know about fashion, I'm only a man."

Touché.

"Father is right, I don't think I look good in purple. No doubt this cut makes my neck longer, I'll look like a swan."

Mr. Westworth sneaked away to return to his office to escape the awkward situation between his daughters. He adored his precious daughters, but was sometimes exasperated by the constant bickering between the two youngest. They were barely a year apart, but it was enough to make them as different as oil and water.

Meanwhile, Margaret sat and watched with amusement as her sisters continued to argue and cheat each other in order to get the dress. It might have been a moment that would have driven anyone out of their senses, but nothing could overshadow Margaret's day, for she had regained something precious to her, and that knew no color, no dress, no muslin.

Dear Henry,

It is several weeks since I have received any letters from you, but I only hope that all the family are in perfect health. We are all in good health at the Westworth, and I hope it will continue so, for I have noticed that my father sometimes complains of a bad back, and I hope it is only a passing complaint.

I'd love to be able to tell you everything that's going on in my life and how hard it is to keep my sanity.

My sisters, now overjoyed to be enjoying the social season because of my recent engagement announcement, argue every moment about their dresses, hairstyles, and even the attention of the maids. They wish to find a perfect husband in their first season, but I tell them they are too young and to enjoy the fun of dances and cocktail parties. I do not wish them to wait as many seasons as I do, but I am sure that the right man will present himself to them when they least expect him, and then they will be very happy.

My father, on the other hand, is busy with his business and has found a new pupil to show the ways of his industry. The truth is that I enjoy seeing him in this new facet, since it seems that he has rejuvenated several years. There is excitement on his face.

However, I am the one who is now on the razor's edge. Too much has happened in my life and in my heart over the past few weeks and I wish I had a map that could guide me through these intricacies, for I fear that inexperience is working against me.

I wish I could tell you all that is going on, but a lady must have her secrets sometimes, though I must confess that I have been only too happy today to regain the friendship of my great friend Thomas. You may remember Thomas from my previous letters. He is a great support in my life since my childhood and a few days ago I hurt his heart and betrayed his trust with a reprehensible act on my part. But affection and friendship can forgive many things and Thomas's kindness is infinite. I value and treasure his friendship as a rare commodity and have vowed never to lose it again.

As to my engagement to Mr. Kingsman, I must confess that it is a joy to us all. My father is thrilled with the idea and you can't imagine Aunt Beatrice's happiness. Everyone seems delighted with the future liaison. I do not know whether you really wish me to discuss this matter with you in our letters. Please let me know if it is too much for you and I will censor it from my letters.

Lastly, I must confess that I still have hopes of your returning to Middleton. Please, if you could come, even once, I can assure you that I should be the happiest woman in the world.

Margaret Westworth

CHAPTER 20

23 July 1876
Middleton, England

Having regained the confidence and friendship of her old friend, Margaret still had much to clear up. She knew that she owed Mr. Kingsman an explanation. She had to confess to him the reasons why she had decided to break off her engagement.

Something very strong was growing in Margaret, but her inexperienced heart was unable to discern whether it was a true and real feeling or whether it was a passing thing born of youth and the summer heat. It was clear that strong feelings were binding her irrevocably to Bright.

However, she knew she couldn't make Kingsman happy, and he didn't deserve a wife who couldn't give him everything he deserved. The breakup had been the sensible thing to do for both their hearts, but not for their reputations. It had condemned Kingsman to social ridicule and her to the reproaches of her family. She had been the one who had given in to the union, and now she would have too much explaining to do that she didn't know if she was willing to reveal.

Margaret had to put her thoughts aside and prepare to approach the town. She had to deliver the letter for Henry to the post office and buy a few things her father needed for the office: some sheets of paper and ink for the inkstand.

The whole service was in an uproar in the house. That very evening, Father wished to have a great feast. He had invited some members of the community, of course, her close friends were among the guests and that encouraged her, for she would have familiar company.

Margaret walked down several roads until she reached the main avenue of Middleton. She greeted every neighbor, stopped to talk to some of them, and before she knew it, a good part of the morning had passed and she still hadn't made it to the parts store.

"Miss Westworth, what a joy to see you on such a morning as this; what can I do for you? "Mr. Weston was a middle-aged man, with some of his hair of a whitish color, but with a very stately bearing.

"My father needs paper and ink, would you have some this week, sir?"

"Well of course I have, my dear. Let me go to the back and get it. It may take a while, the order came in this morning and I still have some parcels to unpack."

"Don't worry, whatever you need."

Margaret watched as the gentleman slipped into the back room to get the spare parts and she waited while he did so. She wandered around the shop and, looking in the display cases, saw some wonderful pens. She would have loved to buy a new one, as hers was a little worn from use, but she didn't want to burden her family with unnecessary or superfluous expenses.

She walked to one of the shelves by the door of the shop and there, spellbound, she gazed at a beautiful binding of a romantic novel that had just been published.

She was passionate about reading and her heart beat for romances between nobles and young maidens. Forbidden loves made her heart race and that made her sigh.

The door opened suddenly startling Margaret who took a step back as a tall, dark gentleman bumped into her as she entered. They both excused themselves and as they looked up after the cordial greetings, they looked at each other.

"Bright."

"Margaret."

They were both silent. A silence that for any spectator hidden behind one of the columns of that small tent would have frozen his breath.

Margaret fought her strong urge to scream and run away. She hadn't expected to meet this gentleman, and she wasn't prepared for it. Bright's very presence upset her in a way she couldn't control, but she was even more exasperated to find that he still wore that mute countenance.

She had not been able to utter a hopeful word in that cabin after her act of passion, and now she was incapable of conversation in a neutral setting. However, her pride and wounded woman's ego would not allow Margaret to make the first step in what would be a tense conversation.

Bright, for his part, fiddled with the hat he had just taken off when he came in and twirled it around in his hands. He was nervous, there was no need for justification. He was unable to look the young woman in the eye, and that surprised Margaret, for Bright always exuded confidence.

"Have you come to see Mr. Weston to buy material for the office? "Bright didn't know how to start the conversation so he figured something trivial and obvious would be appropriate.

"Yes."

"Sure, that's obvious," Bright said, nodding repeatedly. "Mr. Weston has always had a great back room, I'm sure he can help you with whatever you need."

"I know."

Margaret's dry, angry words were frightening Mr. Bright, who now looked at her pleadingly. But she would not yield.

"Margaret... " his voice was tender and soft. Her name slipped through his mouth as if he were pronouncing the name of his mistress. And as he slowly approached her, almost fearing for her reaction, he took her hand without breaking eye contact between them.

He noticed the coldness in the young woman's gaze, but faint warm flecks glowed trying to make their way through the ice and that was enough to make Bright perk up.

Margaret's pulse, which had begun to quicken the instant he had stepped through the door of the establishment, led her to think that her heart would burst with passion when he took her hand. With his other hand, Bright gently stroked her rosy cheek and gently brushed it across her face.

Margaret closed her eyes and breathed in air that smelled only of Bright. It was as if she were drinking from his soul. He called her name again, and she let out a moan.

"You have been lucky, Miss Westworth." Mr. Weston returned to the shop laden with a few bundles of paper and two boxes of pen ink. At that instant they both stepped back, averted their eyes in embarrassment, and played at each other.

"Really, Mr. Weston?" Margaret tried to restore her composure by catching her breath and appearing normal as she walked back to the counter where Mr. Weston was standing.

"On this occasion, I think I shall give you two boxes instead of one. With the season in full swing and your father's business, I'm afraid you'll need to write too many letters. This way, you won't have to come back to town for a while.

"Oh, but it is no trouble at all, Mr. Weston. It is only a little way between the Westworth residence and your shop, and you know I adore walking. Besides, I should hate to believe that you do not enjoy my company."

"On the contrary, young lady. Your enthusiasm for writing is one of the things I admire as the owner of this small business," Mr. Weston confessed as he looked relieved at the young woman in front of her.

Weston prepared the order. With a dark-colored ribbon he tied the sheets of paper with the boxes of ink and handed it to his client.

Margaret knew that as soon as she turned around, Bright's body, which she knew in detail, would be occupying part of the little Weston store. The whole establishment had an air of tension that suffocated the lovers. Margaret prayed that the clerk had not appreciated their touch.

She wanted, she longed, she wished that Bright was still looking at her and that with those eyes that had always been so captivating she longed to meet him again. But at the same time, her brave heart longed to feel free after the slight he himself had caused.

How strange is love!

"By the way, I've included some extra sheets for you. It's been a while since I ordered paper, but I'm sure you'll like the quality."

Since her letters to Henry had no return, Margaret had decided not to burden her friend and to write less frequently.

She didn't feel ready to permanently break off communication with him after long years of friendship, but it was clear that she was no longer a priority for him.

"You are too kind," thanked Margaret as she paid the amount of the order and smiled at Mr. Weston.

"Have a good day, young lady."

"Have a great day, Mr. Weston. Give my regards to your wife."

He turned around and there he was, Bright. His countenance had changed. Fear had given way to hope. Margaret's reaction to his touch had given him strength, encouragement. With a look, Bright smiled at her and tried to tell her to wait outside.

It was that charming, sweet smile, however, that woke Margaret up. She knew that because of his kind words and his manner she had fallen prey to his spell. She had given him everything she possessed and he... The very thought of it filled her with anger all over again.

It was clear he played with her just as she was sure he had played with many other ladies before her.

"Good day to you, Mr. Bright," were the rough, dry words Margaret uttered before she looked away from Bright and hurried out of the tent, barely listening to the gentleman.

"The same to you, Miss Westworth."

Margaret left the tent and, with a quick step, set out on her way home. She wanted to leave the place as far behind her as possible and did not wish to look back. She had to be there in time for lunch, for she was sure the cook would be waiting for her approval of the week's menu.

And so it was, after leaving the parcel in her father's office, Margaret made her way to the kitchen. Mrs. Norton was a little nervous, and her housekeeper kept giving directions to one and all to make everything neat and presentable for dinner that night.

Mr. Westworth's humility led him to admit that his house was modest and simple, and, though furnished in a delicate manner by the late mistress of the house, possessed a large drawing-room worthy of receptions and banquets. Mr. Westworth, however, found it overwhelming to receive numerous guests, and therefore his public functions were confined to small banquets, games or garden-parties, and a few games of cards.

The housekeeper had always been thankful for it, and Margaret, to her eternal rest, too. Social gatherings were always a source of nerves and overwork for everyone. The Westworths longed for a quiet life, though they could not stay out of the busy social life of the town. They knew how to enjoy some of the little pleasures that Middleton life offered.

After the meal, Margaret, as the eldest woman in the house and her mother's heir, helped prepare everything with the housekeeper and cook. She tried to keep herself busy so as not to dwell on the encounter she had shared with Bright. For a few moments, she had let her guard down. She had let the gentleman touch her again, let him make her feel alive. She tried to stay strong, but this man was capable of breaking down all the walls her heart and mind had painstakingly built.

The afternoon wore on and Mr. Westworth found his daughter pacing up and down the house talking about crockery and cutlery.

"My child, you should rest for a second. Our guests will be delighted whatever menu or cutlery we bring out."

"No, Father, we must live up to expectations. This is not just another dinner party. It's a dinner with respected members, friends and neighbors." Margaret was nervous and wanted everything to be perfect. Part of her needed to focus on preparing for the event to take her mind off all the things she was worrying about.

"It's a time to be with family," his father said as he tapped her on the shoulder.

Those words relaxed Margaret. She had always been nervous about visitors, hating to have the normality of her life disturbed by people coming in. But she was willing to do anything for her father.

After the death of his wife, Mr. Westworth did not sink. Although he loved her with all his being and would have wished the lord to take him with her, he devoted himself entirely to the upbringing of his daughters and the welfare of his business in order to leave a profitable and prosperous legacy.

Without a male descendant to carry on the family name, he knew that finding a worthy husband for his three daughters was his mission. And with an older daughter like Margaret, the task was nearly impossible.

But seeing her now, as mistress and mistress of her house, betrothed to a nobleman of good family, he was glad of it. His wife would be proud.

"The guests will be here soon. You should go upstairs to change," her father commented as he took her hands in his, "I've been hearing your sisters screaming from the study for a while now. I promise you that one day they will drive me mad."

"I doubt very much that day will come, father. You're all straightness and patience," Margaret commented as she gave her father a kiss on the cheek and stroked his light beard.

"And how do you think I have managed to be like that? I am very happy that you have found a good husband at last," said Mr. Westworth proudly as he took his daughter's hands in blessing. Mr. Kingsman has great virtues, and from what I have heard, he is skilled in his profession, so you will not lack money to bring up your children.

"Children?" Margaret asked in alarm. It was evident that her father was not aware of the current state of their engagement, but, even if all was going swimmingly, it was too soon for them to be talking about having children at Westworth Manor, "Father, please, it is still too soon to think about having children. We have only just become engaged. I think it would be prudent to wait a while for us to get to know each other, for there to be mutual trust and love before we plan to bring children into this world."

"I wish I had grandchildren, dear Margaret," confessed Mr. Westworth as he smiled broadly at his daughter who had not yet been able to react to such a sudden request. "You see, when you came into our lives, your mother and I did not think we could be so happy. You were protesting and rebellious, but we adored you. Just like I do now."

Mr. Westworth gave his daughter a tender kiss, and she, broken inside and sad to see her father so happy at the idea of enlarging the family, feigned joy. She could not reveal to her father that the engagement to Mr. Kingsman had been broken off and there would be no liaison. There would be no children running around the garden. There would be no children pulling his grandfather's hair or making him lose his mind.

What a disappointment for Mr. Westworth!

One of the maids had left a box on her bed. Her Aunt Beatrice had given her a special package a few days before, but she had asked her not to open it until then.

Now she understood why. If she had seen it at the time, Margaret would have refused to wear anything so suggestive and striking.

The dress for that night was a lovely green color with a somewhat provocative neckline. It was much tighter than any other she had ever had and that caught Margaret's eye. Her aunt had given her a dress that would catch the eye of every man at the party, but that shouldn't be necessary since, in theory, she had already accepted Mr. Kingsman. Did she expect it to catch someone else's eye? Impossible.

She needed the help of a maid to get dressed and after touching up her hair she looked at the person in the mirror. Margaret had to admit that she looked very beautiful. She didn't like to wear dresses that showed too much of her figure or exposed her small breasts, but that night, she didn't care. As he continued to gaze at her face, her waist, the ease with which the color of the dress brought out her flushed cheeks, and the long, slender neckline that showed off her figure, something changed. She had never looked so ravishing as she did on that occasion. A powerful confidence surged from within her to complete the ensemble.

Something had changed inside her. The shame she felt about her body and the embarrassment of showing it had disappeared and in that instant, she thought that there was no more beautiful woman on earth.

With great assurance he went down to the hall just moments before his guests began to arrive.

The Rogers were the first to arrive. Their father's intimate friend, his wife and two children greeted the family and passed into the large dining room. The youngest daughter approached Margaret almost speechless to tell her how beautiful she looked.

Then the Wiltons and the Murrays.

Margaret was not expecting any other guests, so when the door opened to receive another person, she was surprised. One of the servants announced the arrival of Mr. Kingsman, who, with one of the most elegant countenances of the evening, smiled all the while at the female figure who met him at the door.

The romance between them may have faded after Margaret's request to break off the engagement, but the admiration in Mr. Kingsman's eyes was unworthy of censure. So when the gentleman approached his betrothed, he took her hand and placed a sweet, chaste kiss upon it. Margaret smiled delightedly and welcomed him.

Moments later, the doorbell rang again. Margaret took a deep breath so that no other surprises would come through the door, but the Lord must not have heard her prayer, for vivid eyes stared at her from the threshold.

CHAPTER 21

23 July 1876
Middleton, England

Margaret knew from that moment that nothing good could happen that night when Bright's body and his gallantry crossed the threshold of her house. At that instant Mr. Westworth came to meet the young gentleman, and, shaking his hand, led him into the house, unaware that Bright had not had time to greet Margaret and Mr. Westworth properly.

On the one hand, the young girl was glad that her father was so impetuous and ignorant at the same time, of what was really going on there having saved her from an awkward situation.

However, Margaret's eyes strayed several times to Bright's place in the room only to receive a sense of coldness and aloofness in her gaze. It was evident that Bright had witnessed the respectful greeting between the young betrothed and had not liked it.

Several of the servants handed out glasses of wine and brandy to the guests to whet their appetites before dinner. Gradually, the guests began to group together, leading to lively conversation. Mr. Kingsman was chatting with the Rogers and his father, and Bright had come over to talk to the Wiltons, the Murrays, and their sisters.

"I thought it impolite not to invite Mr. Kingsman, Margaret. After all, he will be your husband," Mr. Westworth said to his daughter as they walked across the room to change conversation and guests, "And it is not right that he should not be included in family events."

"Of course, Father," Margaret said, taking a small sip from her glass. She understood why her father had invited Mr. Kingsman, but... "What about Mr. Bright?

"Well, I've found him a very interesting young man from the start and I think he brings a freshness to our meetings. Besides, he was delighted to accept the invitation as soon as I sent him the letter.

Margaret cursed the freshness of blood that her father desired, for he had unknowingly invited her fiancé, her lover, and her best friend into his residence. Nothing could go right. She had earned this tension herself with her decisions, so she thought a few sips from her glass might relax her.

She needed to quell her remorse for cheating on Kingsman and the tension that had been aroused by checking back in on Bright's tense, cold reaction that clashed with the gentleness he'd shown in the parts store.

She couldn't see herself being able to control both feelings as long as the two suitors were in the same room so, in an attempt to show courage and straighten herself out, she went over to chat with the Rogers and Kingsman.

"I'm afraid the price of meat has been out of control for some weeks now" Mrs. Rogers was speaking when Margaret joined the conversation.

"I've heard that a strange disease is threatening the farms in the area and that the farmers have lost cattle, so it's only natural that the price will go up," argued young Margaret after overhearing several villagers talking during her morning walk.

"Certainly, but it must not be to the disadvantage of Middleton's neighbours," said Mrs. Rogers, with a certain severity in her words.

"My dear, the increase in the price of meat also serves to compensate for its loss," explained Mr. Rogers to his wife, "If a commodity is scarce, its price rises because its value increases. It is a basic thing in the market.

Mrs. Rogers had a great heart, and was noble and kind, but sometimes the terms of economics and politics were beyond her control. Her husband came forward to give her a chaste kiss on the cheek, and all the guests laughed when she gave him a light slap on the arm to keep his composure. They were a wonderful married couple whom Margaret admired greatly. After every display of affection between them she understood how Thomas and his sister had been raised with love and gentleness.

Watching these displays of affection, Margaret wondered if, if her mother were alive, her parents would offer the same public displays of affection. A pang of sorrow tugged at her heart and darkened her spirits.

"Tell me, Miss Westworth, what do you think of the loss of the farmers?"

Kingsman, who had appreciated the silence and the subdued look on his hostess's face, looked up before asking for the question to be repeated.

"We were wondering, Miss Westworth, about your opinion of the farmers' misfortune."

"I see this as an evil that affects all levels of the local economy. Of course, the death of livestock affects their owners, who have lost part of their business and therefore their livelihood. I would hate to think that they prefer to profit from rising prices in pursuit of social punishment. I know some of them personally and they care more about honestly feeding their families than ripping off customers. We should take pity and understand their situation and hope that it is temporary."

Margaret wasn't focused on the conversation as her mind was wandering through a thousand possible scenarios of her and Bright arguing in public, the truth of their liaison being revealed, or guests finding a glimmer of doubt in her gaze.

She was the hostess and had to remain poised and polite, show a facility with words, and of course, be kind and respectful to her father's guests. Therefore, she forced herself to remain focused on attending to her guests with enthusiasm and enjoying their company. She should not allow herself to have a bad night because of one particular guest.

"Of course, Margaret, trust in the customer is the most important thing," commented Mr. Rogers proudly. His father's best friend and business partner for the past decades was an honest man. Her father always spoke highly of the humility with which he treated his workers and prided himself on having a person who was able to carry baskets and baskets of food when one of the families in his care went hungry. In that respect Margaret was glad that Thomas had acquired his father's sensible and kindly character.

"Of course."

"Very wise words, my child," said Mrs. Rogers with a smile on her face. Mrs. Rogers had watched Margaret grow up over the years and was proud of the poise and intelligence she displayed in conversation, the confidence she conveyed in sharing her opinion on subjects that were more suited to men, and in her heart of hearts she felt unhappy that her daughter had not inherited a similar temperament.

As the conversation continued, Margaret slowly raised her glass to her special guest and he returned the gesture. The young woman smiled as she saw no sign of rancor in his gaze.

Dinner was soon announced and everyone present walked to the dining room. There was an aroma of roast throughout the house. The cook, a lady with a great talent for turning a turkey into a feast for the senses, had prepared a real feast.

"And tell us, Mr. Kingsman, when will the happy engagement take place?" Mrs. Murray broke off her husbands' business conversation to turn her attention to something that might further entertain the ladies at the table.

Margaret choked on some of the soup she had just eaten and her younger sister lightly patted her back. She apologized as she wiped the corner of her mouth with her napkin and looked up at Kingsman. The gentleman, who was also looking at her in a hurry from the stall opposite, tried to calm her with his gaze.

"We haven't set a date yet. It would not be fair to the rest of the Middleton ladies if the social season were to be overshadowed by a liaison," Kingsman replied politely and immediately, coming to the rescue of his fiancée, who had not yet recovered from the ordeal. Margaret was grateful for his companion's initiative, for he would not have been able to invent a lie commensurate with the circumstances and the guests' level of interest in the subject.

"Of course," said Mrs. Murray enthusiastically in reply as she clapped her delicate finger-tips together. The answer pleased her because she was a great admirer of the social seasons, and also, one of the mothers who endeavor to know all the new things that are going on between salons.

"The most difficult thing has been to persuade Miss Westworth to accept my affections," remarked Mr. Kingsman, returning his gaze to the young lady before him. Margaret could feel warmth and admiration coming from the young suitor who was still skillfully keeping up his charade despite Mrs. Murray's insistence and the curious glances of the rest of the diners who had interrupted their conversations to pay attention to the gossip "The liaison can wait."

"Of course, young people today are entitled to enjoy their lives a little more before marriage," Mrs. Rogers declared. "If I had turned my husband down sometime before we were married, I'm sure our early years of marriage would have been more intense."

"My dear, you turned me down three times," confessed Mr. Rogers in alarm to all the diners as he looked with surprise at his wife as he watched her laugh in delight at the result her provocative remark had caused her husband.

Everyone at the table, including Mr. Westworth and Kingsman, fell into a fit of laughter. It was beautiful to contemplate the complicity and affection that radiated from this couple after so many years together. They were still as much in love as the first day and it was to be admired and envied. Mrs. Rogers was very funny and her youngest daughter had acquired a knack for it.

Margaret thought, at that very moment, if it was so difficult to find a partner as suitable as the one she had in front of her. A gentleman who had lost his mind three times to ask for her hand, and who, after several rejections, still wished to marry her. Margaret gave them a tender look and shared the moment with them.

One of the diners, however, was not paying attention to the amusing moment that had been shared by all present. Mr. Bright was still eating in silence, his head down, as if he didn't care about the conversation. He had not participated in the collective laughter or shown any interest in the topic of conversation.

"And tell us you, Mr. Bright, the most envied suitor in all Middleton; is there no one who has attracted your attention in all our community?" Mrs. Murray's curiosity sometimes exceeded the rules of politeness. To ask a young man where his attentions were directed was to commit him to ridicule if the decision was not accepted by all.

Margaret looked up from her plate with some disguise to observe Bright's reaction and countenance to her ill-advised question. The young man calmly set his cutlery down on his plate and looked up at Mrs. Murray.

"I'm afraid Mr. Kingsman has landed the only young lady with personality in the whole area."

Bright's words were not the most appropriate, for the youngest Preston daughter was also looking for a husband, and though she did not notice the disrespect shown by the gentleman, the rest of the Middleton ladies present and Margaret did. Though she had no close relationship with the young lady, she felt offended as if the insult had fallen upon herself.

They all returned an angry glance at the young man, who had changed his polite countenance into a proud and ill-mannered one. The ladies, speechless, were trying to find the right words with which to reply, but to avoid starting an argument in Mr. Westworth's house, they kept their composure.

Rose took it upon herself to break the tension that for a moment had been in the air, and spoke of Lady Middleton and her suspicions.

She had been analyzing the guests at the social events for weeks and thought she knew who was writing those lines. It didn't take long for her to share her research with some of the guests, and soon rumors began to swirl around the room.

And while the conversation was directed to the ladies, Margaret secretly looked at Bright. He seemed to her to be high-handed, impudent, and ill-mannered. She would not allow him to offend any of her guests.

The dinner was over and the guests went into the great hall for a drink. Grace approached the piano and delighted everyone with a few delicate pieces. She had always had a unique talent for music and when her fingers touched the keys of that instrument, everything changed. It was as if the music transformed the atmosphere into a warm environment that enveloped the hearts of all who listened.

At that point, no one remembered the uncomfortable moment during the meal, nor the irrational and rude behavior of a certain guest.

"Miss Westworth, would it be very rude of me if I asked for a few minutes of your time in private?"

Mr. Kingsman demanded her attention. He had barely noticed how she had approached him while the music was playing.

Margaret agreed and taking her hand to get up, they walked to one of the farthest areas of the room.

"I want to apologize if the question earlier made you uncomfortable." Mr. Kingsman tried to apologize as they both took a place by one of the living room windows.

"No, Mr. Kingsman. I must be the one to apologize to you. I feel that my feelings and my decisions have placed us in a delicate situation that will be difficult to resolve."

"In all honesty, I still hold out hope that you might retract your decision." Kingsman took her hands. "Perhaps it is my fate to be rejected as many as three times as Mister Rogers before you decide to accept me. But in all sincerity, I hope it is only one."

The intensity and hopeful gleam in Kingsman's eyes leads Margaret to take his hands in order to make him understand that their destiny is not to be together. She admired the tenacity with which he showed his affections and insisted on not giving up hope, but she needed to be clear with him about her feelings to avoid hurting him.

"Nothing saddens me more than not being able to make you happy..."

"Well don't refuse me, accept my hand, accept my feelings and marry me." Kingsman's insistence was admirable and the way his eyes expressed affection was intoxicating.

"Oh, Mr. Kingsman. I have searched my heart for deeper feelings for you, but only affection and friendship have emerged. I am not able to feel butterflies or that tension in my body that would drive me to love you the way you want me to. And I know I couldn't live with myself if I wasn't honest with my feelings for you. You deserve so much more than I can give you."

"There is no passion" confessed Kingsman with a certain sadness in his eyes, but without letting go of his companion's hands.

Mr. Kingsman's words surprised Margaret, who had not wished to break eye contact with the gentleman. She owed him a proper explanation as to why she was unable to reciprocate his feelings. However, Margaret knew that a part of that truth must not be spoken since her own reputation would be scarred if it became known that she had accepted his proposal while her mind and heart were thinking of someone else or worse, tarnished if she revealed that she had been with another man.

"I can't deny that I haven't felt it either. I see your heart and I want to take care of it, but you are right, there is nothing deeper. Many elders say that friendship is the basis of passion, but like you, I disagree."

"Exactly, something more primal, something more intimate has to come out of us, don't you think?" asked Margaret hoping that Kingsman would share her opinion.

"I think you have described in just the right words the fire and heat of passion. I hope, my dear friend, for I wish I could call you that, that you find that person who complements your soul and body." Kingsman's words sounded sincere. Each and every one of them was melody to the young Westworth who felt a great relief that her companion was not as wounded in his manhood as she had imagined. It was understanble.

"And I, dear Kingsman, wish you the greatest happiness of all, for I have no doubt that the right lady will challenge you to a game of cricket sooner than you expect, and you will get a worthy adversary to conquer."

Kingsman took Margaret's hands to his mouth and gently, gently, deposited several kisses on them.

"Your farewell."

Kingsman was a noble man. Other gentlemen might have refused to break off the engagement for fear that rumor would punish him, but not he. Margaret knew the man's goodness, and nothing hurt her more than to break his heart by refusing him, but she had taken it with great politeness.

"We should wait until the end of the season to announce the annulment of the wedding. If we announced it now we would be the topic of conversation at all the soirees and we would be too exposed," Margaret proposed.

"I agree, Miss Westworth. We can argue that our personalities were not compatible enough to bind them together for life.

"I hope that can serve as a deterrent to the curious and snoopy."

"It will suffice, I promise you. I will speak to your father to pay my respects and thank him for entrusting me with his hand," Kingsman proposed. Margaret could not believe how lucky she had been to meet such a kindly man as this gentleman, and she blamed herself for being so stupid as to refuse him.

"Don't you think it would be polite if we decided to return with the rest of the guests? I'm sure the lovers will have to share many confidences before the happy union, but maybe it's not the right time."

Margaret turned toward the rude, overbearing, mean voice that had spoken those words. She would know that figure anywhere, even if the light could not bring out its relief. She knew him perfectly.

Bright.

The gentleman stood several feet away from them watching the scene. Kingsman was still holding Margaret's hands, and from the outside it might have appeared that two young lovers were seeking the privacy of home to exchange secrets.

Bright stood in front of them with clenched fists, a scowl on his face and an air of superiority. It was more than obvious that he hadn't heard the conversation the pair had been having because his anger was more than evident.

"You are right, Mr. Bright, we should go back to the rest of the guests. I have robbed them for too long of this beautiful young lady."

Kingsman slowly moved away from Margaret, passing by Bright's side. The tension was evident, but the young woman was thankful that Mr. Kingsman did not understand the source of Mr. Bright's rude behavior. Kingsman was such a good person that he would be incapable of confronting Bright even if he knew the nature of their relationship.

Margaret was perplexed by Bright's rudeness. Angered by his reaction she tried to follow Kingsman into the living room, but Bright stopped him. He grabbed her arm relatively tightly and whispered in her ear.

"Have they finalized the date of their happy engagement yet? Or perhaps they were talking about the preparations for it?" Bright asked in a gruff, commanding tone. It was clear that the rapprochement between Kingsman and Margaret that he had witnessed had succeeded in infuriating him.

"What's the matter with you, Mr. Bright?" Margaret rebutted angrily as she tried to shake off his grip with a hard tug. "You resent someone else taking what you consider to be yours. Then look me straight in the eye and let me tell you something plainly: I am not yours."

Bright was staring at her with a look of disbelief. It was a mixture of fear, anger, and resentment. Margaret knew she should remain unmoved by Bright's provocations, but when he took her hand and led her into one of the adjoining rooms, she knew it would be difficult.

The knight closed the door as they both entered and placed Margaret directly in front of it. Her angry chest was rising and falling uncontrollably and her gaze was fixed on the floor. She did not move. He seemed to be carefully pondering his next steps.

"That was not polite of you to treat Kingsman, you should apologize." Margaret chastised her captor harshly as she tried not to raise her voice too much.

"It is admirable that you still employ formalisms between us and stubbornly stick to it when the intimacy we have shared makes it clear that there is no distance between us?

"How quickly he resorts to mentioning the intimacy we've shared to excuse his behavior." The way Bright was trying to use their memories together to manipulate their feelings was horrible.

"I can't believe you still haven't broken off her engagement to Kingsman after what happened, let alone let him touch you and kiss your hands."

"Do you think I should break off my engagement to him?" At that moment it was Margaret who needed to provoke Bright, she wanted to generate more tension in him that would lead him to confess the real reason why he was asking for such an act.

"Yes, of course I do" Bright replied flatly as if it were more than clear evidence.

"And why should I if you let me ask?"

"Because..."

Silence seized Bright again. Margaret hoped that the gentleman would say a few words of hope that would encourage her to confess to him that her dream had come true, that she had broken off her engagement. But without the slightest hope that he harbored feelings for her beyond the interest of possessing a woman and being able to call her "his," she would not relent.

Margaret moved closer to him. She thought that if she got close enough for him to smell her perfume, feel the warmth of her body or the rise of her chest, Bright would confess.

The knight closed his eyes. He closed his eyes as he felt Margaret's proximity. At the feel of her breathing. At the feel of her body burning from the argument. For an instant he soaked it in but said no words. It was impossible that he couldn't say anything even though the provocation was more than obvious and Margaret grew even angrier at not noticing an initiative.

"You are nothing more than a proud man whose ego has been crushed by not being satisfied. I am sorry, but I have no intention of breaking my bond..."

He could not resist. He captured Margaret in his arms and kissed her. His lips sought her lips with longing and desire. Margaret, who wanted to stay sane in this dispute, tried to break her embrace to escape the stolen kiss, but the resistance of Bright's body prevented her from doing so.

He continued to delight in her kisses and to tighten his embrace as he felt her resistance. Bright, who had lost his composure and politeness several times during the evening as he watched Margaret's continued pursuit of marriage to another man, couldn't help but kiss her. He wanted to remember what it felt like to hold her in his arms. To love her.

With her eyes closed and the tension growing between them, Bright felt Margaret's arms stop resisting and her demeanor mellow. Her efforts to appear indifferent and tough were fading, and so were the defenses she had set up between them.

Their lips embraced each other without hesitation. Desire. That thing that Margaret had tried to explain to Kingsman that was missing from their relationship and now, devoured her like liquid fire coursing through her body was the only thing she could surrender to. She felt everything turn to flames between them.

Bright tried to further entrench the kiss by grabbing the young woman's hips and pulling their bodies even closer together. Margaret could feel the hardness growing inside Bright's pants and felt her body begging for release.

"You can't get married, Margaret, please."

"Tell me why.... Tell me."

Margaret pleaded with him between kisses, but his response was not forthcoming. He felt that the intensity of the encounter was clouding his judgment and he did the most appropriate thing, he broke the moment.

They were both breathing hot and heavy trying to figure out how their bodies worked if they weren't together. Margaret raised her arm to mark the distance between them and prevent Bright from coming near her again. This man was confusing her in every possible way and she felt like she was losing all reason around him. But on this occasion, she had to hold herself together.

If Bright was unable to express his feelings and make it clear that he had intentions for her that went beyond carnal desire, she would not give in again.

"I told you in that cabin, and I tell you again, Mr. Bright. I will not be one more of your conquests. Not any more. I will marry Mr. Kingsman unless you give me a compelling reason why I should not."

CHAPTER 22

24 July 1876
Middleton, England
Newsert, England

The rest of the evening passed off without further mishap. Margaret had time to chat with her friends, with Mr. Kingsman, and even, on one occasion, addressed a question to Mr. Bright. She didn't want her father or any of the other guests to think her rude or a bad hostess for not paying equal attention to all the guests.

The gentleman begged for her gaze from across the room. He wished that the young woman would look at him, that she would heed his pleas and confirm that the engagement was broken.

Margaret had left the room triumphantly, leaving behind a confused Bright who had expected the young woman to fall at his feet. Margaret's rightness of will had come to her at the best possible moment. Her engagement to Mr. Kingsman may have been broken but she would not give in to Bright's wishes and her own body's desires if he did not declare his love or at least his sincere intentions. She had noticed a certain deeper need in Bright's request not to marry, something beyond manly pride, but there was no promise in his words.

Margaret wanted a love marriage or nothing.

Margaret, for her part, was more than ever committed to forgetting that odious gentleman. She was convinced that Bright would quickly recover from his disappointment in love, if it could be called that, for he would not be without affection from other women if he was open to attention.

That was why Bright's silence pained her, his inability to offer her what she so desperately needed. But without it, Margaret would be evoked to justify to her prospective husband that her virtue had been sullied or resigned to admit that she would never marry.

She had given herself to Bright without hardly knowing him, and with that she had rejected Kingsman because she believed it was the honest thing to do for everyone. But at that moment, she regretted it.

The next morning, Margaret was still thinking about the argument with Bright, so she picked up a pen and paper and plucked up the courage to put her feelings into words, something she had mastered to perfection, and share them with the one person she loved most in the world.

Henry.

She couldn't believe that the one person she trusted the most had abandoned her at such a crucial time in her life. He hadn't answered any of her last letters after suggesting that marrying another man would be best for her.

How could he be so insensitive or so foolish as to be unaware of Margaret's feelings for him?

The young woman had to get to the bottom of everything.

Dear Henry,

I am aware that I only sent my last letter a day ago, but I miss our conversations and I would hate to think that in this time I have done anything to damage our friendship.

For this reason, and in order to be able to talk face to face after so many years, I have decided to go to Newsert to see you. I hope to be able to arrive in several days. Although it is possible that, at the reading of this letter, I will already be there.

Sincerely yours,
Margaret.

When she had finished writing the letter, she folded it neatly and went downstairs to the living room to hand it to one of the servants. The latter left the house to contact the postman before he could leave for the delivery.

Margaret's decision to seek out her friend had been hasty and prompted by her encounter with Bright. She considered herself a sensible, thoughtful woman, but on this occasion the man had managed to get on her nerves, and she needed to clarify once and for all what was going on with Henry. She couldn't pretend that his indifference over the past few weeks wasn't hurting her.

She couldn't broach the subject with Bright now, since everything was too delicate and the thought of it was obfuscating, but she needed to understand the reasons for the estrangement she'd noticed in his friend Henry. At first she thought the announcement of their engagement would have hurt, but the letters stopped coming just before the social season. So she needed to clear up the mystery in order to move on.

Of course, Margaret was also nervous and excited to see her childhood friend again, and that cheered her up.

She announced to her father that she was going for a few days to see her cousins in Pollton, a village near Newsert. It was a long time since she had seen them, and she thought it would be a great opportunity. Her father frowned in surprise at his daughter's sudden decision and asked if it was appropriate for her to leave while the season was still in its infancy.

"Father, I am already engaged. For me, dances no longer make sense," Margaret tried to explain patiently to her father as he looked at her in annoyance.

"You're right, have you checked with Mr. Kingsman to see if he thinks it's suitable?"

"I think Mr. Kingsman will be able to do without my attentions for a few days."

Her father nodded, but he sensed that something wasn't right. He remembered that the first moments with his late wife were intense but tense. Two young people who barely knew each other and who were driven by emotions only wanted to be together at every moment to get to know every detail about each other.

However, his daughter decided to go away after the announcement of her engagement. He didn't understand what was happening but accepted it, he trusted his daughter.

In just a few hours, a small trunk, some belongings, and a lady-in-waiting and Margaret herself were ready to leave. She bade farewell to her sisters and apologized for not being able to accompany them to the next society ball.

"Please listen to Aunt Beatrice, she will take care of you."

"Don't worry, dear sister. We are sure we will manage to enjoy the dance even without you. You may find us both betrothed upon your return."

"I'm afraid so."

Margaret's answer provoked laughter among them. She didn't expect her sisters to follow her example of putting off the decision to marry until eternity, but she didn't want them to accept the first man who asked them to dance, either. Marriage was a complicated decision, even if she wasn't the best example of sanity at the moment.

The drive to Newsert took two days. Margaret and Susan, her lady-in-waiting, stayed in a small guesthouse in one of the county's outlying villages. During the buggy ride, Margaret had time to reflect and collect her thoughts.

She longed to finally meet his friend again. She knew that the decision to leave was the right one, and she blamed herself for several hours for not having taken the initiative years ago.

She had always hoped it would be Henry who would come to meet her, but the road always goes two ways, and now she understood that.

But she also wanted to scold his friend for his silence. Because he had abandoned him at a delicate moment. Their friendship deserved more than the absence of letters.

The last letter she had received from him may have been just before the social season and she may not have known the intense details that had transpired since then but it wasn't her fault. He had decided to break off contact for weeks. And though she knew in her heart of hearts that there was a logical and rational explanation for it, all she could think of was that maybe she had lost Henry.

At last, at the beginning of the third day, Margaret and Susan arrived at Newsert. Secretly and carefully Margaret had put some of the last of her friend's letters in her little handbag. When the time came, she took them out and pointed the coachman in the direction. The area was unfamiliar to her so she asked for directions.

The village had charm. From the window of the buggy you could see the people going from one side to the other, a tasty smell of freshly baked bread conquered the air and of course, some knights and ladies strolling around the area.

The coachman finally stopped. He opened the door on Margaret's side and offered her his hand so that she could alight safely. Once on solid ground, she arranged her headdress and dress and looked up. The house before her was modest and humble. Nothing compared to the splendor of the house Henry's father once ran. Poor Henry.

He knocked on the door.

"Good morning to you, Miss, how can I help you?"

A middle-aged lady in a white cap and apron appeared with a smiling face on the other side of the door.

"I am looking for Mr. Henry Williams, am I correct in saying that this is his address?"

Margaret was anxious. Just as nervous as she was on the first day of school. She felt that at any moment Henry would appear and recognizing her voice would smile at her.

"I'm afraid you are mistaken, miss," replied the lady in a melodious voice and with sincerity. She seemed like a good person.

"I beg your pardon?"

"Mr. Henry Williams was the previous tenant of this house, but he left some time ago and my lord occupied his rooms. I am afraid he no longer lives here."

"And by any chance, would you know where I could find him? Do you have any reference to him?"

"I'm afraid not, miss. He spoke to the village estate manager about putting the house up for sale as soon as possible, and it was Mr. Gerald who arranged all the papers with my lord. But if you wish, in case I see the master again, I can tell him that you are looking for him."

"Yes, that would be wonderful. Margaret's smile danced between gratitude and disappointment when the owner of the house did not match the sender of her letters.

"Could you tell me your name, miss?"

"Miss Margaret Westworth."

"Good day to you, Miss Westworth."

Margaret bade her a courteous farewell, but she had her serious doubts as to whether she would have a good day or not, and all the more so after such dire news. It had brought a certain uneasiness to her heart.

The housekeeper had indicated that Henry had left without leaving any information with his new tenants, or with the property manager or a neighbor. Nothing in Henry's letters hinted at his desire to leave or to settle elsewhere. Had he really left?

Her friend had twice moved in search of job opportunities for his family to pay off debts, but had always sent her a letter to refer her to his new location as soon as he could.

That time, nothing. Nothing since he left. The letters had stopped the moment he left that house.

Saddened and frustrated by a trip with so few results, she alerted her lady-in-waiting to help her inquire at various shops in town. Someone had to know something about her whereabouts.

First, she went to the shop where he could get paper and ink for his letters. For several years he had kept the same address, so perhaps the owner of the shop could give her a reference to his whereabouts.

For nearly four hours, the two ladies asked several of the more respected and some of the more suspicious establishments for Henry's references, but no one could come up with anything.

The evidence was clear, Henry Williams was gone and had left no trace behind him.

When it was time for lunch, they both went to one of the guesthouses and there, they ordered some dishes to eat. The sadness of her unsuccessful search had robbed her appetite. Her stomach was clenched and she had hundreds of questions in her head.

"Are you Miss Margaret Westworth?" asked a man of her father's age very politely. The gentleman was carrying a knapsack across his back.

"Yes, it's me."

"I think this is yours."

The gentleman held out a set of envelopes neatly tied with string. She looked at them carefully and turned pale. They were her letters. Each and every one of the letters she had sent to Henry in the last few weeks.

"The housekeeper of the present master of the house was returning the letters to the post office. I have been watching the correspondence between you for years so I thought it wise to keep them in case either of you returned to claim them. In carrying the mail today, the lady indicated that you were in town and I felt the desire to bring them back."

"That's very kind of you. Thank you."

The gentleman took his leave, and Margaret stared at the bundle of cards that now rested on the table. She felt an irrepressible desire to cry. She did not understand what was happening.

She indicated to his lady-in-waiting that she needed to rest and went to the room they had rented. There, on the bed, she cried.

Margaret's heart was a jumble of senseless emotions and every day that passed in her life they became more complicated and entangled with each other. Too much was happening in too short a time and she hardly knew how to sort it out.

At this very moment, more than ever, she missed her mother. Mrs. Westworth was a sensible and cautious woman, though at times she could also show a certain impulsiveness. She was sure that she would have advised her on whether or not she should marry Mr. Kingsman, whether it had been wise to give her body to Bright, or even whether it was childish to go in search of Henry.

Margaret realized that her heart and mind were divided by three men. All her life she had only had Henry and now Bright and Kingsman were complicating things.

She had never acknowledged that her feelings for Henry went beyond the barrier of friendship, but she had always secretly believed that, when the time came, he would come to rescue her from the pressures of her social position and the obligation to marry. Perhaps too childish a thought for a woman of her age. But to acknowledge that the way she saw her friend had become something different was honest.

But her heart did not deceive her.

Bright and Henry had disappointed her. Henry, her closest friend, had disappeared without a trace.

For a moment she thought that perhaps something serious had happened to him to prevent him from contacting her for weeks on end, but she concluded that, given their relationship, his family would have sent that bad news.

Henry had said goodbye in a resounding way. Perhaps the letters were a reminder of the past, a sign of his childhood and that moment, maturity was calling to the fore. Perhaps the waiting had become unbearable for him and he had come to the conclusion that we could never meet again.

Whatever Henry's decision, Margaret felt that given their years of friendship and the sincerity that had always characterized them, he should have confided in her. He hadn't, and for that, she was devastated, sad, and angry.

Bright was another matter. She knew that when she returned she would have to face him. Or, rather, she hoped he would come to finish a certain conversation that he was unable to finish.

Night soon came and Margaret, tired of so much thinking and crying, let herself be carried away by dreams.

Middleton Post. July 26, 1876

Dear readers,

It is possible that, during these days of absence, my most loyal fans have come to think that I have abandoned them. No, dear ones, I just needed to confirm my suspicions. This will undoubtedly be one of the most disturbing columns of the last few months.

Everything seemed to indicate that Margaret Westworth, the great Middleton spinster, was going to star at the end of this season in one of the most awaited marriages by all. Well, not without effort, we've all been working hard to make sure that this young lady would get married. However, according to my sense of smell, this marriage may not take place. There are suspicions that the heart of our young lady is committed to another gentleman.

Lady Middleton

CHAPTER 23

27 July 1876
Middleton, England

Back in Middleton, and as expected, Margaret heard the news of her own break-up from the pen of the blissful Lady Middleton. It seemed that the lady whose identity was a mystery to all knew details of her engagement to Kingsman, and even of her possible affair with Bright that had left her exposed to the opinion of all in the county.

Despite her anger at the tactlessness the vile woman had shown in revealing her secrets for the amusement of others, Margaret made an important decision. If they themselves would not confirm the end of their liaison, no one would listen to Lady Middleton. She would try to live a normal life without men around. Bright did not seem inclined to make a proposal of engagement either, and Henry had vanished without a trace.

For years she had been adamant about not getting married and now, at last, she found the perfect reason not to comply.

Henry had decided to forget her, and she felt betrayed by Bright. She had no hope left in the honest intentions of men.

Though exhausted by the journey, Margaret agreed to accompany her younger sisters to the ball at the Rogers' house. They were like members of her family and, first and foremost, she knew she would feel very comfortable among them. She needed to feel comfortable and at home in those moments. With some help, Margaret got ready for dinner. When she looked in the mirror, she barely recognized herself. There was something very different about her, something she thought she had lost over the last few weeks. Strength and confidence. She would live her life her way.

Once at the Rogers' house, he went over to greet his friends warmly. Thomas was nervous, for it had been quite some time since they had welcomed so many guests into their home, and the sight of so many people watching him as a prospective host made him nervous. One of the things Margaret loved about her friend was his simplicity, his humility and modesty. He would be the heir to a great fortune, but he would still prefer to live modestly in a country house. However, he valued his father's hard work and sacrifice throughout his life and his attempts to ensure that they lived an affluent life, so Thomas had accepted the family legacy.

"Thomas, if you don't calm down I'm sure your nerves will come alive." Thomas's hands were shaking too much and Margaret wrapped them around her own to try and instill calm in him.

"I'm not able to find calm but now that I know you're here, I'm sure everything can get better." Thomas looked more confidently at his friend and she smiled delightedly at him.

"Let's go dancing."

"Are you sure?" Thomas asked in confusion and after seeing the look on his face, Margaret understood why. An engaged young woman should always reserve the first dance for her future husband otherwise she might give away that her intentions for him were not noble or that she had a lover. Margaret blamed herself for not being able to keep up appearances. In her friend's eyes, the engagement was still going on, and she could not embarrass Mr. Kingsman.

"You're absolutely right. I must fetch Mr. Kingsman first, how absent-minded of me! I sometimes find it hard to take in that I am to be a married lady." Margaret apologized for her carelessness to her friend, but she knew it was not necessary.

"Book me the next piece, please." Thomas eagerly requested his friend.

"That I can assure you."

Margaret searched among the guests for her fiancé, Mr. Kingsman. Luckily, the search did not take too long as the gentleman was in one of the rooms having a glass of brandy with several guests. Upon seeing her, Kingsman smiled, apologized to his companions and broke away from the group to approach her. He held her gaze the whole time. It was so warm that Margaret regretted her decision at that moment.

"May I tell my fiancée how radiant and wonderful she looks today? She is certainly going to be the most envied woman of the evening," Kingsman said aloud so that the guests could hear his comment. The tone of his voice changed completely when he spoke to her. It was warm and melodious as if his palate was filled with sweetness. There was no double-meaning in his words, only true admiration.

"I'm ready for our first dance" said Margaret presumptuously.

Kingsman smiled as he heard Margaret's bold words, Margaret realized the pride she had shown in her words and tried to apologize. "I mean, if you wish it, Mr. Kingsman. I do not wish to force you to..." Margaret's voice trembled with embarrassment at the arrogance they had shown. She cursed herself inwardly for being so rude as to continue to offend Kingsman's feelings in such a manner.

"Calm down Margaret. I know our situation is tense at the moment, but I have understood your joke and have wished to share it. If I can't get to hold your hand, I wish I could be your friend."

Kingsman's comment allowed her to breathe a sigh of relief. He was too good a man to deserve her friendship, and Margaret looked at him with benevolent, loving eyes.

"That I guarantee."

Those words managed to calm Margaret down and even Mr. Kingsman was able to steal a smile.

Margaret held out her arm for the gentleman to take and with a wink she encouraged him to lead him out onto the dance floor and back into the dining area. Kingsman gave a small bow which Margaret repeated and arm in arm they walked down the corridor and then into the dining room.

When the new piece began, the two of them shared a joyful dance full of complicit glances. He might not be her husband, but she would share a great friendship with him.

When the song ended, they applauded the band and Margaret and her escort returned with the rest of the couples to the far ends of the room allowing new dancers to come into the area.

Margaret and Kingsman chatted with Kingsman's sisters, and amidst laughter and some sighing from her sister Grace, Margaret noticed something strange in her belly. She felt the air take on a warm tinge. The hair on the back of her neck stood on end as she heard a loud voice.

"Miss Westworth, would you have the honor of sharing the next piece with me?"

She knew, without turning around, who the owner of such an invitation was. For a moment she thought of refusing his offer, for she had every reason to do so, but she did not wish to give rise to malicious remarks that would brand her as ill-mannered.

"Of course, Mr. Bright. It will be a pleasure."

"Thank you."

The minutes that followed until the start of the next piece were interminable for Margaret Westworth. She counted every second without taking her eyes off Bright. The gentleman, who stood on the other side of the room waiting his turn, watched her without blinking. And almost without realizing it, and with the miracle of not bumping into anyone on his way to the center of the room, the two met.

That was a terrible mistake, too big a mistake. Unforgivable.

She couldn't afford to lose his temper and giving in to his charms could be fatal.

Bright was incapable of being honest and sharing any feelings he might have for her, but he felt worthy of challenging her wherever she went as if he owned her body and the reactions she caused in him.

The rest of the couples got ready to begin the piece while the musicians prepared themselves. Margaret kept her head down, trying to remain calm.

She found Mr. Bright obnoxious but irresistible, and she was sure that to look up at him would mean falling back into his nets. She had decided not to succumb, and she needed to be strong.

One beat and Margaret knew it was the end of her.

He took a step forward and their hands touched for only a few moments, but to the young woman it was as if a bolt of lightning passed through her body. She felt more alive than ever when Bright touched her. Couples circled around each other, and danced hand in hand, intertwining with other couples. A beautiful, coordinated dance.

When Bright put his arm behind her back and with the other, held her hand, Margaret felt herself die. Her body burned from the inside out. She could feel Bright's touch making her skin sensitive. She wished with all her might that he would brush against her neck, that he would kiss every inch of her body and that she could forget all about it.

Margaret felt envious and jealous every time her partner's smile was directed at one of the other ladies on the dance floor. And so, she decided to claim Bright's attention.

She was sure that, on this occasion, Bright was not doing it with malice or for the purpose of making her jealous or provoking her, yet he was having that effect on Margaret. She wanted the gentleman's attentions to be for her alone.

And when their bodies met again, Margaret captured Bright's gaze and would not allow him to look at another lady. Bright was surprised and pleased by the determination in her dancing partner's eyes and accepted the power in her gaze.

No one in the room was paying attention, for if they had been, they would have noticed the fury in Margaret's eyes and the inordinate attention the gentleman was showing her.

How their chests had matched despite the distance and how the desire in their bodies was a tension that could be felt in the air.

He finished the piece, they both took a little bow and Margaret, looking mischievous and playful, blinked several times, slowly closed her eyes and began to withdraw from the dancing area. When she had separated several yards, she stopped, turned her face to see a still confused Bright standing in the very spot she had left, and with a simple, decisive gesture, Margaret invited him to join her.

Just a few moments later, Bright had walked with a determined step on the track to reach one of the farthest rooms of that area that had the door ajar. He finished opening it carefully and quietly and there, in the dark, he found a slender and mysterious figure.

He knew, in fact, who was the owner of that perfume, of that sensual and unprotected neck that he was delicately touching. To whom that fine face and strong chin belonged. He knew that her mysterious face would be linked to breasts that he knew and craved like an animal that needs to hunt, and then, her long legs that fit perfectly with her body.

Margaret had betrayed her promise to herself but she couldn't help it, this man was her weakness and his eyes her undoing. She knew that, like the times before, he was not going to give her emotional relief or commit himself to her with hopeful words of a possible love match. But Margaret was prey to those eyes.

The young woman allowed herself to be touched and he, eager to prolong their furtive encounter, whispered her name several times before she let out a moan.

Carefully, Bright began to slowly unbuckle the corset that squeezed those small breasts that were screaming to be released. Her chest was heaving up and down, nervous because she sensed what was coming next. Tenderly at first, then hungrily, Bright captured one of her nipples with his mouth eliciting a moan that was lost in the secrecy of the night. The young woman pulled her body closer to his to ease the contact with her breasts. She desperately wanted this encounter, Bright could tell in the way she had accepted his fierceness, in the way she arched her back and gripped his hair tightly to keep him from releasing her.

Bright, bold and confident that he would not be rejected, broke away from the young woman and invited her to make them both comfortable on the carpet that could be felt at his feet.

She kept gripping his arms so that he wouldn't pull away from her, which she interpreted as an invitation to deepen their encounter. He slipped his right hand under her skirts and with lightning speed but like an ostrich feather, he ran up her legs until he reached her inner thighs. She was wet, warm. She was perfect. She wanted it. Her whole body wanted him. He fiddled with the curls that protected the entrance to paradise and when he felt she was about to lose her mind, he slipped one of his fingers inside her.

Her legs began to tremble and Bright could feel what his skill was doing to her. Her breathing was getting faster and faster and as she tugged at his jacket so that he could pull her up and kiss her. But he didn't. He wanted her to lose her mind. He wanted her to know the virtues of letting herself be loved by him. He wanted them both to meet again in the fire of passion.

They had no fear of being caught in the middle of something so daring and objectionable. When Bright sensed that she was ready for him, he broke away, not without feeling the reproach in her, and quickly pulled down his pants. She, complicit in the desire that had bewitched them both, hiked up her skirt and waited anxiously for the gentleman.

When Bright was ready and prepared to enter her, and he found himself not a nervous or lost young woman, but a woman who wanted to be loved. She was as willing as he was to be carried away by the heat of the moment.

And so it was, Bright thrust precisely into her and captured her lips so as not to alert the guests. She circled Bright's back encouraging him to continue and he took her into the sky.

Bright didn't want to play. He wanted to love her. So even though her eyes couldn't be seen in the dark, he refused to take his gaze from her and gazed at her in silence. He let himself be carried away by the moment and sped up his thrusts more and more. The young woman tried to remain silent despite the pleasure she felt every time Bright came all the way in.

"It's mine, Mr. Bright.

The young woman pulled her legs even tighter around Bright's back so she could feel him even deeper and deeper. This intensified their contact even more and she arched her back to make penetration easier. The determination in the young woman completely seduced Bright who couldn't resist loving her more intensely. Their bodies burned and the heat in the room was overwhelming and suffocating, but neither of them noticed. It was just the two of them.

When the young woman thought the sky couldn't be any closer to her fingertips, Bright instructed her to turn around. She obeyed and deftly lifted her skirts and waited.

Bright caressed her buttocks, grabbed them hard, caressed them again. This disconcerted, alarmed and seduced Margaret even more. The young woman reached back to grab Bright by the jacket and with a strong tug, she told him what she wanted. She wanted him to come inside her.

He shifted his hips a little to make an arc and when he was ready, he came back inside her. After several more lunges, Bright stopped with a guttural groan. Out of gentleness, he didn't drop on top of her, but rolled to the carpet. She, turned around and wet for him, tried to pull down her skirt, however, he managed to grab her arm and stopped her.

"I'm not finished with you."

Those words drove her to the brink of madness as the gentleman repositioned his trousers and leapt without warning onto her breasts. He loved them again with intensity. And she let herself. Bright wanted his companion to enjoy that moment as much as he had. So he went back to playing with the curls between her thighs and teasing the entrance to her mons pubis. She trembled and her legs twitched with his every tease.

She, oblivious to the reality around her, could only feel Bright's burning hands, the fire they had made her feel, and how they adored her body. After several moments that for the young lover seemed the most eternal and pleasurable of her life, her body collapsed and tensed. She had never felt anything like this before. Grateful for the beauty of his partner's body, Bright climbed up to her face and kissed her again and again.

"It's glorious, Margaret."

When his body responded, Margaret moved over to Bright and lying on her half side, she hugged him.

For a few moments, silence reigned between them.

Only her heaving breasts and the accumulated heat in the room bore witness to what had happened in that room.

Bright was sure that if the light could bathe his lover's face he would appreciate a rosy hue to her cheeks, bright eyes and breasts aching with desire.

He knew how lucky he really was. Not that he had such a willing young woman by his side, but that her whole body and heart accepted him. He had loved Margaret again and they had both enjoyed it. Bright didn't understand how they were unable to understand each other with words when it was clear that their bodies spoke a common language.

Yet there was something inside him that still gnawed at his soul and kept him awake at night: Margaret was not his. He had accepted another man's marriage proposal, and despite knowing that Margaret's whole body was screaming his name, he couldn't find a reason why Margaret hadn't broken her promise. He couldn't think rationally. It was as if a ghost called jealousy haunted him relentlessly.

Thinking that the young woman would irretrievably belong to another man, together with the tension he felt because of what he had experienced with her, he made a big mistake in commenting on the following.

"I hear from your father that you've been away for a few days to visit some relatives. Has it been to your liking?" The silence was broken by Bright's comment.

"Yeah, right." Margaret's body tensed. She didn't understand why Bright was bringing that particular subject up right after what had just happened. "It was strange. I wanted to visit my mother's brothers. It had been a long time since I'd seen them."

Liar, Margaret told herself. She had rehearsed a convincing excuse for any curious inquirer who asked about her unplanned trip.

"Curious that you decided to leave Middleton in the middle of the social season, without your fiancé and without your father having any idea of your plans. It would have been better to wait until autumn so that the sweltering heat would not prevent you from enjoying walks in the open air.

These words were enough to break the magic and the moment they had shared moments before. As if it were the spring of a spring, Margaret broke her embrace.

Margaret sensed that Bright's comment was a double-entendre, a hint of resentment or a lack of trust in his word. It was clearly not the best time to talk about her unexpected trip, even more so when she was still waiting for Bright to say a few words from the bottom of his heart that would show her a modicum of affection.

She sat down on the carpet and, with sloppy, awkward gestures, repositioning her skirt, tried to keep her composure. How had he been able to mention her fiancé at a time like this? Had he been thinking about her engagement to Kingsman during their whole moment of passion?

Bright didn't understand how those words had come out of his mouth and he regretted it from the first moment. He knew she wouldn't appreciate his concern but the audacity to provoke him and remind him that even though they had shared something so intimate between them, she belonged to another man.

"Do you think I'm lying, Mr. Bright?" Margaret challenged him angrily as she tried to calm her breathing and get her thoughts in order.

Indeed, Margaret had been angry.

Her grumpiness was matched only by the pain she had made him feel by making him believe again, that this encounter had meant nothing to him. He had decided to abandon the familiarity and affection her body was showing for the coldness of politeness and protocol.

"I don't know what to make of your actions, Miss Westworth. You clearly has no respect for your fiancé or your father, else you would have stayed at Middleton."

"Do you think it convenient to remind me every moment that I belong to another man?" Margaret commented in a dry but sharp tone showing her more than obvious anger at Bright "You asked me to break off my engagement to Mr. Kingsman, but I don't understand your motive as the obvious and decent thing to do would be to send a proposal."

"A proposal?" Bright looked at him in shock and surprise. That comment had taken him by surprise. He may have been a knowledgeable gentleman in the art of love, but he made it clear that his forte was not speaking or using words to express himself sincerely.

"You just want to play with me, that's clear. I shouldn't have trusted you. I knew it from the first moment we exchanged a few words and you made your interest in the opposite sex clear. If you were so decent, you wouldn't play with me."

"But it was you who provoked me to come here. I think it is you who should reflect on the morality of your behavior. It is unbecoming of a committed woman to meet another man in this way."

Margaret was silent. Those words struck her dumb, but Bright was more right than ever, but to hear it as a reproach hurt her to the core.
It was true that she had seduced him on this occasion to force a meeting, despite being engaged and repeating to herself countless times that she should forget about him, it was neither proper nor gentlemanly for her to tarnish her morality in that way.

"I didn't mean that, Margaret" he tried to apologize quickly as he moved closer to her. He wanted to get closer to stop himself from storming off in anger, but it was obvious that he had hurt her.

"Your intentions are all too clear, Mr. Bright. From now on, you will be a stranger to me, and don't worry about my lack of morality, it won't happen again. I assure you of that."

She couldn't explain where she had found the strength to answer with such serenity and sobriety to that hurtful comment, but as much as it hurt her that she had been treated that way, she had been the cause and that made her chest tighten even more. She had brought this on herself.

Margaret settled the discussion by getting up from the carpet and walking towards what she thought was the door to that room. As she walked, she was able to make out the voices coming from the living room, how the music and the party went on without being aware of what had just happened.

CHAPTER 24

※

27 July 1876
Middleton, England

Her body still trembling from the intensity and passion shared with Bright and from her lover's shameless question, Margaret stepped out onto one of the balconies of her friend's house in search of some calm. She needed the air she had so sorely lacked in that darkened room. She would never see Mr. Rogers's office with the same eyes again, knowing that her body had been loved on the carpet he held so dear.

She placed her hands on the balustrade and tried to calm herself. She chastised herself over and over again for having made the mistake of believing that this time she could be strong, that she could control her feelings and let Bright take her body without risking her heart and soul. But she hadn't. Stupid was the word she kept repeating over and over again.

She had been unable to keep the promise she had made to herself. She needed to feel free, she didn't want to be under the sway of any man or let anyone control her, and that night, she had proven the opposite.

Bright was right, for it had been she who had provoked the meeting. She had tempted him with that dance and with her gaze at the moment when his walls and defenses had fallen to the ground and she had told him to follow her into that office. She alone was the cause of her own misfortune and ruin.

However, Bright was also to blame for keeping her in a period of continuous anger and tension by being unable to show any real emotional interest in her.

The night was perfect. A shy full moon lit up Middleton and all that Margaret did not yet know of the world. Watching that immense star made her feel small and slowly her breathing relaxed. If anyone found her in this state she would undoubtedly attract attention, so she needed to relax.

Suddenly, she felt a presence behind her.

"Margaret."

He spoke her name with such gentleness and need that she was tempted to turn and run into his arms. But she didn't. She gripped the balcony stone tighter and closed her eyes violently, wishing Bright would disappear.

"Please," the gentleman pleaded in a whisper. He did not want to arouse the interest of the rest of the guests, but his soft, guilt-ridden tone caught Margaret's attention.

He had hurt her again. She had sacrificed far more than she was capable of admitting for him, and Bright was again emphasizing that she was a betrothed woman and that she had broken her word.

Instead of pleading with affection and affection for her to break off all engagement with Mr. Kingsman, it had been her possessive and boastful side that had dominated. And that, Margaret, she could never forgive him.

Was so few words of affection and love capable of awakening in a man after making love to him? That question made Margaret feel dirty and hateful. There were no words the gentleman could utter that would soothe

the mood and sadness that plagued the young woman's heart. She felt rejected and humiliated.

When Bright realized that Margaret wasn't going to respond to his pleas and wouldn't let him near her either, he said goodbye quietly and walked back to the party. She felt the footsteps slowly recede and releasing the feelings that had been trying to come out during that whole moment, she dropped to the floor.

Just then, Mr. Kingsman came to the balcony and helped her up. In spite of the nervous state the young woman was in, Kingsman didn't ask any questions, just took her in his arms and carefully helped her inside. He found chairs for both of them and motioned for her to take a seat.

He was worried about Margaret and his heart just wanted to comfort her. He wanted to hold her hands and make her feel that nothing bad was going to happen. He wondered inwardly what had happened to her to put her in this state but he didn't want to be indiscreet if she didn't say anything.

"It is not for me to ask questions, Margaret, for we well know that I have no right over you. But I do want to tell you something.

She looked up and watched carefully.

"My mother has always told me that love is like a storm. It is unpredictable, indomitable, treacherous and violent. It tides the waters, twists the forests and impresses with its lightning. But there is also beauty behind it. It helps the fields to grow and nature to run its course, it produces special and brilliant sparkles in the sky and captures everyone's breath."

"I don't understand you."

"Everything may seem complicated now, but don't forget that after the storm there is always a calm.

Kingsman took Margaret's hands in his and with light touches tried to reassure her. The young woman couldn't quite understand

Kingsman's words, but something inside her told her that he was trying to help her.

"I will always be by your side, Margaret, as your friend, if you so desire. And if at any time you wish to share with me your thoughts or sufferings, I will be ready to listen to them."

"It would be a real pleasure for me."

Her companion's eyes looked sad, but when he took her hands to his mouth and placed a kiss on them, Margaret caught a slight gleam in his eye. It pained her that she had not been able to love this man. She was sure he would have been the perfect husband, but she didn't crave the perfect husband, she needed a husband who made every day feel like an adventure.

I needed fucking Bright.

For a while, the two friends remained in the hallway until, calmer, Margaret took the initiative to ask Kingsman to dance, who gladly accepted.

They shared not just one dance, but three. Thomas, his friend, claimed the fourth and again, she took Kingsman's hand. Both young men had made her smile again and enjoy the night she had thought was completely lost after her argument with Bright.

She willed herself not to look for his eyes in the audience, but, in a moment of weakness, she found them. They were leaning against one of the windows of the room, a full glass in one hand and whispering words in their conversation partner's ear.

At first, Margaret chalked up the loud noise caused by the music, voices, and revelry to their proximity for conversation, but when he placed his hand on her chest, she became enraged. She gently grabbed his hand and pulled it away from her torso, giving Margaret hope that soon vanished as quickly as Bright drained the drinks.

The evening was coming to an end and part of Margaret was glad to be going home to rest, but another part needed to stay with her friends and Mr. Kingsman a little longer.

She hadn't been the best of company that night and had even disappeared from the room for a sinful while, but she couldn't forget how much she had enjoyed dancing carefree with her fiancé, her friends and her sisters.

Climbing into the buggy with her sisters, her father and her Aunt Beatrice, they all bade a fond farewell to their hosts and wished them rest for the rest of the night.

CHAPTER 25

※

28 July 1876
Middleton, England

Her whole body was sore. Not just from the hours and hours that Margaret had enjoyed on the dance floor dancing with other guests at the Rogers' party, but from the passion that Bright had shown her relentlessly in that office.

She had recreated that moment many times. Her sweet caresses, her intense kisses, how he had loved her breasts and the fierceness he had shown when he had entered her. Far from frightening him by such bold, carnal behavior, she had encouraged it. She had begged Bright to make her his.

That was why she couldn't understand how things had gone so wrong and how they were so incapable of understanding each other when it was clear that their bodies loved each other. During the night, Bright had once again demonstrated that haughty, presumptuous, conquering demeanor he'd bragged so much about with another young woman. And maybe this time it was to hurt her.

I didn't understand anything.

She needed to put an end to this matter forever or else she would end up losing her mind and her heart. And so she summoned all the courage she could muster, dressed herself, and, with determination, asked her housekeeper to send for the coachman. She was to visit Bright at once.

Henry Williams had decided to interrupt his communication with her and now also for Bright, he needed to know if it was her fault.

"May I know where you are going in such a hurry, Margaret?" asked her sister Grace curiously and impudently.

"I'm sure Mr. Kingsman has come to fetch her and she, as usual, is late," commented the youngest of the sisters with a certain jocular tone as she finished stitching the new picture she was painstakingly embroidering.

"Do you think Mr. Kingsman is coming?"

"Of course, he is our sister's fiancé, he must be seen in our house often, otherwise the rumors could start. Besides, they danced several times last night, and I'm sure you noticed Margaret's smile, she was in high spirits.

"Sisters, you are nosy, stubborn, and snoopy." Margaret scolded as she finished picking up the small fan that lay next to the table.

Margaret was in a hurry to leave the house as soon as possible, or she was afraid of losing the courage that was now vibrating in her heart. But, on the other hand, she was glad of the ingenuity which her sisters breathed in the face of all the maelstrom of feelings, encounters, and disaffections which were present in their elder sister's life.

"But, still, you adore us."

"And how could I not? Now, if you will excuse me, I have something very important to do.

At no time did guilt punish Margaret for setting out to wake Bright, since it had been a good part of the morning, and it was a more than prudent hour for a social call. Perhaps, however, the excess wine he'd ingested the night before had kept him lethargic. Margaret didn't mind.

When the coachman stopped in front of his house, he helped down the young lady who had asked her lady-in-waiting to stay at home on this occasion, and with a determined step went to the door.

She knocked politely and a middle-aged lady appeared on the other side.

"I am Miss Westworth, I would like to see Mr. Bright, please."

"Of course, please come in."

The housekeeper invited Margaret to follow him down the hall to a modest but warm room. As she entered, her heart stopped.

There was a young woman sitting on one of the small sofas.

It was the same young woman who had dared to put her hand on Bright's torso the night before.

What was she doing at Bright's house?

The young lady, seeing another lady enter the room, rose to her feet and gently bowed to Margaret. Politeness made the difference between the savage and the civilized, and though Margaret wished to go up to her and shake her for touching a torso she considered hers, she lowered her shoulders and her body.

Margaret couldn't help but compare herself to that young woman. She was undoubtedly younger than her, and it might have been her first year as a debutante. Her face was delicate, her gaze innocent, her hands seemed soft and her figure sculpted to be adored. She felt envious of her virtues which of course, were more exuberant and attractive for a gentleman.

"Good morning, I'm Alice. " the lady introduced herself.

"I'm Margaret Westworth, pleased to meet you."

"The pleasure is all mine, William has told me about you."

William? Was that Bright's name? She couldn't remember. The closeness and affection with which that young woman spoke Bright's name made her retch. It was clear that she knew him in a much more intimate way than Margaret herself did, and that made him feel horrible.

The intimacy they must have shared must have been overwhelming for such license to be allowed to be taken.

The confusion that her presence and the way she had referred to Bright had caused Margaret was not lost on young Alice who tried to regain her education.

"You wish to see Mr. Bright?" Alice asked eagerly taking a step forward to approach the newcomer.

Margaret's face must have turned into an expression of terror when she appreciated the naturalness with which the young woman felt herself master and mistress of that house. She was not there as a guest, but felt that she had the right to summon or ask for the master of the house to be summoned. That revelation provoked a reaction in Margaret.

She felt small, broken and confused. The conclusions her mind was drawing evidenced a remarkable loss of her reason, evidenced a lack of knowledge of the person she had thought she had shared so much with, and of course, forced her to censure her debauched behavior.

"No, that's not necessary. I understand that Mr. Bright is not available for visitors. Don't worry, I just realized that I have several errands for my father that I have not yet been able to accomplish. Excuse me, have a nice day," Margaret replied in a dodgy, uncouth manner, forgetting all about protocol.

She said goodbye to the young woman, trying to escape from the overwhelming feelings that her presence in Bright's house had caused him, and ran out of the house.

She wasn't Bright's only lover.

There was another young woman, much younger than herself, who enjoyed his attentions and caresses and even dared to call him by his first name. Not only was she skirting all the rules of politeness, but she was exiling the decorum between a man and a woman to oblivion by allowing her to be in his house without him being present.

Such was the tension she felt, that she began to feel short of breath. She put her hand to her chest and trying to muster what little strength she had left, she ordered herself to find enough composure to climb into the buggy that waited a couple of yards ahead and not make a scene in public. She felt a retch rise in her throat and did her best to make it go away.

Sitting inside, she began to cry as at that moment she realized how deeply and painfully in love she was with Bright.

CHAPTER 26

28 July 1876
Middleton, England

Margaret asked the coachman to take him to the Rogers'. She wanted to ask Thomas to go riding together, and this time, without running away or disobeying him. She needed to breathe fresh air, to breathe, to regain part of herself.

Thomas, who was usually up with the first rays of the sun, was helping some of the ladies of the service to clear the tables and chairs. Although it was not his responsibility and his mother repeatedly reminded him that the service should take care of it, his friend's goodwill was unwavering.

"Dear Margaret, a very good morning," greeted young Rogers with a big smile on his face as he saw his friend approaching in such a hurried manner. I hope you have been able to rest. The truth is, my feet are sore."

"Good morning, Thomas. Yes, I have been able to rest. I wondered if you would care to take a ride on horseback with me," the words came out of Margaret's mouth with hardly any time to think them over.

"Only if you promise me that this time there will be no surprises and that you won't run away."

"I promise."

Thomas's eyes opened wide and with a frown he doubted Margaret's promise, for on another occasion she had promised the same thing and had ended up in the forest lost for hours. Intuition and years of knowing his dear friend led him to recognize her moods and though he trusted her after their renewed restoration of friendship, he couldn't help but appreciate the nervousness and alarm that overpowered her.

Thomas could sense that something was going on with his friend, even if she did not have the courage to tell him, nor could he find the right words to ask her to share her concern with him. If there was one thing he had learned in his role as brother and friend, it was not to pressure the ladies, for they were entitled to their secrets.

"I promise you, for the long years of friendship we have, that I will be good."

They both laughed when she promised to be good, for it was ridiculous for Thomas to play the role of a father. They walked together to the stable and, with the stable boy's help, saddled two horses. The beautiful mare Margaret had ridden last time was glad to see her, for she gave him a slight nudge with her muzzle as she passed him. Thomas helped her up and then mounted his horse. With a leisurely pace they rode out of the stables and into the woods behind the property. On the way they talked about the party, the guests, the gossip they had both heard about.

They rode deep into the forest, and all that time, Margaret had relegated Bright to the back of her mind. She didn't want to think about him again and how painful it was that it hadn't taken him long to replace her or how little he'd valued her giving. It gnawed at her insides not knowing if during all this time she'd gone out of her way to forget him with the only result of finding herself hopelessly in love with him, he already had another lady to share his intimacy with.

Margaret forgot that pressure that compressed her chest and drove her headlong into a sadness from which she did not know how she could extricate herself. Her friend's smile and his good intentions kept her from the memory of Bright and his caresses, and she had to be strong and do more than her share in trying to forget him. The thought that only hours before she had been in his arms and now another lady was waiting patiently for him in his living room was completely shattering her.

Mrs. Rogers invited Margaret to join them for the meal. She sent a missive to Mr. Westworth's house, that he might not be troubled by her absence, and Margaret tried to enjoy herself.

"Tell me, dear Margaret. We are all very anxious to know have you and Mr. Kingsman fixed a date for the engagement?"

"Mother, do not fall under the spell of that Lady Middleton's gossip. I think we owe Miss Westworth respect." Thomas reproached his mother's question. Mrs. Rogers loved Margaret as a third daughter, and therefore, knowing the young lady's future was one of her concerns.

"I am not gossipy, Thomas, I care about Margaret and her future and if she has chosen Mr. Kingsman I only wish to see her married and happy."

"We haven't set a date yet, Mrs. Rogers, but I'm sure we will soon," Margaret replied so as not to offend Mrs. Rogers even though it was a lie what she was telling her.

"That's very nice. It will be one of the most eagerly awaited liaisons in all Middleton, of that there is no doubt. Your father and aunt must be overjoyed at the situation," said Mrs. Rogers as she clapped her hands enthusiastically.

"Of course, you know Aunt Beatrice. She is more than devoted to the noble task of betrothing her nieces, and of course, much to my regret, I have presented a real challenge."

"Well, well, that's a thing of the past now. All young ladies have to beg if they want to find the right person. I only hope my daughter finds a gentleman as noble and distinguished as her betrothed."

When the meal was over, Margaret accompanied her hosts to the small parlor to enjoy refreshments along with an amusing game of cards. Mr. Rogers was skilled in the art of cards and his son had inherited his virtue, so competing against them was difficult. Sometimes, however, they let the ladies win. And between games, the afternoon flew by.

"Thomas, I think I must return home. I have abused your hospitality too much."

"You know you are always welcome here," said Thomas trying to calm his friend who, in truth, did not wish to be an inconvenience to the natural course of things in the Rogers household.

"I know."

"Margaret, forgive me for being so nosy, but... you're happy, aren't you?" Thomas asked confidently and using a low tone of voice to keep the rest of his family from overhearing.

He was glad that his friend had decided to share that day with him, it made it clear to him how important his friendship was to her, especially knowing that something was bothering her. Knowing that she found serenity with him made him feel flattered.

"Of course" -despite saying those words with a smile, Margaret hesitated and realized that her friend had appreciated it. It was impossible to hide the sadness in her eyes, no matter how exciting her card games with Mr. Rogers were.

A little later, after bidding farewell to the Rogers family, Margaret borrowed Mr. and Mrs. Rogers' buggy at the express request of the master of the house and drove home.

She had to learn not to be so transparent with her emotions or everyone would soon start to notice. It was clear that the social season was coming to an end and the announcement of the breakup of her liaison with Kingsman would soon be made public. That would draw stares, comments and jeers and Margaret had to be prepared. Of course, it would attract the stares of all the Middleton women and perhaps even her hated Lady Middleton. Her viperous tongue would taint her already tarnished reputation and they might scrutinize her behavior or the possible motivations for the breakup by blaming it on a scandal with another possible man. At last, her home was in the distance. The Westworth residence was one of the finest properties in all of Middleton and Margaret was more than grateful to live in it. If her future was uncertain and in the end she did not get a husband for whom, if indeed she felt the impulse to abandon spinsterhood, Margaret was happy to remain at home with her father. All her memories and passions resided in that house.

She opened the front door, and when she reached the living room, she found something that completely threw him off. Her father and Mr. Bright were playing cards in the living room.

"My dear, my dear, how glad I am that you have come! When Mrs. Rogers's note came I was glad to hear you would spend the day in such kind company," said Mr. Westworth, as he laid his letters on the table, and rose to receive his daughter.

She, for her part, let herself be hugged by her affectionate father who gave her a kiss on the cheek. Their relationship had always been very close, and given the tension that was beginning to build up in her body after seeing Bright, she needed his affection.

"I'm here now, father.

The words came out of Margaret's mouth trembling, nervous.

"And you do not know how glad we are," remarked Mr. Westworth, enthusiastically, as he waved his daughter into the room. Mr. Bright arrived shortly after you left this morning, with the intention of calling on us. Will you join us in our departure?"

Her father, unaware of what was going on, was only forcing an already tense situation. Although she enjoyed a great game of cards, especially with her father, who was a natural gambler, she had no desire to share a room with Bright. The scent of his body intoxicated Margaret's senses and would keep her from thinking clearly.

For most of the day she had managed to put him out of her mind and out of her thoughts and now there he was, in the middle of the living room sharing a drink and some cards with his father. Almost as if she accepted him as her son. It made Margaret more tense.

She could see an exciting combination in Bright's eyes: tension, need, and guilt. Feelings Margaret punished.

"No, thank you. I think I should retire before dinner and take a bath, Thomas and I have been riding and it would be disrespectful to your guest, father.

These words spoken, Margaret turned and began to walk straight to the front door.

"Margaret."

"Bright."

"I am sorry you could not enjoy Margaret's company." Mr. Westworth apologized to his guest. He understood his daughter's possible need for rest before dinner, but not the sudden impoliteness of not wishing to attend to a guest who seemed willing to share his company.

"Do not trouble yourself, Mr. Westworth. I shall return home with my sister, Alice, whom Margaret has already had the pleasure of meeting this very morning." said Bright, raising his voice a little at a time so that the lady who was about to leave the room might hear him.

Margaret paused with her hand on the handrail of the staircase. Her breath stopped. Her heart stopped. Her sister? Was the young woman William had so affectionately called his sister? Margaret didn't know if she believed it, but the truth was that it made sense of some things.

"Yes, my sister came just a few days ago for a visit. It is curious, but last night she accompanied me to the soiree at Mr. and Mrs. Rogers'. I feel guilty that I have not had the pleasure of introducing her to you properly.

"Why, Mr. Bright! You're a box of surprises. I didn't know you had a sister. In that case, we must make amends for this situation.

Margaret continued to listen silently to the conversation in the room between the gentlemen without turning around, without looking at Bright, and without knowing what to do. It was as if her world was falling apart and taking shape by the second.

"Of course, of course. How about we remedy that situation and you join us for dinner tomorrow?" Bright's invitation was enthusiastic and sincere which Mr. Westworth appreciated with a big smile on his face as he saw the young man's kindness to make amends for his mistake. " It would be a very natural occasion to introduce you to my dear sister, I'm sure her daughters are looking forward to meeting her. Though I would ask you not to expect a grand menu, our cuisine and resources are not so...."

"Don't worry about that, Mr. Bright. It's the least of it. Of course, we accept the invitation."

Mr. Westworth seemed indeed delighted at meeting more of the Bright family, and at the dinner which was to take place the next evening. He was always pleased to meet new neighbors, and all the more so if they were related to people whom he already respected.

Having settled the details of his next visit, Mr. Bright politely took his leave and made his way to the front entrance of the house where he could see that Margaret was still there. He picked up his hat, placed it on his scalp, and for a split second, waited.

At that instant, Margaret plucked up her courage, turned her face to look at him and gave him a shy smile before losing herself in the upper floor of the house.

Lying on her bed with one hand on her chest, Margaret breathed a sigh of relief as she heard the front door of the house close.

She was his sister.

CHAPTER 27

29 July 1876
Middleton, England

His sister.

Alice was his sister.

Margaret apologized to herself, saying that it was only natural that such confusion had occurred. She hardly knew Bright, let alone his family, so mistaking young Alice for a mistress was understandable. There was no reason to think he had a sister as it hadn't been mentioned in any meeting they had shared and she didn't have to look for similarities in their features either. It was that thought that had allowed Margaret to rest for the entire night. The relief.

The relief of seeing the sad, pleading look on Bright's face when he was playing with his father in the living room and how he waited to say goodbye to her at the front door.

That mystery that had so plagued Margaret may have been solved at dinner that night, but there were many other secrets Bright seemed to be keeping.

That breakthrough didn't mean she forgave Bright for his bad manners and boorish behavior during their encounters, but it certainly gave her a better opinion of him in that regard.

Throughout the morning, Margaret was in high spirits. Her mood changed completely and it was not lost on her sisters or even the servants. Margaret was happy. This very night, she would get to know Bright a little better through Alice. She planned to talk to the young woman all night after apologizing for her strange behavior the day before. And, furthermore, she would try to get as much information as possible.

The house was prepared for dinner. Margaret's sisters, as usual, were more nervous than usual. Alarmed by such an impending unannounced visit, and with no new dress to wear for the occasion, they tried to find something beautiful to dazzle in. They were going to meet a lady who was a complete mystery. They didn't know if she was close in age to them or if she was younger or too old, they didn't know her tastes, her favorite topics of conversation, what dishes she enjoyed most, if she had already fixed her eyes on any desirable Middleton suitor that they themselves had in mind....

Margaret spent little time dressing. The maid had prepared a very simple emerald dress for the occasion that she thought was just right.

The buggy was ready when they all went out to the entrance of the house, showed the coachman where he was to go, and started on their way.

Margaret looked out of the window and smiled. She wanted to feel the sun bathe her face, for it had been several weeks since she had allowed herself to enjoy such a simple moment as this.

Her sisters, Grace and Rose, fought in the car incessantly. And Margaret, oblivious to it all, began to see Bright's residence in the distance. Her nerves began to gather in her stomach and slowly came to life until her mouth went dry and her hands trembled.

The carriage stopped and everyone got out with the help of one of Mr. Bright's servants who was waiting at the entrance to the residence. The housekeeper escorted the guests into the parlor, where Bright and his sister Alice were sitting.

At that moment, as Bright's eyes rested on her face and gently lowered down her body to admire it, Margaret felt a blush creep across her cheeks. So intimate and precious had been the smile with which she had acknowledged him that she thought she could never give him another such smile.

She saw the young woman in front of her with different eyes. She reproached herself for having been unfair to her. She had judged her identity and the relationship she shared with Bright out of jealousy. Margaret felt like a little girl who wouldn't allow her toys to be played with, and for that, she felt ashamed. Someday she should apologize to the young woman.

"Welcome, Mr. Westworth, Mmes Westworth. I would like to introduce you to my dear little sister, Alice Bright.

The young woman rushed up to Margaret and, taking her hands in hers, gave little jumps of joy. Something that was quite striking and imprudent since they had just been introduced. An overly effusive reaction that caught Margaret off guard.

"You must forgive me, Miss Westworth, but I was so anxious to meet you at last. It is a real pleasure that you have accepted my brother's invitation to dine with us. This house is too large for the two of us to enjoy.

In that moment that Margaret was so close to young Alice she could see the small glimpses or similarities to her older brother. They shared a similar facial structure and, no doubt, the eyes were the same. The hair, untamed in both cases, was more subdued in Alice's updo than in the gentleman's lightly groomed mane. But it was undoubtedly her eyes. Eyes that were lively and full of energy.

"Your brother has been very generous in his invitation," Margaret thanked her with sincerity and affection. She loved Alice's spontaneity and the naturalness with which she had welcomed him on his arrival, as if there were a certain familiarity between them.

"It is, I can't deny it," she said turning her face and giving her brother a beautiful smile. That touched Margaret's heart. She could tell that Alice adored her brother and it made her happy.

"If you wish, we can play a game of cards while the ladies get acquainted." Bright addressed the invitation to Mr. Westworth who gladly accepted but not before Margaret noticed the reproachful look Alice was giving her sister after the suggestion. Margaret felt strange to detect this silent remark between siblings, and was overcome with a sense of curiosity.

The four young women sat on various couches and began to talk about the main topic of conversation, the social season. Alice was excited about their arrival.

On his first day in the county he had been able to accompany his brother to the Rogers' house, not without first begging him until he agreed.

"You can't imagine the emotion I felt when I saw that room and all the guests dancing, it was thrilling."

"In Middleton there are dances or concerts every week during the social season, and if you come from a respectable and well-connected family you are likely to get an invitation to all the events."

"Though it is also true that it is tedious," Rose said with a certain mocking tone in her words.

"Don't talk rubbish, Rose, we've hardly been to a couple of dances during this social season and it's all thanks to Margaret's engagement.

Those words caught Alice's attention and she turned to look at Margaret with wide eyes. It seemed that Grace's comment had taken Alice by surprise and she was eager to know more details.

"Are you engaged, Miss Westworth?"

"Yes, I gave my word to the gentleman," Margaret answered with her eyes lowered to prevent any of the young women from reading the lie in her eyes. In the face of the world she was still betrothed to Mr. Kingsman and even if she had her lover's sister in front of her she could not discover the truth. Until the right day came she must continue to defend the lie she was trying to make all Middleton and Bright believe. Bright in particular.

"We are all very excited because it has been several years of waiting, no one seemed to be that good for Margaret. I don't think I'll be that good myself, I don't expect to wait years to get married, I'm sure I'll meet the right man before long," Rose commented excitedly as she touched up her skirt again and again so that the others wouldn't notice how she was blushing.

"I am sure of it, Miss Westworth, you are very agreeable, and have a facility for words. You will soon attract the attention of the right young man."

"We all hope so," Grace confirmed as she held her fan to her face to cover the hearty laugh that her sister's comment had caused her.

"Yes, but remember, Miss Westworth, sometimes the wait is worth it. It may be that your knight in shining armor will be longing and waiting for the right moment to appear. There may be certain impediments that make it difficult for him to approach you freely and confidently enough to make his love public, and the wait may be bitter. Will he have the patience to wait for you?"

Margaret didn't know if that comment was directed at her younger sister or herself, but everything she had said could apply to her relationship with Bright. Perhaps Alice was unaware of the close relationship she had established with her brother, or perhaps, on the contrary, she had been alerted to her engagement to Mr. Kingsman when she knew that she and her brother were lovers.

It was impossible for a gentleman to share such intimacy with his younger sister if decency and chivalry reigned in his temper, though it was evident that they had exchanged some secret concerning their relationship. For a few seconds, Margaret was lost in thought, remembering Alice's last remark as she watched her father and Bright playing cards. Her father was in high spirits and she could tell he was enjoying the card game. Bright, on the other hand, didn't seem to quite understand how the cards should be placed in his hand or how to play his trick, which brought a slight smile to Margaret's face.

"William is incapable of denying me anything. He is the best brother there is, I assure you." Alice was silent for a second as she looked at Margaret and then changed the subject. "I'm sure I can talk to you at the next ball, though. Do you think I'll be invited? I can't wait to accompany William to more parties but I don't know if it's acceptable for me to attend."

Grace noticed Alice's glance at the distracted Margaret and lightly tapped her knee with the closed fan to catch her interest again. Margaret apologized to her conversation partners and refocused.

"Certainly Mr. Bright, your brother, has been very well accepted at Middleton, and I am sure the hosts of the next parties will extend the invitation so that you may also come," Grace assured young Alice, who, excited and beaming, clapped her hands in delight.

"I hope so; I have read so much about Middleton in William's letters that I was dying to be able to come as soon as possible to visit him."

"Does your brother write letters?" Margaret asked curiously. She didn't know that side of Bright, but she found it adorable that the two siblings kept up a steady correspondence during the weeks of separation. Away from the possible business missives Bright might have to exchange with his suppliers or workers, she couldn't imagine him dedicating a few lines of affection to someone else.

"Of course, he's a great writer. I can never admit it, but our father never encouraged William's desire to write for no reason. He wanted him to continue the family business, but in the end he had to resign himself to it.

On several more occasions, Margaret turned her gaze from her conversation with the ladies to the gaming table. On several occasions Margaret met Bright's gaze. Two furtive glances in the bustle of the room.

Margaret smiled and blushed at the thought of Bright with her again. She opened her fan again and began to wave it. The air soothed the warmth that was pouring out of her.

"We've moved several times because of our father's business, but we've never minded it too much."

"It must have been hard for you, Alice, to find friends in every new place." Margaret was troubled by young Alice's sudden confession. So many moves for such a young lady might mean her permanent backwardness in society. She felt sorry that Alice had been deprived of the pleasures of a lively society more so even though she seemed to be a cheerful and charming spirit.

"Yes, you're right about that. But I think it was harder on my brother. He's shy and reserved. He doesn't really enjoy talking to people and has trouble making friends. I'm surprised he's been as welcoming as they indicate."

"Are we talking about the same Bright?" Rose asked confused "Mr Bright has always been open and charming at Middleton and doesn't seem to have any trouble socializing. In fact, he is the centre of attention at many a gentleman's gathering and quite popular with the ladies if I may confess."

"Oh, yes, indeed," Alice assured her guests again, "I know my brother better than I know myself, and I can say that he had only a few real friends in his childhood, and nothing else."

Poor Bright, Margaret thought. Changing surroundings at such a young age made it very difficult to establish real relationships or friendships. It was certain that the fear of losing them when he moved led him to close himself off. To refuse to meet more people. But none of that matched the identity of the Bright she knew. Not that she could say for sure that she knew the gentleman as closely as her sister did, but she was certain that Bright showed no problems interacting, least of all with the opposite sex.

"Yes, but at the beginning of the summer he said we weren't going to travel anymore, that he had made up his mind and would fight to find a happy home for both of us.

"That's so beautiful. He has such a tender heart." Rose said holding her hand to her chest. Margaret watched as her younger sister watched Alice with a laughing look on her face. Margaret knew that her younger sister was in love with any man who could show her affection and it was obvious that Bright had provoked feelings in her.

"Dinner is ready, sir."

The conversation was interrupted by the announcement of dinner time.

"I would like to continue our game further, young man. I think you are rather more skillful than you appear to be," said Mr. Westworth, accusing Bright of cheating. "If I find that you have let me win, I may be offended," remarked Mr. Westworth, accusing Bright of cheating.

"I wouldn't want anything like that, Mr. Westworth, but for now, if you would be so kind, join us in the dining-room.

"Yes, please. We don't want to hear Mrs. Robbinson's screams if dinner gets cold," Alice commented amusingly as she stood up and encouraged the rest of the ladies to follow him into the property.

The young hostess took her new friend Margaret by the arm and together they walked towards the dining room. Miss Westworth had never been beyond the drawing-room before, so to walk the corridors of such a simple but warm house seemed a delight to her. It was strange, but even though they had occupied that residence at the beginning of the social season, everything about it was welcoming and conveyed a feeling of peculiarity. Family.

All the diners settled around a modest dining table and gladly waited for the first course to be served. During the wait, glasses were filled with water and wine.

"Tell me, Mr. Bright, do you intend to undertake business at Middleton after the season?" asked Grace.

Margaret was surprised that her sister, who was usually more reserved when she had to talk to men, would initiate a conversation by asking Bright without hesitation.

"It is my firm intention to settle in Middleton for a long season, and with that, if possible, to be able to set up a small business."

"In that case, don't hesitate to consult me," offered Mr. Westworth with a smile. Mr. Rogers and I will be happy to advise you whatever the nature of your business."

"Father has an exceptional eye for math, accounting and opportunity," said Rose proud of her father.

"I know a winning horse when I see one. Although my eldest daughter, Margaret, is of vital importance to my business, she has a good eye for them," he remarked, raising his wine glass to Bright and Margaret.

"I thank you from the bottom of my heart, Mr. Westworth. But for now I think I'll focus on restoring normalcy to our lives and enjoy myself.

There have been too many changes in too short a time. Alice has just arrived in Middleton and I would like her to get used to the county before I am away for a few seasons on business trips. It wouldn't be fair to her to leave her alone after we get reacquainted. I would love for her to accompany me to upcoming social events and meet other young women her age to befriend.

"Wise words. Enjoying the moments of calm is fundamental to establish priorities."

"And wife? Do you expect to find a wife?"

Margaret kicked her sister Rose under the table for the recklessness and impudence of her question. How could she be so bold?

Such questions were not asked, especially not in the host's own home. Margaret thought that at some point she would have to talk to her sister about how reckless her behavior was on occasions that showed her lack of maturity.

"You are direct, Miss Westworth. I don't know that yet," he said, avoiding looking at Margaret so that her situation would not come into debate as he took a sip from his wine glass. The social season is not over yet. One never knows."

"My brother's heart already has a mistress," Alice commented nonchalantly as she gave her brother a smile.

Margaret's heart skipped a beat. Did he already have a mistress? Did he secretly mean her? Was it possible that her suspicions about Bright sharing the nature of his relationship with her sister were real? Part of it made Margaret blush, for she had shared a conversation with her sister, and to think that she knew more than she had implied made her feel vulnerable. But if she was referring to another woman....

"Alice, I don't think this is the time to share such things." Bright scolded his sister in a subtle way, but without raising his voice or seeming crude. The scolding was understood by young Alice who, embarrassed, but with a mischievous smile on her mouth ducked her head and apologized. It was as if she enjoyed the provocation she had just caused.

"Come, come, let us enjoy our dinner," encouraged Mr. Westworth to restore serenity to the table.

Several times during dinner, Bright sought Margaret's gaze to try to convey calm and try to connect with her and for a split second, their gazes connected. There were no words. Just a sincere smile.

The conversation over dinner cheered everyone at the table and even Alice surprised everyone with spontaneous and affectionate gestures to everyone. It was clear that the young girl had grown up without a governess to tell her what the rules were or what behavior was allowed depending on the situation, but for once Margaret put all politeness aside and enjoyed the sweetness and brightness of this young girl.

Maybe I envied her. She envied her for having such an affable character, for being so transparent, for loving her brother so unconditionally and for being so affectionate. Sent her vitality.

After dinner, Alice suggested that everyone enjoy a walk around the property. It was still daylight and the weather was nice, so everyone gladly agreed.

Alice, accompanied by Rose, Grace, and Mr. Westworth, set out. The young hostess wished to show her beautiful gardens to her brother's guests. Taking Rose by the hand, she led her to run through the grove.

Margaret lagged behind, and realizing that this would allow her some private time with Bright, she became nervous. After a few moments, a voice came from behind her.

"It's nice to see you smiling like that," commented Mr. Bright enthusiastically, and he held out his arm to Margaret, "Will you join me?"

"Sure.

Margaret took Bright's proffered arm and they walked together at a fairly safe distance from the rest of the group. The walk led them to a secluded area within the small grove of trees that was on Bright's land. An area that afforded privacy.

Although they both had a lot of things to say to each other, neither dared. For the first few minutes, the silence fell over them and the awkwardness was evident.

"Margaret, I..."

"No, I must be the one to speak first. My reaction yesterday was neither polite nor rational. I jumped to conclusions, and along the way, I mistook your sister for...."

"With who?" Bright asked curiously, but with fear in his eyes. He wished he knew what the confusion was about, but he was afraid he had made a bad impression on the young woman.

"With another lover of yours," Margaret uttered these four words as her heart tore just remembering what she felt the first time she called herself a "lover" thus demeaning her identity and her body.

Bright instantly stopped the walk, broke away just an inch from her and looked Margaret in the eye. The latter, embarrassed, was looking at her shoes and the floor. The gentleman took her face in his hands and gently forced her to look at him.

For that instant, the air stopped. Margaret couldn't hear the birds chirping, or the wind rustling through the trees.

"Listen to me, Margaret. There was, is, and will be no one but you. I am able to imagine that seeing my sister in the drawing-room yesterday and not being properly introduced led you to think that she might be my mistress, but she is not. I do not want you to think that there is another woman in my life, and I do not allow you to call yourself by that despicable word. You are not my mistress."

With some speed, Bright led Margaret by the hand into the shelter of the cluster of trees and, hidden from prying eyes, kissed her.

She responded eagerly to his caresses, which soon merged into an intense kiss. Their hands roamed each other's bodies as if their lives depended on it. Bright intensified the kiss to the point where they both lost their minds.

"Please say you won't marry Kingsman and I can breathe. I feel like I'm a prisoner of all this and I need you to set me free."

"I won't "Margaret said with some pride as Bright still loved her lips passionately. She let herself be enveloped by his every kiss and allowed Bright to take him.

"How?" he asked in exasperation breaking the kiss. He couldn't credit Margaret's refusal to break their liaison when it was more than obvious that there was a very strong attraction between them. Bright was infuriated because he didn't understand the young lady's reticence when it was clear that they both desired each other. It couldn't be more obvious.

"I spoke to Kingsman after our first meeting at the cabin and asked him to break our promise. We're not engaged," Margaret confessed with a beaming smile and an excited look in her eyes while Bright, in disbelief, didn't know how to react. His large hands were still wrapped around her face to keep the moment from ending, and that reassured Margaret.

"Is it true, Margaret, what you say?"

"As sure as I wish you'd keep kissing me."

And so he did.

They did not care that the rest of the guests were strolling in the garden, for the distance and safety of that secret hiding place gave them license to indulge their passion. Nothing could disturb them at that moment. There was only them and their two bodies.

Bright took control of the situation and taking advantage of the intimacy offered by those hedges, he quickly unbuttoned some of the strings of Margaret's corset until one of her breasts was free. In that instant, they both looked at each other with intensity and Margaret's gasp as he took her breast in his hands was enough to break the magnetism that bound them together.

The young man caught her breast and played with it as he ran his other hand amusedly up and down Margaret's leg. He wished she was ready for him. He slowly lifted her skirt as she was enraptured by the light nibbles Bright was leaving on her erect nipples.

Modesty had left Margaret's mind and body days ago, and so when Bright's playful fingers neared her thighs, she trembled with impatience. She wished from the depths of her being that Bright would insert his fingers inside her and he did. Margaret arched her back as she felt Bright inside her and with a moan that the young woman tried to stifle, Bright deepened his hold on her breast that much more.

Margaret's body burned against that tree. She was fascinated by the secrets of the love she was discovering with Bright and how easy and sensational everything seemed to be between them.

When Bright felt the time had come, he pulled away from her but not before noticing how his lover's body was clamoring to have him close again and began to pull down part of his pants.

Margaret, trying to get a sense of the space between them, grabbed Bright by his jacket and pulled him closer to her to take his lips.

When they were close, Margaret brought her curious hands to his trousers and silently asked him to free her own throbbing member. The young woman could feel how hard it was and needed to touch it.

Bright felt how the lady in his arms had turned into a lioness as he took that initiative and started kissing her body, nibbling on her ears and driving her crazy the way Margaret was making him feel.

When the young woman released his member she took some time to play with it. Carefully she stroked it gently as if it were something worthy of veneration.

Bright brought his hand to Margaret's and showed her how to caress him to give him passion. And she continued alone for a few moments.

Bright couldn't hide the pleasure he was feeling and after a minute he asked Margaret to stop, he moved much closer to her and lifting her skirts again he sought her pleasure center to make her his. The madness had reached Bright's mind who could only think of Margaret and she, for her part, was surrendered to the passion they were sharing and daring after having given pleasure to Bright, she was ready to continue.

The young man took one of the young woman's legs which he placed on one side of her body and with a little skill entered inside her. Margaret knew she couldn't scream or make any noise as she might alert her family or the servants, so she reached for Bright's shoulder and bit down on it to quell the pleasure she felt with each thrust of the young lover's thrusts.

Bright was loving her right there, next to a tree in the middle of his property, and she couldn't have been more overjoyed, for her heart and body were about to reach heaven.

When the time came, Bright asked her to turn around, and with her back turned, he lifted her skirt again and inserted his member. Margaret noticed that bending part of her back forward and separating herself from Bright's body made access easier, so leaning against the tree she felt Bright's member much deeper.

After a minute, Bright gave one last thrust over Margaret's body and stopped after unloading his heat inside her. Bright gently stroked her body before carefully pulling out his member and helping her up.

Margaret turned around and looked at Bright's big smile. Bright, who was trying to put his pants back in place, couldn't take his eyes off her. For her part, the young mistress was repositioning her breasts and her corset to return to normal, but her face and her whole body still burned with desire.

"I couldn't be happier right now, Margaret."

CHAPTER 28

31 July 1876
Middleton, England

Two days had passed and Margaret's legs still trembled at the memory of that tree, of Bright's kisses and his touch. Of how her body reacted to his as they complemented each other, and how she missed him now, not being able to hold him close.

Confessing to Bright that she'd broken off her liaison with Kingsman had been revelatory. She couldn't have waited for a more propitious moment, just as she hadn't expected such a bold reaction from Bright. Taking her in the garden of his house, in broad daylight and with guests and servants around. It was the forbidden element and the tension of the moment that heightened the passion between them. Margaret blushed as she remembered it and confessed, to herself, how much she had enjoyed it.

Bright had scolded her for calling herself his mistress, and that pleased her because it showed certain feelings on his part.

She felt powerful as she took Bright's member in her hands. She was skipping all the rules of modesty and prudence in an instant and she didn't care. She wanted this with all her soul and her body was burning in his arms.

She didn't know what she was doing, but she needed to try to give pleasure just as she was receiving it from her lover. Bright had taught her how to do it and seeing the way her body reacted had been gift enough.

During those minutes in the bushes, the two of them had given themselves completely to each other. Margaret had felt a very special bond between them that required no words, and she knew Bright had felt the same, for their kisses showed devotion and not need or hunger.

Margaret came to feel something like love welling up in Bright's body, but she could not be sure of his feelings if he did not convey them to her in words or confirm them in deeds.

After that moment, Bright grabbed her arm and asked her to follow the rest of the group as quickly as possible to avoid the rumors. That puzzled Margaret and since then, her mind hadn't stopped thinking about his comment.

Bright's concern about the rumors or comments of the other guests confused her, especially after she had confessed to him the end of her engagement to Kingsman. The gentleman had shown his most vivid enthusiasm in that grove, and yet he had made no proposal at the time, and that confused Margaret too much.

What did he want from her?

It was the question that kept crossing Margaret's mind, and all she could think of was a warm and affectionate answer.

Perhaps he was waiting to meet her father, Mr. Westworth, first, after learning of the annulment of the betrothal, to ask for her hand, or perhaps, just perhaps, he did not care enough for her to make the fantasy she so longed for come true.

Wasn't it obvious that Margaret was processing deep feelings for the young man? Was Bright so blind that he didn't realize it? Or perhaps he was aware and had decided not to do anything about it?

After that beautiful evening, the time was ripe for an engagement, and yet Margaret returned home single again, unmarried and unpromised. Over the next few days, Margaret tried to return to normality while still taking time to reminisce. She accompanied her sisters to town to run errands, picked flowers from the garden, decorated some centerpieces, studied some political and economic papers that had been recommended to her, and even tried to focus on embroidering, without much success, a small doily.

Tired of reminiscing and punishing herself or trying to find an explanation for everything, Margaret went down to the common rooms and there, had breakfast with her family. Her sisters were quieter than usual and barely lifted their faces from their plates. Silence. Margaret worried.

"Rose, what's the matter?" Margaret asked worriedly as she saw such a scene in the dining room. The silence was so suspicious that it caught Margaret's attention instantly.

"Nothing," the answer was quick and blunt.

"Nothing is the matter, why should anything happen? Nothing is the matter." Her sister Grace's stammering and hasty way of justifying her sister led Margaret to suspect that something was wrong. Had something happened to her dear father or Aunt Beatrice? She could not bear it.

"Rose, look at me right now."

Margaret ordered her sister, and slowly, with a sad and desolate look, she looked at Margaret. There was something in her look that did not please her.

"What are you hiding? It's rather unusual that you're not shouting, jumping up and down, or commenting on some rumor or gossip. Maybe...

At that moment Margaret noticed that on the table beside Rose was the town newspaper. When Grace realized that her sister had seen it, she scrambled to her feet, grabbing the paper tightly and trying to hide it behind her. But it was too late.

"Give me that paper right now," Margaret ordered angrily. There was something in the pages of that paper that they were trying to hide from her, so it was about her. Would it be Mr. bloody Middleton?

"There's nothing interesting about him."

"Then why are you hiding it?"

After chasing his sister across the living room, she managed to catch up with her and take the newspaper from her. She knew that her sisters were only fans of one particular page in that archive of stories, so he looked for the woman's signature without delay.

Middleton Post. August 1, 1876

Dear readers,

Just when I could not think that the season could bring us any more news, I can at last confirm some rumors which for some weeks have troubled the Middleton ladies and mothers: Mr. Kingsman and Miss Westworth have broken off their engagement. Sources close to the family have confirmed this tragic news and reveal that no reproach should fall on the noble gentleman.

Therefore, and as a lady of my talents is always on the lookout for any warning sign or small detail, I may venture to confirm that perhaps the rupture is due to Miss Westworth's having decided to give her heart to another man.

What a scandal! Indeed, it is a scandal and perhaps, one of the most important scandals of the decade in Middleton and of course, a source of embarrassment for some and amusement for others.

How unhappy Miss Westworth will be, however, when she finds that her sweetheart has left Middleton with no return date! We shall not discover the name of so handsome and fiery a gentleman, but no doubt the doors of his residence were closed yesterday morning, and who knows when they will be opened again?

Lady Middleton

The piece of paper slipped through Margaret's hands and fell to the floor before the watchful eyes of her sisters. It couldn't be true. Bright was gone? Had he abandoned her? She could barely move or think. Her whole body had turned to stone. It felt numb and didn't respond to her commands to sit back in the chair. She couldn't. She couldn't breathe. She couldn't breathe.

Her sister Rose tried to approach her, to comfort her silently, but she wouldn't let herself. The moment Rose touched her, she turned away and stood at the side of the dining room fireplace. She picked up the piece of newspaper and reducing it to small scraps of paper threw them angrily to the floor.

She walked through the dining room until she reached the central hallway and from there, to the entrance of the house. She continued her walk to the stables where she spoke to the foreman and asked him to saddle her horse. He, concerned about his mistress's condition, refused to prepare a horse for her for fear that she might have an accident. So Margaret herself took the saddle, tied the straps and with great effort, got on the horse.

When he spurred the horse, it was clear to her where he should go. He could have asked for the family buggy, but he didn't have the time or the inclination to wait or answer awkward questions from his father. Riding a horse was the quickest way.

It went out the main entrance to the property and lost its way across the road, kicking up a great dusting of dirt. Margaret shook the reins firmly to get the animal to pick up speed.

She needed to get to Bright's house as soon as possible and prove with her own eyes that Lady Middleton's words were not true. To prove her wrong.

She needed it not to be true.

She needed to check it, again, he had left her.

When he arrived at Bright's house, a butler, who had heard the young woman arrive, was waiting for him at the door. She stopped the horse with some fear and waited for the man to help her off the animal.

"Is Mr. Bright at home?" asked Margaret hurriedly, with hardly any breath in her body and breathing hard.

"No, Miss Westworth. Mr. Bright left for town yesterday, and we have not yet received any news of his return."

"And Miss Bright, is she at home?"

"Yes. I will announce your visit."

It was true. Bright was gone. He had left her there. Margaret clenched her fists and with tremendous anger followed the butler until she was announced into the house.

Miss Bright was embroidering in the sitting-room, taking advantage of the natural morning light. At sight of her, the young lady sprang to her feet. She was nervous. They both bowed and fell silent.

She barely looked at her.

"Is it true, has she gone?" asked Margaret at last, trying to catch Alice's attention, who, to her shame, was unable to look at her.

"I'm afraid so, but...."

Margaret didn't want to listen any longer. That confirmation was what her heart needed to finish breaking. In short, she had thrown away her future and her hope of a respectable marriage for an undesirable man who would abandon her after making her his own.

He had done it every time. It wasn't the first time he had left without leaving a note or promises, it was the second time.

She had to be prepared for it, but she believed, deep down she believed, that after the conversation they had had two days ago it had become clear what their interests were.

Miss Westworth began to pace up and down the room nervously. She repeatedly put her hand to her mouth and chest, and this alerted young Miss Bright.

"Margaret, please sit down and let me explain about my brother. I'm sure that..." Miss Bright was raising her arms, trying to reach out to Margaret and calm her down.

"It should not be you who should give me those explanations, but your brother.

Hadn't Bright confessed to her that he couldn't be happier than she was at that moment? Hadn't it been proof enough of love on her part to give herself to the young man again in the face of the clear threat of discovery? She had broken off her engagement to Kingsman to be true to her heart and to what she was feeling, but little by little, her feelings were turning dark.

Bright hadn't rated them.

He had insisted at dinner on his interest in staying at Middleton for a while to keep his sister company before he went away on business, but he had broken his word.

It was evident that Alice was aware of the relationship her brother and Margaret shared because she tried to excuse her brother's behavior and decision to leave. But there were no words or excuses that would comfort the grumpiness and regret that had now devastated the young woman's heart.

Margaret hadn't realized it until that moment, but in a subtle way, Miss Bright had walked over to the desk by one of the parlor windows and stood in front of it.

It was striking because instead of sitting down after being unable to calm Margaret she had given up the comfort of the armchair to stand in front of the warmth of a window.

It reminded him so much of his sisters and how they always tried to hide things from him when they knew they had done something wrong. The elusive way she avoided his gaze, her hands behind her body resting on the desk....

"Miss Bright, what are you hiding?"

Margaret understood that not only were her sisters hiding something from her, but Miss Bright was also covering up her brother's misdeeds. When Margaret reached her, she grabbed his arms tightly and tried to move him, but the young woman would not allow her to do so.

This only made Margaret's desire to know what the young woman was hiding behind her body even more intense. What was so important?

Feeling vehemence in her attitude and a reprehensible lack of politeness, Margaret felt guilty for upsetting and hurting Miss Bright, but she could not rectify it if she wished to know the truth.

When she managed to pull Alice away from the desk she saw him.

On those wooden boards which had so skillfully constructed a beautiful desk for a room of that size lay dozens and dozens of letters. And on all of them, in a delicate handwriting almost inspired by angels, was Henry's name. And on the back, his own.

Margaret didn't understand. What was Mr. Bright doing with all those letters? Why did he have all the letters he had written so lovingly to his friend Henry? Had he stolen them? What was his purpose in doing so?

He took several letters and checked the dates. The first one was dated a year ago, the next one several months earlier. She unscrambled all the letters and the dates went back years. There was all her history, all her conversations with Henry, all her experiences and her heart.

Next to those, some more recent ones that didn't look as worn or manhandled as the previous ones as if they hadn't been read several times.

Margaret had put so many thoughts and memories in those letters that she felt vulnerable that they were in Bright's hands.

If it was true that Bright had had them in his possession for some time, it was understandable that he knew Margaret so well and that she felt such a special bond with him. He would have had time to read and reread those pages. To get to know her, to know what she longs for, what she likes and what she expects from life.

Margaret didn't know what to feel. Tears tore at her eyes and clamored to come out, but rage held them inside. She didn't understand anything that was happening, and Bright's disappearance made the moment even more complicated. She needed so many explanations.

He wanted to know why those letters were in her possession. She wanted to ask her why she had gone and left him behind.

He wanted to know if what they had shared was real or just a joke or the whim of a vain man.

Poor Henry.

Henry.

Margaret uttered that name aloud, and as if a bolt of lightning had passed through her body, she fainted and fell to the ground.

Miss Bright rushed to his side to try to help him and shouted for someone from the service to come to her aid. Carefully and gently they carried the young woman in their arms to one of the sofas in the sitting-room and laid her on it until she awoke.

The young lady understood that the heat of the day, the intensity of the moment, and even the tension the young woman was giving off had brought her to the brink of collapse. But deep in her heart she knew there was another reason why the young woman had fainted.

After a few minutes, young Margaret began to wake up and Alice carefully helped her to stand up straight. Margaret held her head, trying to regain some order in her thoughts, and took the glass of water her companion offered her.

Alice did not want to force her guest to know what part of her brother's secrets she had been able to discover on her visit. She knew that her brother would be angry with her the moment he knew that she had left the letters so much in view. But she could not help reading them when her brother was not at home, they were so beautiful that she became enraptured with reading them.

When Margaret pulled herself together she slowly got up from the couch and began to pace the room. She needed to think and turn off the faint black lights that still appeared in her mind. Alice and one of the maids followed close behind in case she fainted again, but as they saw the strength return to Miss Westworth's body they left her to walk alone.

As he paced back and forth across the room, unanswered questions and doubts plagued his mind.

Henry stopped answering his letters at the start of the season coinciding with Bright's arrival.

What if he had caused Henry to lose interest in her? What if Bright had caused the letters between them to stop? Had he persuaded her to abandon our friendship? Was he withholding Henry's letters, or perhaps worse?

But those questions only led to more and more questions, and each time she asked one, Margaret was drawn into a deeper and deeper pit.

"What if...? " Margaret wondered aloud. Miss Bright watched her guest carefully and waited for any reaction on her part so she could help her. Seeing her in that state hurt her, but she had to give her space.

At that instant, Margaret put her hand to her mouth and caught her breath and froze. She felt as if a knife was going all the way through her chest. She lost her breath. Her life was drained from her.

Tears burst onto Margaret's face and she couldn't stop crying. Among so many unanswered questions, Margaret had discovered the truth about Bright. It was at that instant that young Alice rose quickly to comfort her guest.

"Please, Miss Westworth, don't hate my brother. " Alice begged in shock. "He's a very good person. He just wanted to...”

Trembling and with some difficulty, Miss Westworth walked step by step unaided, and leaned against the desk. In one of the drawers were several letters, handwritten and signed by Bright. Margaret looked at them carefully. She was surprised to recognize the neat handwriting at once. The way he was careful to recreate the capital letters. The curvature of his letters.

Margaret took those letters and some of the ones she had sent to Henry and holding them up in the air looked at Alice.

"Henry didn't stop writing to me, did he? " Margaret asked resolutely, directing her gaze at Alice.

"Margaret. "She didn't want to say anything that would confirm the truth that she already suspected, but it was her silence that finally revealed the secret.

"He didn't stop writing to me because he was here with me.

"I...”

"Henry is Mr. Bright.

CHAPTER 29

※

August 2, 1876
Middleton, England

Margaret was as fond of romance novels as she was of mystery novels and had read countless times about important revelations that are discovered in the precious moment and help solve a case, an investigation, or clear up a mystery. There was her epiphany.

Looking carefully at the letters she had so lovingly written to her faithful friend, she held forward one of the sheets of paper that lay on a block of paper on the desk. It contained Bright's farewell letter to his sister Alice. But it was not the words that caught her attention, fors he felt sorry for young Alice and the sudden news of her brother's departure without explanation, but the handwriting in which they were written.

A calligraphy that he had so admiringly enjoyed for years. A style so characteristic that it would almost confirm that it was special and belonged to a sincere, honest and generous man. The handwriting of her good friend Henry. Her Henry.

There was the truth that Bright had worked so hard to hide. He was Henry.

What did it all mean, had Henry grown tired of his cards and decided to play with her? Because that's how Margaret felt, like a doll he had played with. She couldn't imagine that her best friend had approached her without revealing his true identity when for years she had begged and pleaded with him to come for her.

At that moment she noticed a detail that had subtly caught her attention but now seemed significant, Bright's eyes. From the first moment she saw them she felt something familiar, something close. It had been him all this time and he hadn't deigned to tell her who he was despite her pleading words.

Margaret tore up each and every letter she had access to before she was stopped by Alice. Margaret's tears streamed down her face like a waterfall on the loose. She felt as if two parts of her heart had been ripped out of her.

I loved Henry as a friend and I loved Bright as a lover and now, neither was real. All an invention.

"Listen to me, Miss Westworth, I promise you by the Lord who so lovingly watches over us that Henry meant you no harm. You must let him explain himself. I'm sure when he comes back..."

Alice tried to calm Margaret, but Margaret was in a state somewhere between anger and the most wrenching pain.

She had found out the truth about her brother, and she knew it wasn't the best way to find out, for her brother had planned to reveal everything at the right time.

"I think he's wrong."

Gathering all the strength she had left in her body, Margaret left the house, leaving behind Alice Bright and all the lies that the house seemed to harbor.

The butler, who had taken Margaret's horse, immediately hurried to the stables to fetch the animal. He helped the nervous young woman onto the horse and watched her run away.

Margaret came home and without a word locked herself in her bedroom. Her worried sisters were not aware of the nature of their sister's distress, but they understood that, if it was connected with the breaking off of her engagement and her possible affair with Bright, they must be with her if it was true that the young man had gone away. They followed her upstairs, and through the closed door they heard their dear sister weeping.

They had not realized that their sister had shown deep feelings for Mr.Bright, for they were predictably thrilled that she had accepted Kingsman as her husband.

There on the bed, Margaret wept inconsolably until she allowed her sisters to enter the room and join her.

Grace and Rose did not ask the reason for her grief, but understood that these were matters that concerned their sister alone, and that they must not press her to reveal them, even if they were dying to know what was going on, but like good sisters, they comforted her.

And so the days and nights passed. Young Margaret Westworth would not leave her bedroom at any time. Her sisters had told the servants that she was not fit to take her meals in the dining-room, and had asked her to have her dishes served in the dormitory.

She had scarcely strength to get out of bed, and after the fourth day of sobbing and negative thoughts, her tears dried up. Grace and Rose thought that no woman had ever shed so many tears for a man as poor Margaret. They both secretly wished they had not suffered for love as their sister had.

She had not spoken a word in the many visits she had received from her aunt and sisters. And even Thomas's sister had come to see her, expecting to share a merry walk with her friend, and had been obliged to return because the elder Westworth was unwell.

Margaret felt sunk and abandoned, deceived and humiliated. She had trusted her friend Henry with all her heart, and after that season, she had given her body and her heart to Bright, but they had both betrayed her.

As much as it pained her to admit that she felt something special for them, their betrayal and the lies that had surrounded that charade hurt her more than anything else in the world.

Henry had not been brave enough to confess to her that he was coming to Middleton to see her, and when he was there he had invented a whole story of lies and a lifetime of falsehoods in order to get near her. And she, like a lady in love, had fallen into his nets. She didn't know when her old friend had decided to use those tricks to get close to her when she was the person who knew him best in the whole world. For years he had revealed to her the secrets of his heart in thousands of letters and had used them to charm her in the name of another gentleman.

Young Margaret felt an emptiness in her chest so great that she didn't know how she would be able to go on living without what was once the shape of a heart.

Not only did Henry's or Bright's betrayal pain him, but now she must bear the shame that Lady Middleton had revealed the truth about her engagement to Kingsman and her feelings for Mr. Bright. The thought of the shame her esteemed Mr. Kingsman must be feeling crushed her even more, for the poor gentleman was blameless, and now he would be the mockery of the entire community as he was replaced by another man.

The day gave way to the beautiful night that Margaret watched from her window. And at dawn on the fifth day, the young woman decided to clean herself, ask one of the maids to help her get dressed and leave that sad room.

She needed to regain some of the dignity that Bright or Henry or both had stolen from her. For days she had cried for them, but now, she had to get over it and face the world.

Grace and Rose were overjoyed when their sister came into the dining-room looking as if she were human. The young girl had large bags under her eyes from the previous days' tiredness, crying, and lack of sleep, but to her sisters, that she had left the room was a sign of triumph over sadness.

The two stood up and with a tight hug surrounded their older sister. They were happy to see her out of her room.

"Okay, okay. If you don't let go of me I think I'll start to get short of breath. "Margaret said with a smile on her mouth. It made her happy to see the reaction it caused in her sisters and it was very tender that, for once in their lives, Grace and Rose agreed on one thing.

"Excuse me, Margaret. We are so happy to see you at last."

"Yeah, it's about time you got out of that room. It was starting to smell pretty bad down the hall," Rose said jokingly trying to make her sister laugh.

"But how do you say that to her, you idiot?" Grace scolded her younger sister. Grace didn't understand how her sister could be so insensitive, but when she gave her an angry glare, Margaret burst out laughing.

"Yes, you're right Rose, you don't know how much good a bath did me. I feel so much better now." commented Margaret to try to resume the conversation peacefully and show them that she was feeling a little better.

"You're telling me. And now that you're among the living, what do you say we go for a walk in the garden? We could pick some of the vegetables that have ripened in the garden. We're sure you'd like that."

Grace knew her sister inside out and knew that getting involved in things that made Margaret happy would be the best way to help her recover. It saddened her to see her sister with so much grief in her heart and she needed to help her, so if she had to get the skirts of her dress dirty by getting down on her knees in the dirt to pick some tomatoes and peppers, she would do it.

"That would be fabulous. Will you join us, Rose?"

Margaret giggled like a little girl when she saw that her younger sister had a huge piece of hard-boiled egg in her mouth and was unable to bite into it. She had been unwise not to break it in half before putting it in her mouth and now she looked like a squirrel storing food. Soon Grace followed her.

At the end of breakfast, the three sisters left the house but not before passing through the kitchen to collect some aprons, scissors and knives, some baskets and some gloves.

Ready to gather the produce of the land, the young Westworths made their way to the orchard where one of the maidens was picking a bush of tomatoes.

"Don't worry, Emerald, we'll take care of it today. You can go get some rest."

"Thank you very much, Miss Margaret. I am glad you are feeling better."

First, Margaret showed her sisters how to cut the stalks so as not to kill the plant and allow more fruit to grow. Rose was shocked the moment a little soil stained her skirt, but she soon recovered and, to Margaret's surprise, proved to be a skilled gardener.

The three of them spent much of the morning in the sun, filling the baskets several times and making trips to the kitchen to hand them over to the cook. They were not to pick all the fruit because it was always better to pick what would be eaten during the day than to hoard it and risk it rotting. At least on the bush, they could continue to grow.

Margaret found peace and calm among her plants and she had to admit that the presence of her sisters and the sacrifice they were making for her had brought a smile to her face.

On several occasions her mind had returned to the harsh truth that awaited her behind the walls of that estate. She wished she could stay locked up forever and not have to face the gossip of the people or the truth of her feelings, but she knew that sooner or later she would have to go out into the world and that the gazes would inevitably censure her.

When they returned home, Margaret asked them both to clean their shoes carefully before coming in to avoid giving the maids more work to do. So they all obeyed. They went through the back of the house into the kitchen and left everything they had collected there.

They entered the house and came into the drawing-room, where their aunt and father were waiting curiously by a large jug of lemonade.

"Your aunt has made some delicious lemonade, and I suggest you have some, you have been working in the orchard all the morning," Mr. Westworth's tone was an enigma. Margaret had not spoken to him since the note that had been published in the village paper, and she needed to know if he also reproached her behavior as she herself did.

"Yes, in the orchard! A most unbecoming place for ladies, I might add, dear brother-in-law," Aunt Beatrice reproached in alarm as she fanned herself to soothe the heat that had begun to condense in the room. "I can't believe how you've left your dresses. You look like beggars."

Aunt Beatrice seemed very angry at their ill-advised behavior in the garden, but their aunt's harsh words only caused the three sisters to burst out laughing. No one could take away from the fact that they had shared a great time together.

"I won't allow you to laugh at me like that, young ladies!"

"Come on, Beatrice. They were just having fun," Mr. Westworth tried to calm his sister-in-law, but she did not approve of her nieces' behavior.

Rose and Grace sat exhausted in one of the armchairs as Margaret reached across the table for several glasses and the pitcher of lemonade. She felt indebted to her sisters, so she served them refreshments under the watchful eye of her aunt.

"Well Margaret, I'm glad to see you back in charge of those things that make you happy, but I think the time has come to...."

"Now is not the time, sister-in-law," said Mr. Westworth, interrupting his sister-in-law. "Things will be talked over at the proper time."

"But..."

"Now is not the time," Mr. Westworth insisted sharply as he looked at his eldest daughter. He knew his sister-in-law was eager to reproach Margaret for the rumors that had been swirling around Middleton for days, but Mr. Westworth did not wish to subject his daughter to more pain than her eyes already conveyed she was enduring.

"All right." Aunt Beatrice resignedly agreed as she gave her niece a less than affectionate look that indicated they would talk later.

After a long, awkward silence, Rose and Grace excused themselves, for they had to go up to their room to change their skirts for clean ones, and asked Margaret's help. Margaret, delighted with the new relationship restored between them, agreed. Margaret was thankful to find herself in any room in the house but the little parlor, where her aunt seemed more than willing to coax the truth out of her.

"Wait, Margaret," said her father as he got up from the couch and walked over to the door of the parlor where she stood. He reached inside his jacket and handed her a letter. "I must give this to you. It is for you."

Margaret took the envelope her father handed her and was afraid to look at the handwriting on the return address. Her father gave her a big kiss on the cheek and then hugged her to encourage her.

She had not spoken to him during the last few days. Mr. Westworth was not acquainted with all that had taken place during the last few weeks, but he would not interfere with the designs of his daughter's heart. He trusted her, and knew that when she was ready and willing, she would confide to him what she wished.

The young woman left the room and slowly made her way up to the upper floor of the residence. There her sisters were scurrying about, looking for their skirts and calling for the maid. When they saw that her elder sister stood silently on the threshold of her bedroom, they noticed that she was carrying a letter in her hand.

"Margaret, don't worry. We'll take care of it."

With that dispensation, Margaret closed the door of her room and with a tremor in her hands sat down on the bed and read.

My dearest Margaret,

I am sorry in the depths of my heart that I cannot be in front of you revealing these words that are born of the purest truth. Cowardice and shame have been inseparable companions throughout my life and now that I have finally managed to overcome the rumors and the darkness, I am unable to tell you how sorry I am.

Your gaze, being what I adore most about you, scares me. I'm afraid of your rejection, your indifference, that I'll disgust you and you'll hate me.

I know I am not worthy to beg your understanding and forgiveness after all that I have kept from you, but I would like the opportunity to explain myself.

You may destroy these sheets as soon as you read my name on the envelope, but my heart and soul cannot live together if I am not honest with you. My love.

I was born under the name of Henry and without a doubt my surname is Williams. I am the eldest son of Lord Williams. It pains me to admit that the family fortune was burned between card tables and parties as you well know. My late father not only lost the family fortune, but owed money to other families who enjoyed his trust. My mother could not live with the humiliation and we left the county. I didn't even get to say goodbye to you, my great friend.

For the last two years I have been trying to regain the family heritage and prestige. I could not return to your side, to the side of my beloved Margaret, to the side of the girl who would now be a woman, the owner of my heart, as a fraud. I wanted you to be proud of me and I wanted to give you a reason to accept me.

On more occasions than I can remember I prepared my trips to return to Middleton, but each time, doubt and embarrassment sapped my enthusiasm.

Your sweet letters were the cloth of my long nights alone in exile. I didn't enjoy gambling or women like other young men, I longed for your words, your letters. Through them I could see how you grew as a person and a woman.

The strength of your convictions, your refusal to enter society and be part of this spectacle that we both hate and, above all, your noble heart encouraged me to stay by your side, caring for you. I took refuge in words.

Your boldness in arguing with me proved me right, you owned me. Only you, Margaret. There has never been anyone else in my life and there never will be. I myself may have caused our hearts to never meet again, but know that I love you beyond measure. Always.

When you revealed to me that you had received a request from a young nobleman to marry, I was devastated. My Margaret was to be betrothed. However, you confessed that you did not wish to share your life with him. You could not abandon your sisters after your mother's death. That made me love you more.

That is why, the first day I had the pleasure of being in your presence in that room, I trembled. I trembled like a little child. You were so beautiful. It had been too many years without seeing your face, but you were so much more than I remembered and dreamed. Your harsh words were true, I lied to you. I did not reveal my true identity to you.

I could have told you my name and that I was the recipient of your letters, but I was afraid. During these years we have grown up together and I have always known that you had feelings for your childhood friend, but I needed to know if as a man, you could love me too.

But at the same time, I was afraid that the whole community would recognize my true identity and I would be the laughing stock of Middleton. But most of all, I was afraid that you would reject me as unworthy of you.

I secretly adored you for weeks. The dances, which had always been boring, were the only thing that allowed me to be close to you. You were so perfect that it killed me inside to see that other eyes could watch your body move to the music. I could feel how your soul responded to mine, how your body matched mine. I couldn't pretend next to you.

But even though I love you, I abandoned you. You gave me the greatest gift a man can deserve, a woman's heart. You gave me your body and soul and there are no words to describe how blissful I felt when you revealed to me that you had broken your engagement for me, for us.

However, I had to leave you and I need to explain why. It was not shame on this occasion, but a reason of force majeure, I swear.

My younger brother has not been able to eliminate the dark hobby that consumed my father. On more than one occasion I have had to save him from a violent situation. Much to my regret, upon arriving home from our meeting my housekeeper revealed to me that Marcus had been seen in town seduced by drink and gambling. My heart could not be divided and even at the risk of losing your love and trust, I had to save my brother. Marcus.

You may not remember him because during our childhood he was sent to boarding school to control his temper.

He received neither fortune nor father's title, and that dishonor plunged him deeper into misery. But I could not abandon him as our father had done. I had to take care of him, even if it meant sacrificing our love.

I understand that there are too many reproaches that fall on me and thousands of questions that will be dancing in your mind, but I just want you to know that every caress and kiss I have given you, every time we have loved each other and every letter we have exchanged have been the greatest gift I could receive in life because I will always be yours.

May the day come when I can explain to you that Henry and Bright are two pieces of an incomplete puzzle for they lack the one essence to hold them together. You, Margaret.

I'm sorry I didn't show enough courage to reveal to you myself who I really was. I swear that in each of our meetings I wanted to tell you the truth, to be free with you at last, but the words wouldn't come out. I know that every moment you expected something from me, however, my words were trapped in my throat without knowing how to get out. It hurt me inside that you thought I didn't love you or that I was using you when the biggest truth is that I have been yours for years and I love you with all my heart.

I will be back to Middleton shortly, I promise, and I only wish you could take a moment to listen to me and express how sorry I am.

Yours always,

Henry.

Margaret's heart had stopped. She recognized Henry's handwriting from the first instant, and like a decanter of liquor, she drank his every word to completion. In its pages she could recognize the sincerity of Henry's sweet heart, but also Bright's impetus.

It pained her to discover that Marcus, Henry's brother, whom she barely remembered, had developed the same pernicious fondness as his late father. And it had been his love for his brother and his duty to protect him that had led him to absent himself on several occasions without explanation.

That repulsion to gambling which Bright had shown her on the first day that Mr. Westworth had invited her to share a game of cards with him was a hint of his identity which Margaret did not see because she did not know that she ought to look for it. She only hated herself and blamed her father for encouraging Henry to play at something that had brought him so much misfortune. In the same way, she understood the look Alice had given him when Mr. Westworth had encouraged him to play cards in his own house.

That resignation and the smile he always wore on his mouth with every hand he played with Mr. Westworth only showed the young man's true interest in sharing and making memories with her' family. He was flattered.

At that moment, with the letter still warm in her hands, Margaret began to notice small details that had hitherto been unnoticed.

The moment they had shared in the cabin when Bright had admired her freckles, the little spots that sculpted her face and that Henry had admired so amusingly when they were little, came to mind.

The way his body had always felt comfortable next to her without feeling foreign. As if it had always belonged to him.

But it was his eyes that brought those two people together. They were the same and he had not known how to see it.

How unfair Miss Westworth had been to poor Bright! The coincidences of destiny had meant that he should justly be absent after crucial moments in their relationship, but she could not blame him for it, knowing the truth now, for a note or reference to the reason of his absence would have been either to reveal the truth, or to fall into a lie.

Margaret wondered if she could love him, if she could love them both. Two sides of the same coin that undoubtedly now owned her heart. Admitting that she had always secretly loved Henry and his letters had been the reason she had put off finding a husband for years. None of the young gentlemen she knew was equal to the deep affection she already felt for the young man behind her letters.

And, on the other hand, she couldn't deny that her whole body and soul had been given to a man she loved without reserve and who managed to drive her crazy at all times.

Henry and Bright were a great mystery that she had to think about if she was willing to venture to know.

Amidst all the maelstrom of thoughts that were racing through his mind, the door rang several times.

"Margaret, my dear, can I come in?" Mr. Westworth's deep voice called out to her from the other side of the door.

"Of course, father."

Mr. Westworth entered his daughter's room with a decided step, and, closing the door, sat down beside her on the bed. From his pocket he drew another letter.

"I have received a rather interesting letter from Mr. Bright, and it has not been possible for me not to be more astonished at its contents." her father began to relate as he laid the letter on the side of the bed and looked at his daughter with a mixture of astonishment and confusion.

"You too father?" Margaret asked confusedly as she turned to see her father's face and expectant that he would reveal the contents of it to her as soon as possible.

"Although I imagine this one on your bed has a very different content, Mr. Bright has confessed his true identity to me and expressed his sincerest apologies for the inconvenience caused."

Mr. Westworth's voice was neutral. It showed no anger, nor, indeed, any joy at learning the truth. However, Margaret could see a certain disappointment in his eyes. She knew that her father had trusted the young man from the first moment he had seen him. He trusted his intentions, his plans for the future, played cards with him on several occasions, and even dined at his house. Mr. Bright had earned his trust, and now he had stolen it by revealing the truth.

"Oh, father, I don't know what to do," Margaret said through her tears as she threw herself into her father's arms. He tried to soothe her with a few light pats on the back, but he knew that nothing he could say would clear up the tangle of feelings that were now in his daughter's heart.

"Your aunt had suspected for some weeks that your relationship with Mr. Kingsman would not end in marriage because she had detected some behavior on your part that indicated you had a predilection for another gentleman." Margaret broke the embrace with her father as she recounted details that had transpired over the past few weeks that she had not been aware of. "So I decided to dispel those suspicions myself and observed you for some time."

When Margaret heard that her father had been watching her for weeks she felt the heat rush to her cheeks and immediately covered her mouth. How many secrets did her father know? Shame possessed her because she didn't want her father to witness the conversations or even the encounters she'd shared with Bright.

"Shame on you!" said the young woman covering her face with her hands hoping that her father wouldn't suspect that her relationship with Bright had reached a physical level.

"No shame, daughter. The devotion with which that man watched you removed any doubt as to his possible intentions for you so much so that I expected him to come to my door with a proposal any day now. The patience with which he waited for you to finish dancing with all the men and of course, Kingsman, only alerted me to the temperance of his person."

"Yes, but he fooled us all, father. In my letter he says he needed to know if I could love him as a man and not just as a friend, and so he introduced himself under another name."

"And tell me, if he had come to you as your dear friend Henry, would you have loved him the way your body is confessing to me? You knew the boy and have grown up with him, but what of the man he has become?"

Mr. Westworth asked the right question, which left Margaret silent. Henry had always been her friend, and though for years she had taken refuge in his letters and believed that no one could ever replace him, it had always been a feeling of friendship, nothing like what her heart and stomach felt every time she stood before Bright or talked to him.

"You're right, father."

"Henry needed to abandon the boy and become before you a man."

"I feel so confused I don't know what to think."

"Your mother thought the same thing when I confessed my feelings to her, my child. Love is like that. It is overwhelming and confusing, but also, it is the greatest of adventures and you have been lucky enough to meet two people so different and so special that they have captivated you. Not everyone is this lucky. Now you have to think about whether the lie you've been caught in is greater than the feelings that have grown in you, or if on the contrary..."

Margaret sprang out of bed like a spring and grabbed the hat that was on one of the chairs and ran out the front door, leaving her father speechless. When she reached the stables, the caretaker handed her saddled horse to her.

"Your father warned me to have his horse saddled at all times because he suspected you would need it."

The young girl couldn't help but smile and let herself be helped to mount and as if the animal already knew the way, she headed for Bright's residence."

She was proud of the father she had, of his understanding and how he had encouraged her to follow the dictates of her heart when everything seemed dark and confusing. There was no reproach in his words but encouragement, strength and courage.

So she needed to get to Bright's property as quickly as possible and see if he had arrived. On the way, Margaret didn't notice, but several of the neighbors watched in amazement to see her riding that way on the horse. To see a lady on a large animal like that instead of enjoying the comfort of a buggy was not an everyday occurrence.

After ten minutes, Margaret crossed the gate that separated the property from the road and headed for the house. On her arrival, the butler took the horse's reins and another helped her down.

"I regret to inform you that Mr. Bright is not at home."

"I'm aware of that, but, still, if you don't mind, I'll wait for him inside."

With a determined step, and without waiting for directions from the servants, Margaret Westworth opened the door of the house and lost herself in it.

CHAPTER 30

August 20, 1876
Middleton, England

A week had passed since Margaret had decided to wait for Bright. She went home several times during the day to be with Alice and to wait patiently for his return. She didn't know if it would be a week, two weeks, or a month. Nothing would keep him from that house and from getting answers to all his questions. Miss Alice was delighted to have company, and during long conversations she answered Margaret's innumerable questions about their past.

All the summer that Margaret had hidden her true feelings from the people she loved most for fear of their reproaches she now felt at peace in being able to speak freely. Those days, some memories of little Alice came to Margaret's mind. But they were faded images in her memory because of Margaret's young age when the family left Middleton. She remembered her little brother less clearly, but even so, if she had seen him come to Middleton she would not be able to recognize him.

She found Alice's company and friendship comforting. The young woman had nothing but good words to say about her dear brother and how much they had missed Middleton, its people, and her, Margaret.

Alice explained that she was one of the main topics of her conversations with her brother because he couldn't stop talking about the things he had told her in his letters.

For her part, Margaret was pleased to construct their past through Alice's eyes and how she had experienced the family's humiliation, Henry's efforts to restore his family's honor, and, above all, the affection with which she wrote each of her letters.

Margaret refused to participate in the rest of the season's social events until Bright returned home so she could talk to him. She needed to clear up this whole situation and convey to him how angry she was about his deception.

Together, like sisters, Alice and Margaret took long walks around the property, rode horses, enjoyed the company of Grace and Rose, and even Thomas's visits. Margaret watched as the days passed and Bright did not return home, and though she feared he had regretted his request to wait for her, Alice insisted on the honesty of his words.

"Margaret, my friend. I cannot speak for my brother, but if I could, I could only confess to him the deep feelings he has for you. I wish I could forgive him and myself for our deception."

"Alice..."

"I know it wasn't fair to you and honest on our part, but..." the honesty and sorrow that trailed Alice's words only evidenced the deep pain that being complicit in her brother's lie had caused her.

"Don't worry, Alice. I understand the motive that led you to conceal your true identities and pretend to be newcomers in Middleton. I myself blush because there was a time when I thought you were lovers after seeing you together at a ball and finding you at Mr. Bright's house the next morning, and I even reproached him for it."

"Yes, Henry confessed to me the next day. I couldn't stop laughing and he just cursed at our audacity and how deceitful we were. He felt so bad, poor Henry."

"It's funny. You call him Henry and I call him Bright."

"Does it make any difference?" Alice asked sincerely.

"No, I suppose not."

Alice was right, there was no difference between Henry and Bright. They were the same person who had appeared before her at different times in her life and had somehow complemented her as a girl and as a woman. It was up to her to figure out if she was willing to overcome the feelings that had led her there.

At dusk at the end of another week, Margaret and Alice were returning home from one of their rides when several horses approached the property.

"It's Henry and Marcus, thank heavens they are back. Look, Margaret, it's Henry," said the young woman as she ran to the front of the house forgetting the rules that should govern a lady.

Of course Margaret was watching. She was watching as the figure of the man who had made her experience such intense things during the last few weeks galloped up beside her brother. When Bright became aware of the young woman's presence, he quickened his pace to get ahead of his brother in the race. Margaret was trembling. Her heart stopped the instant Bright's dark eyes rested on her face. It was Bright.

When the knight was close to her, he dismounted with alacrity, grabbed the reins to prevent the horse from escaping, but both of them were breathing in a hurried manner. They stood scarcely five feet apart, not taking their eyes off each other, but not uttering a word. Alice, who stood beside him, greeted her brother, and he returned her embrace warmly. The young girl was excited about her older brother's return and when Marcus dismounted from his horse she also threw herself into his arms.

"Be thankful that I'm your little sister and that you're twice as big as me otherwise I'd smack you upside that silly head of yours that gets you into so much trouble." Alice scolded her brother as she gave him one and a thousand hugs and pinched his arm to cause him the tiniest hint of pain.

"Alice, I..."

"Home, without complaint" Alice brought out a temper that caught Margaret's attention as she ordered her brother to go to the house and stop causing trouble.

At that moment, Marcus noticed another female silhouette complementing the beautiful scenery and recognized her features.

"You must be Margaret. A pleasure to meet... I can't say meet you because in truth, we already knew each other, perhaps it's better to say met again."

"A pleasure, Marcus." Margaret greeted sincerely.

"Come on, Marcus, you'll have time to talk to Miss Westworth another time, you can't realize that our presence is superfluous at the moment."

"Of more? What do you mean?" Marcus asked incredulously as he was dragged away by Alice and looked back to watch as two stone statues stood motionless behind them.

"Take the horses and let's go home."

It was only a few steps that separated their bodies, but to Margaret, it seemed like miles away. The young woman couldn't help but stare at Bright's countenance, how his chest heaved, his hair tousled from riding, his eyes bright and eager. And of course, she realized that Bright's body was waiting for her to be the one to take the first step.

A few seconds pass and soon, Bright's nervousness turned to fear. Margaret had appreciated the change in her partner's face, but she wants to stay away for a little while longer. She wanted to watch him, every nuance that hadn't caught her attention before and check the fine lines that separated Bright from Henry or Henry from Bright.

"You're late, Mr. Bright."

Margaret spoke those words with a serious face and barely moved. Bright dropped his shoulders in surrender. All was lost. The young man, who had bared his heart and soul in that letter, was crushed by the harshness of Margaret's words. She had not forgiven him. Margaret had found no comfort in his words.

"Listen to me carefully, Mr. Bright."

Margaret finally took several steps toward Bright, bringing him to within inches of her face. The proximity of their bodies caused a reaction in Margaret's body. Her legs began to tremble, she felt as if her voice would be consumed by a spontaneous stutter, but she tried to summon all her strength to control herself as the hairs on her body stood on end. Bright's presence captivated her.

"From this moment on, no more unanswered letters, no more lies, no more card games with my father. For I alone will own your heart as you, Bright, own mine."

Bright threw himself at Margaret the moment he noticed how forgiveness and love flowed to him from those words. Margaret was smiling at him now as he caught her face in his rough hands. She kissed him, kissed him as she had never kissed him before. Lovingly and sweetly. Her forehead, her cheeks, her chin, her lips, her eyes-no corner of Margaret's face was left out of Bright's devotion.

"You must know, Margaret, that my intentions have always been honest in spite of my deception and please know, do not blame or grudge Alice for being my accomplice, she only longs to see me happy."

"Bright."

"Wait, let me finish. I know I'm not worthy and I may never be worthy of your love and your heart, but if you let me, I will take care of you and protect you with my life because that's what you are to me, Margaret. I want us to write together the greatest love letter ever."

Margaret couldn't help but feel her eyes water at those beautiful words. She felt Bright's warmth and the sincerity of his words, and all the doubts she had harbored for weeks about Bright's true intentions dissipated with the sunset.

"Margaret, I wish to speak to you with affection and closeness."

"I allow it."

"Can you ever forgive me?"

"Yes, the day you dare ask my father for my hand."

"I did it a week ago."

Middleton Post. September 20, 1876

Dear readers,

This has undoubtedly been the busiest and most published social season in the history of the Middleton paper. While I must admit defeat in not being able to discover what has been the enigma between Mr. Bright and Miss Westworth, it ends today with this footnote announcing their marital dispensations for the first time.

I feel a certain sadness in saying goodbye to one of the most sought-after and talked-about bachelorettes in all of Middleton, but something tells me, and I'm sure my instinct confirms it, that a new lady will soon emerge in Middleton capable of catching my eye.

It only remains for me to wish the young couple the greatest of congratulations and to remind all ladies of marriageable age that Mr. Kingsman is a great catch.

Lady Middleton

EPILOGUE

March 14, 1877
Middleton, England

"Let me tell you, Mrs. Bright, I find you radiant on this winter morning."

"Cheeky, deceitful, a liar. After all this time you should have learned to tell a more credible lie, or rather, not to lie to your dear wife."

"But it's the truth, my dear."

"By the creature I carry in my womb, how can you tell me I am beautiful when my size has increased so much, my feet are swollen and I look like Mrs. Pullbright?" pouted Margaret as she touched the bulging belly that had grown over the last few months from their love.

"Then I should write a letter to Mrs. Pullbright to tell her that I find her beautiful," Bright remarked mockingly as his wife tapped him hard on the shoulder with her delicate fists.

"You won't be able to, Mr. Bright." Margaret's challenging look brought a smile to her husband's face, who, embracing him from behind, placed gentle kisses along the length of his neck.

"I love the way you say that."

Bright's kisses still lingered on Margaret's neck. Gone were those tense moments between them. As Bright continued to embrace his wife, voices began to be heard from outside the house.

None of them were able to tell whose they were until a hurricane blew through the entrance of the residence and into the room where they were standing, forcing them to regain a more presentable position for their unexpected guests.

"I'll go first." shouted Rose exaltedly entering the Bright residence with hardly any respect for the rules of politeness or being properly introduced.

"No, I want to see our sister first. I want to feel our nephew, Grace."

Margaret's sisters burst into the room and came to where their elder sister and brother-in-law were. They were not privy to all that had happened between them, for it was a secret that concerned only the husband and wife, though deep down the two young women were still in love with young Bright, and nothing he could have done would tarnish his image.

"How do you feel, sister?" Rose hurried over to touch Margaret's tummy, and all the while Bright and Grace admired the spectacle from their places. It was a very tender sight that would soften the heart of any rough man.

"I trust little Bright is healthy." Grace said as she looked at her smiling brother-in-law.

"Little Bright? You take it for granted, dear sister-in-law, that it will be a girl. Is there not also the possibility of it being a boy?" asked Bright with a chuckle.

"In case you haven't noticed, the Westworth blood has raised three healthy and complicated women, therefore, and I'm sorry to disappoint you, it is likely that my sister has a girl inside her.

"It doesn't matter his sex, the important thing is that he is born healthy and strong," confessed the proud father as he admired how lucky he was to have a family again.

"That goes without saying."

"I must warn you, dear sister-in-law, that next season you will be the target of the eyes and the desires of the marrying mothers. You are the next heiress to the Westworth fortune."

"That remains to be seen." Grace commented in a tone of voice so loud that it alerted her sisters who were still chattering with amusement at Margaret's bulging belly.

"I am sorry to inform you, sister, that you will soon have to start thinking about marriage."

"I'm looking forward to it!" cried Rose delightedly clapping her hands. Her elation was infectious.

"I meant Grace, dear Rose. For the next season you will be the centre of attention of mothers in search of a suitable wife for their children. " confessed Margaret, winking at her sister.

"That will be if I let myself."

"I said the same thing, and look," Margaret said, touching her belly and pointing at Bright. "Someone once told me that love is like a hurricane. It blows you around, it's devastating but a great gift. It will be fun to see how it captures you."

"That won't happen, I'm too proud to let any man think he's entitled to me."

No one present could suppress laughter at Grace's remark. All her stubbornness had been Margaret's own for the last few social seasons, and at last she had fallen a prey to an intense and boundless love.

As the three sisters talked about the preparations for a little trip Rose and Grace were taking to visit relatives on the coast, Bright couldn't help but stare at the picture before him in silence.

Bright couldn't hide the passion and affection he felt for his wife, for the confidence that the person he'd always been in love with would look back at him with that intensity and love him. Margaret had been what he had always wanted, what he had always loved, and now they were expecting the first of what was to be a long line that would carry on the Bright name.

The knight had left behind the shame that his family name had instilled in his heart for years, thanks to his new family and the new life he had begun with them.

It amused him when his wife would challenge him with her eyes, teasing him and calling him Bright in their intimate moments. He loved to find little notes on his desk every day in which his wife expressed her undying love. For over the months he had learned to reconcile the two halves of the man he was.

And at last, he was ready to say each and every day of his life to Margaret those words of love which for months he was not be able to utter but which in his letters were hidden in every line for years.

For Margaret was and will be the sole mistress of his heart.

AUTHOR'S COMMENTS

Dear reader,

I want to thank you from the bottom of my heart for giving "Letters to Middleton" a chance, the first story with which I start a new path in historical romance literature. It has been a complicated and exciting adventure, but as if it were a black hole, I have no escape and from this moment, I am prey to romances that arise from the most tender of my heart.

I hope you have enjoyed every one of these pages and that, together with Margaret and Bright, you have experienced an intense romance.

Therefore, I invite you and would heartily appreciate it if you could write a short review or comment on the platform to encourage other readers to enjoy this story.

From the heart and always,

Patricia

ACKNOWLEDGEMENTS

I want to dedicate this story, mainly, to the person who day by day supports me to continue fulfilling my dreams, gives me wings and allows me to fly as high as my mind wants to go. Thank you for everything you give me.

And I can't forget that little person who without knowing it has already changed my world completely.

To Elena, my dear sister, who book after book, is there at the foot of the cannon living my adventures.

To Alba López, my friend, my confidant, my writing sister. Thank you for all these years by my side and for continuing to fight by my side.

To Elena Castillo Castro, one of the best people that the world of writing has allowed me to meet. Thank you for believing in me, for giving me strength and for always being a source of inspiration.

As always, to Inma and Sara, two fundamental pillars of this adventure that for months have helped me to convince myself that this is my genre.

And of course, to you, Jane. I know you'll never be able to read this dedication, but I owe you more than you could ever imagine. You have inspired me as an author and as a person. Thank you for discovering a new world for me and for allowing me to be a part of it.

And I can't forget you. Thanks to all of you who have been appreciating my literary projects on the blog, YouTube and networks for years and who have also decided to support me in my new adventure as a writer.

BIOGRAPHY

Zaragoza, 1990.

Patricia García Ferrer, better known as Little Red, began to read before she walked, and her love of writing began between classes in economics and literature. For more than eight years he has created two great literary projects: "Little Red Reading Hood" (literary blog) and "Little Red Read" (literary channel on YouTube) with which he was able to share his opinion on readings with other people.

Her writing debut took place in May 2018 with the publication of "The Ice Dome" and eight months later she published "Daughters of the Shadows" in 2019. Two novels belonging to the juvenile fantasy genre and which are currently being enjoyed by readers of all the world.

Now, Patricia focuses her narrative activity on the historical romantic novel from the Middleton Series that began with "Letters to Middleton", a story that has reached thousands of readers and with which she began an exciting adventure to show how much treasures and adores period romances.

You can follow their progress on social networks.
Twitter, Instagram and Facebook: @littleredread

AUTHOR´S NOVELS

The rest of the books in the Middleton series will be published in English shortly.

Meanwhile, I have several books published in Spanish.

Serie Middleton

    Cartas a Middleton

    La rosa de Middleton

    Escándalo en Middleton

Youth fantasy

    La cúpula de hielo

    Hijas de las sombras

Printed in Great Britain
by Amazon